**WE
NOW
RETURN
TO
REGULAR
LIFE**

WE NOW RETURN TO REGULAR LIFE

A Novel

martin wilson

Dial Books

Dial Books
An imprint of Penguin Random House LLC
375 Hudson Street | New York, NY 10014

Library of Congress Cataloging-in-Publication Data

Names: Wilson, Martin, date, author.
Title: We now return to regular life / Martin Wilson.
Description: New York, NY : Dial Books, [2017]
Summary: When fourteen-year-old Sam Walsh returns home after three years in the
custody of his kidnapper, his older sister Beth and childhood friend Josh must deal with
their survivors' guilt, their memories of what really happened the day Sam disappeared,
and with the fact that Sam is not the boy they remember, but a troubled teen struggling
to re-adapt to normal life.
Identifiers: LCCN 2016032500 | ISBN 9780735227828 (hardcover)
Subjects: | CYAC: Kidnapping—Fiction. | Emotional problems—Fiction. |
High schools—Fiction. | Schools—Fiction. | Gays—Fiction.
Classification: LCC PZ7.W6972 We 2017 | DDC [Fic]—dc23
LC record available at https://lccn.loc.gov/2016032500

Printed in the United States of America
1 3 5 7 9 10 8 6 4 2

Design by Nancy R. Leo-Kelly
Text set in Janson MT Std

= For Avery =

"Something was wrong with a world where people came and went so easily."

—Anne Tyler, *Saint Maybe*

CHAPTER *1*
THAT DAY

Beth

We'd been studying on his couch, our Advanced Chemistry textbooks sitting on the coffee table, suffering through questions about alkali metals and noble gases, when Donal made a joke about gas being *ig*noble. And I'd laughed, like I always did at his dumb jokes. And then our knees touch and our shoulders bump and suddenly we start kissing each other. Like, a real kiss, deep and forceful, sending gentle sparks up my back. I'm wondering how in the world this happened when my cell phone starts ringing.

It's Mom—I know from the ringtone, I don't even have to look. The one day I cut out from school early. The one day I break routine. I pull away from Donal, instantly wishing I hadn't. I let out a little laugh and instantly feel this ridiculous mix of nervousness, because Mom is calling, and regret, because we stopped kissing too soon, and then confusion, because why were we even kissing to begin with?

"Damn," Donal says. "Let's not stop."

I stare into his blue eyes, which look a little dopey right

now. He isn't my boyfriend. He's my friend, just my friend, ever since freshman year. Why did I like kissing him so much? I wipe my lips, but I also have the urge to lean into him again and start all over.

But the phone keeps ringing. I can't ignore Mom. I'm her dependable daughter. And if, for once, I'm not, she'll freak out.

I scoot away from Donal and make a move to go to my purse on the floor at the end of the couch, but I stop.

Did he plan on kissing me all along?

"You gonna get that?" Donal asks. "Or can you just ignore it," he says, breaking into a smile while raising his eyebrows again and again in a silly way.

It must be close to three o'clock. I'm skipping sixth-period soccer practice. We both are. I hurt my ankle last week and have a doctor's note—a light sprain. I'm not out for the season or anything. But I'm still supposed to sit on the sidelines and physically be there—you know, be a team player, rah-rah-rah.

But I snuck away with Donal. He's on the boys' team, but his coach had the flu and their practice was canceled. It was his idea, skipping out. "Let's get this chemistry assignment done," he'd said. And then he added, "at my place." He knew I didn't like to spend a lot of time at my own house. So yeah, maybe he planned this. Makes total sense. Except it doesn't. And now my phone won't shut up.

I finally hop from the couch and grab my phone from my bag, squatting on the floor. I don't answer, I just stare at the word "Mom" flashing on the screen. Then the ringing stops. "Great," I say. Somehow she's figured out that I'm not at school. Maybe Coach Bailey called her. All I can think about is my mom's worried face, the thoughts that must be swirling through her brain.

Donal runs a hand through his red hair then leans forward, his eyes on me, but he's not making the funny face anymore. Then the phone starts ringing again, and he leans back on the couch, laughing.

I try to gather my thoughts. Okay, quick—what's my excuse? Screw it. "Hello," I say after the third ring. I brace myself. But I don't hear any words. I just hear something like a moan. "Hello?" I say again.

The moan turns to some sort of heavy breathing, and then I hear Mom's voice: "Beth?" It sounds like she's been crying.

"Mom, I'm here," I say, feeling sick to my stomach. I was worried about being in trouble. But now I'm just afraid.

"Thank God I found you!" Mom says. I hear her take a few deep breaths. She sniffles and says, "They said you weren't at school. I thought, I thought—I didn't know what to think."

I'm used to hearing my mother cry. For over three years it's been a fact of life. She can be laughing one minute and then, wham, she's leaking tears. Like she feels bad for ever having fun. I'm so used to it, it hardly ever phases me. I'm always there to hug her, rub her back, play the good daughter. But the way she sounds now is different. "Mom, I'm okay. I'm at a friend's—"

"Just come home. Come home." Then she makes some kind of gurgling noise.

"Mom?" My heart is revving up. I hear a voice in the background—my stepfather's, probably. I think I hear him say *Tell her.*

Oh God. I look over at Donal, but he's still staring up at the ceiling, smiling in an exasperated way.

"Beth," Mom says, her voice sounding shaky.

I hold my breath, close my eyes.

"They found Sam."

I let out my breath, or maybe it's a gasp, but I don't say anything, and I keep my eyes shut. Because when I open my eyes I'm not sure what the world will look like.

I've been waiting for this moment for three years.

"Beth," Mom says, speaking carefully now. "He's alive."

I open my eyes. The world looks the same as before. But it shouldn't. It should be brighter, more colorful, like a wondrous land of make-believe. I must be in some weird dream now.

Because what Mom is saying isn't possible.

"They found him this morning, honey. And now he's

home, he's home with us." She starts crying again, and then I realize why she sounded different. This is a happy cry.

My brain can't make sense of it. Sam + Found + Alive + Home = Sam is found, Sam is alive, Sam is at home. *Our* home.

It's all wrong. Sam is dead. Sam is gone. He disappeared three years ago. No, more than three years ago. Vanished. Like one of those kids on the milk cartons. You never see them again. You just don't.

"Beth, did you hear me?" Mom says.

Donal is looking over at me now with a concerned expression. He mouths something but I'm too foggy to read his lips.

"Beth?" Mom says.

I press the phone back against my ear. "Yes," I say.

Mom says, "Wherever you are, just come home."

"Okay," I say. "Okay. I'm coming." I end the call and drop the phone back in my bag. I just stay there, frozen. I should be screaming and jumping up and down. I should be the happiest person alive. But I don't feel like I'm in the real world.

"Beth? You okay?"

Donal sits up and I stare over at him and that's when I realize that I'm not dreaming all of this. "I have to go." I don't say good-bye or hug him or anything. I grab my stuff and rush out of his house into the overcast October day. It's not cold, but I'm shivering when I take out my car keys. I can hear Donal shouting my name from the front door of his house, but I don't look back. I steady my hand and get in my car and drive. I manage to obey traffic laws. I manage to get back to the southern side of the city, where we live in Pine Forest Estates, in the same house we lived in back when Sam went missing.

My stepdad, Earl, had wanted to move. But Mom was adamant that we stay. *What if he comes back and doesn't find us? How will he be able to find us if we move?* Ridiculous. Earl thought so, too. Ridiculous that she could even think that might happen, as if Sam were some stray dog who had simply lost his way.

But now we're the ridiculous ones.

Sam. I can see him. Brown hair, brown eyes, stubby little nose, sharp dimples. A classically cute kid. And he knew it. Even at that young age, he had the cockiness of a good-looking older boy. Mom always said he was going to grow up to be a heartbreaker. He's eleven in my mind. Always eleven. But of course he'd be fourteen now, wouldn't he? He *is* fourteen now.

I'm driving, getting closer and closer to our neighborhood, approaching a future I never knew existed.

That day in July was hot and sticky. A day when you just wanted to stay inside, which is what I was doing the day

Sam disappeared. The AC was on, but Earl was tight with money, and he didn't like us to run it too low. So basically we all suffered, with useless ceiling fans blowing the stuffy air around. At least my room faced the backyard, which was mostly shaded by a big oak tree. So it was a little cooler in there. But I remember the heat, because it became one more unpleasant thing about that day.

Mom and Earl were at work. We'd been fighting a lot back then—Earl and I. About the AC, about how late I stayed up, too late, about how I talked to Mom ("Don't be smart," he'd always say). She had married him the year before. He was fine, but I still didn't know him that well. Like, who was this guy living in my house and telling me what to do, pretending to be my real dad?

On *that day*, Sam pushed open my bedroom door, around two in the afternoon.

"What?" I said.

He was always barging in, which I hated. Normally I locked my door but that day I must have forgotten.

"What do you *want?*"

Let me pause to take in Sam that day: He was tall for his age. He played soccer, basketball, sometimes football, so I guess you can say he was an athletic kid, but he was too young to be muscular. He rode his bike, played video games. He was active, loud, energetic—a boy. That day he was wearing cargo shorts and a Superman T-shirt, looking flush, his dark hair slightly sweaty and stuck to his forehead.

"Josh and I are going to the mall." Josh Keller was our neighbor, a kid Sam's age. "We're gonna ride our bikes."

"You're kidding?" The nearest mall was two miles away along a busy road. It was a dying, crappy mall. And it was hot as hell out. "Why doesn't Mrs. Keller drive you?"

"She's too busy studying or something. We want to buy some new video games."

"Mom will kill you if she finds out."

"But she won't find out," he said, smiling that dimpled smile. He knew he could get away with anything. "You want to go with us?" he asked. Maybe he was trying to rope me in so we'd both get in trouble.

"No way," I said. The idea of riding a bike with two eleven-year-old boys, all the way down Skyland Boulevard as cars zoomed by, was too embarrassing to contemplate.

"I wish *you* could drive," he said.

I was fourteen, but turning fifteen that September, and I could get my learner's permit then. "Me too," I said.

"If I'm not back by the time Mom gets home, will you cover for me?"

I rolled my eyes and he gave me a pleading, innocent look—always performing, hamming it up. I have to admit, sometimes he was hard to say no to. We were brother and sister, after all. Even if he bugged me, we still had some kind of pact. Especially after Dad had left, when Mom's bad moods could strike us like thunder.

I sighed. "Fine."

He cracked his impish grin and gave me a thumbs-up. Then he shut my door.

I almost yelled, "Be careful!" or something like that. But I didn't say anything.

That was the last time I saw him.

Two or three hours later, I was still in my room. I'd fallen asleep while reading *Forever* for the millionth time. I'd been trying to read *My Antonia*, because it was on our summer reading list—this was the summer before I started high school—but, sorry, it was too hot for fine literature. It was the knock on the door that roused me, the sound of it whooshing open.

"Where's your brother?" Mom asked from the doorway. She was in her work clothes, but her hair—light brown like mine, but with gray roots because she wasn't good about coloring it—was sort of messy and wilted.

"I don't know," I said, feeling groggy. I rubbed my eyes and was almost surprised to find her still standing there. "He's probably at Josh's house." I looked at the little pink digital clock on my bedside table. It was just after five.

"I just saw Josh. He was riding his bike around. I didn't see Sam."

I thought about what Sam had said earlier, about how I should cover for him. If Mom found out he was riding his bike out of the neighborhood—one of many things that was strictly forbidden—then he was toast. Part of me wanted to rat him out right then and there. *Precious Sam disobeyed you.* But he always broke the rules, and it never mattered. Plus, if he got grounded he'd be in my hair a lot more than he already was. So I decided to play dumb. Let Mom figure it out on her own.

Besides, I didn't think anything was wrong. Bad things didn't happen to Sam. He'd fallen off his bike once, flipped and rolled, and all he had was a scraped elbow. When most of the kids in his third-grade class got the flu one winter, Sam was fine, not even a sniffle. He seemed invincible.

"Call his cell," I said. Mom had given us cell phones, but they were meant only for "emergencies."

"His phone's in his room. I checked."

"I don't know then."

Mom stared at me, folding her arms across her chest, which is what she always did when she meant business. "You're supposed to watch your brother," she said.

"He's not a baby."

Mom shook her head and walked out of my room without even bothering to pull my door shut.

A few seconds later I heard the front door slam. I went down the hall to the living room—the room we never used, with its white carpet and fancy furnishings—and looked outside and saw Mom marching across the street to the Kellers' house. Josh was riding his bike around his driveway in tight circles, but he stopped when he saw Mom approach. Josh was Sam's friend, but I knew Sam kind of thought he was a tool. A sissy. He had sandy blond hair and fair skin that freckled in the summer. He looked delicate, not like the rough-and-tumble type of boy that Sam was. He was quiet, polite, careful. Josh was the only kid who was Sam's age in the neighborhood. They were friends of convenience more than anything else.

"Josh hasn't seen Sam for hours," Mom said when she came back into the house. "He said they rode their bikes on the trails in the woods, but he went home and Sam stayed there."

The trails? What happened to the mall? "Yeah, I'm sure he's just still goofing around out there."

Mom nodded, pulling her hair back away from her face, barely pushing back panic. It's like she knew. Mother's intuition or something.

I went back to my room, but I didn't stay there long. I felt an uneasiness gnawing at my insides. I put *Forever* down again and went outside into the heat and over to the Kellers'. I felt better, doing something, instead of sitting around. Josh wasn't outside anymore, so I knocked on the door and Mr. Keller answered, the cold air from inside whooshing out at me. Mr. Keller was tall, blond going gray, wearing jeans and a blazer. "Hi, Beth."

"Is Josh here?"

"Yes, he is. You want to come in?"

"Can he just come out for a second?"

"Sure," he said. He yelled for Josh, who came down the stairs to the foyer and seemed to pause when he saw me. He came outside, and Mr. Keller shut the door and left us alone.

"Sam's not home," I said.

"I know. Your mom already came over here."

"Did you two ride to the mall earlier?"

He hesitated. "Yeah, we did. Did you tell your mom that?"

"No. She would flip out if she knew."

He seemed relieved. "We did start out together. But I came back."

"Why?"

Again, he hesitated. "I don't know. He was mean."

"What did he do?"

"Nothing."

"Josh, you just said he was mean. What did he do? You can tell me." I felt a twinge of tenderness for him. I wanted to say: *I know how he is. He can be a little brat.*

"Someone drove by and threw, like, a Coke at me. It got all over me and I fell off my bike and Sam . . . he just laughed. He laughed at me." He rubbed his elbow and I saw a scrape. There were a few scratches on his knees, too.

"Are you okay?"

He shrugged. His face reddened as he looked down at the ground.

"So you came home after that?"

He nodded. "I was all scratched up and all covered in dirt and stuff. So I rode my bike home. I—never mind."

"What?"

"I just rode off. I was mad at him. I didn't look back."

"Well, maybe he rode on to the mall. I'm sure he'll turn up soon."

Josh nodded again. "Yeah."

"I'm sorry he was mean to you."

"It's okay."

"I'll just tell Mom what you told me. That you were riding in the woods."

"Okay, good. I just didn't . . . I don't want to get him in trouble."

We were both protecting him. Or so we thought.

"He'll turn up," I said again, like if I said it enough it would come true. Josh looked at me then, relieved. He believed me. And, right then, I still believed myself.

Panic didn't truly set in for another hour or so, when Sam still hadn't shown up. Outside, the daylight was fading.

"And tell me again, what did Josh say?" Earl asked Mom when he got home and she started explaining. She'd already called him on his cell, which she hardly did when he was at a construction site job.

"He said he left him in the woods."

"So let's go look there." He was in his jeans, a sweaty white T-shirt, and his boots. He looked sunburned and overheated from the long day.

"I can help." That unease was gnawing at me again, and I wanted to do something to keep it at bay. Still, deep down I thought Sam would turn up eventually. Just like him to cause us so much worry.

"No, you stay here in case he comes back. Call my cell right away if you hear from him," Mom said.

I could tell she blamed me for this whole mess. Somehow it was my fault, and not Sam's. I almost told them right then that he had gone to the mall—that he had totally broken the rules. But then I'd be in trouble, too, for letting him. And anyway, they were already out the door, carrying flashlights for when it got dark, which I realized would be soon.

Where the hell was he? The idea that he would have vanished seemed ludicrous. Little girls were the ones who went missing. Boys knew how to take care of themselves. Nothing could happen to a tough boy like Sam.

I sat and waited, tried to distract myself with my book, then with TV. But nothing really worked. The unease spread through my whole body like a fever. I couldn't get my mind off Sam. As it got darker out, I started to get scared. I finally walked over to the Kellers'. I knew I was supposed to stay put, but I had to speak to Josh. He answered right after I knocked, like he was expecting me.

"He's not back yet?"

"My mom and my stepdad went to the woods to look for him. Josh, we have to tell them."

A voice floated from the living room. "What's going on, Joshie?" It was Mrs. Keller. She walked down the hall toward the foyer, barefoot with a pencil tucked behind her ear. She was in law school.

Weird, for a woman her age, my mother always said. But maybe she said that because she was jealous. Mrs. Keller was pretty—tall, with long dark hair, an elegant and smooth face with hardly ever any makeup on. She was going to be a lawyer, *a fancy rich lawyer,* Mom would say. We'd always been friendly and neighborly, but I could tell that Mom didn't feel totally comfortable around them. Maybe because Mom believed the Kellers thought they were better than us. Mr. Keller taught geology at the University of Alabama. Earl was in construction—the foreman, in charge of a lot of elaborate projects and renovations, a good job, but still. Mom was a secretary at an insurance company. She had never finished college, because she'd gotten pregnant with me. So everything was always my fault.

"Sam's missing," I told Mrs. Keller.

"What? Since when?"

"Since this afternoon." I looked at Josh, and I could see his blue eyes widen. *Don't tell*, he seemed to be saying. "Mom and Earl are looking for him in the woods."

"Can we help?" She turned then and shouted, "Hal!"

"Josh may be the last person who saw him," I said.

"When, Joshie?" she asked, stooping slightly and zooming her focus on to him. "When did you last see Sam?" She was normally a distracted person, kind of spacey, maybe because she was always thinking about legal cases and writing papers and stuff. But now she was giving us her full attention. I knew then that it was serious.

"I dunno. Like, at three maybe? We were in the woods." He looked back at me, like he was checking to see if we were still going to continue with this. But I knew we couldn't.

"You're sure it was three?" Mrs. Keller asked.

He stood there, sort of staring into space. "I dunno."

"Think. This is important."

Mr. Keller walked up then. "What's going on?"

I rehashed the whole situation.

"Josh? You sure it was three?" Mrs. Keller asked again.

Right then, as if under a bright light, Josh began to break down, started crying. "I dunno," he said, and then choked out the story, the truth about heading to the mall. "I came back home. I . . . left him."

Mrs. Keller was calm. Mr. Keller, too. They looked so

kindhearted and understanding, and I envied Josh for that. Not the glares and tears and accusatory tones that would normally come from Mom, not the put-upon looks from Earl.

"And what did Sam do?"

"He kept riding, I guess. He shouted at me to come back." He wiped a tear away, sniffled. "He yelled he was sorry. But I just kept riding."

I didn't know Sam had said he was sorry. I felt a pang then.

Mrs. Keller rubbed Josh's head, touched his cheek. "It's okay, it's okay."

"I'll go find your parents," Mr. Keller said, heading off toward the woods.

Beyond him, I watched the entry to Pine Forest Estates, hoping against hope that, right then, Sam would ride up the little slope on his bike. I was ready to yell at him, and hug him, too.

"We'll find him, Beth," Mrs. Keller said, putting her hand on my shoulder. I stepped away, staring off in vain toward where I hoped Sam might appear.

I sometimes later wished that I could do that moment all over. I wish I would have just stood there and enjoyed the touch of her hand. I sometimes wish I would have turned around and hugged her and let her comfort me. But instead I stood there, apart, clutching myself like I was cold, waiting. It's like I knew it was the beginning of a new sort of life—a new life for all of us—and I was bracing for what was yet to come.

Mr. Keller told Mom and Earl what had happened when he found them in the woods, and by the time they got back to our house they were frantic. We all trekked back to our house. Earl called the police, who seemed to ask a ton of annoying questions. Finally, an hour later, when it was full-on dark, the police came, a man and a woman. The man was tall with thick brown hair and matching thick eyebrows, and he was chewing gum, which seemed inappropriate. The woman seemed much more like someone official—she had dark skin, and her black hair was pinned back, and she smiled at us before putting on a serious, let's-get-down-to-business face. They talked to Mom and Earl and the Kellers. Then they spoke with Josh and me.

Josh was first, with all of the adults looking on in our living room. That room we never used, which was so quiet and undisturbed, now violated by all of this activity, by all these people. I stood and watched from the foyer, waiting my turn.

Josh didn't tell them the entire truth. For one thing, he didn't tell them that I'd known all along that they'd both gone off on their bikes to the mall. He covered for me. He'd started crying again, and I almost wished I was sitting next to him, holding his hand. But it was his mom sitting with him on the couch. It was her hand he was holding. I was leaning against the wall in the foyer, by myself.

When the policewoman, Officer Redmond, sat me down on the couch to go through *my* version of the story, I told her what I had told my mother. That as far as I knew Sam had gone off with Josh to ride their bikes in the woods at around two or three. She had this calming smile that made me think that everything was going to be okay.

Mom sat watching across from me on one of the boxy upholstered chairs, her eyes strained from fear. My hands were clenched fists at my sides. After Officer Redmond had finished with her questions, Earl came and sat next to me on the couch. He put his arm around me and said, "It's okay, Beth. It'll be okay."

I nodded, feeling the heft of him next to me. Feeling a little stunned by it. He'd never shown me this type of affection. I looked over at Mom. I wanted to see something in her eyes—forgiveness, or even anger. But she just looked blank.

The Kellers finally left, Josh giving me one last sad glance before they returned to their home where no one was missing.

Later, I crawled into my bed and fell asleep. I woke up sometime in the middle of the night. It was cold. I guess Earl finally decided to run the AC on low, to spare us from feeling hot on top of everything else.

I sensed someone was in my room. I could hear quiet

breathing. I adjusted my eyes to the darkness and saw Mom standing by the window, looking through the blinds, her form slightly illuminated by the moonlight outside. I watched her for as long as I could, and I almost said something—*Sorry, Mom, I'm so sorry*—but then I sensed her turn to look at me and I shut my eyes quickly. I listened as she left my room, shutting the door softly behind her.

I kept my eyes closed, but I never fell back asleep. Sam was out there, somewhere, and I was mad at him for doing this to us. And then I was scared for him. And then I started crying, wishing I could go back in time and grab him and tell him there was no way he was going to the mall. He was going to stay right here in this damned stuffy house with me.

When I drive up to the house, I expect—I don't know, a scene? But there's nothing like that. Mom's car is there, and so is Earl's. There's an ugly gray sedan I don't recognize. And a police car. That's it.

I park and sit in the driveway for a minute. I grab my phone from my bag—three texts from Donal, one asking me what's wrong, the next saying sorry if I got in trouble, then the last one just three question marks. I put it on silent and throw it back in my bag. I get out of the car, and right then I feel a chill, like I have a fever.

I don't want to go inside.

But I have to. I have to see him.

I don't know where Sam has been. Where do you go for three years? Without getting in touch, without letting us know you are alive? What happened? I can't even imagine what he looks like now.

I slowly open the door and walk into the kitchen. I hear voices from the den. I could turn around, go back outside, and drive away. But Earl walks into the kitchen, his eyes puffy. I don't think I've ever seen him cry. He comes to me and pulls me into a hug. "He's come back to us," he says, his voice cracking. I sink further into him, holding on tight. "Come see your brother."

I pull back and look up at him. "Where—I mean, what—"

Earl puts a finger to his lips, shakes his head. Now is not the time for questions, he seems to be saying. All of that can wait.

In the den, I see the police officer—the same one who interviewed me when Sam vanished, Officer Redmond. When she sees me, she smiles. There's a man in a suit, too, with thick black hair, and Officer Redmond's partner, that same tall, slouchy guy who's chewing gum, like last time. They're all standing around like they're unsure what to do. On the couch I see Mom sitting up straight. Her eyes are closed, a content look on her face, like she's having a pleasant daydream. She's clutching a teenage boy with shaggy brown hair who is sitting next to her, his eyes closed, too, his head resting on her shoulder.

I feel a tightness in my chest, because at first it's like I'm looking at Mom with some stranger. With his eyes closed, it's hard for me to get a good look at him. He could be anyone.

I notice something shiny on his eyebrow, visible even in the fading afternoon light of the room. I squint—a piercing? For a moment, I wonder if this is someone else. Maybe Mom finally lost her mind and grabbed this random kid off the street and won't let go of him, and that is why the police are here. It would almost make more sense.

"Sam," I say, barely croaking it out.

His eyes open. He lifts his head from Mom's shoulder, his eyes widening now, his mouth forming an oval, as if I'm the one who's suddenly reappeared.

He looks the same, but not the same. He's older of course. Gaunt but also muscular, filled out. His face thin and angular, a more pronounced jaw, and bulging Adam's apple. And yes, his eyebrow is pierced, and so is his lip, the right bottom corner. It hurts to look at it.

"Beth," he says. His voice is deeper than the last time I heard him. It sounds so strange. And it all happens so fast: He stands and staggers over and hugs me, and I hug him back, resting my head on his shoulder because that seems the natural thing to do. He's tall now, taller than me. I can feel the broadness of him. "Beth," he whispers. "Beth." I hold on to him, maybe a little too tightly, but it's like I have to make up for all the years that have gone by, all the hugs I've missed.

Finally, he pulls back gently and just stares at me, his dark brown eyes glassy. He's wearing a checked flannel shirt, unbuttoned, over a black T-shirt. He has on ratty jeans, sneakers.

Someone bought him these things, I realize.

Mom stands and comes over to us and pulls us all into an embrace, a clump of three. And soon I feel another hand on my shoulder—Earl's. I think I might suffocate, held in this group hug.

Once we all break apart, Mom looks at me with that relaxed expression and says, "I told you he'd come back to us," like I was so silly to ever doubt that.

Mom had spent almost all of her waking moments searching for him, even after the years went by. She started a website. She made calls. She focused almost all of her energy on this hope that he was out there.

She was right all along. And I was wrong. A cold kind of shame creeps through my body.

"The news conference will start in about twenty minutes," the man with the thick black hair says. "So we might want to get going."

"The what?" I ask.

"News conference," Earl says.

"About Sam?"

Earl grabs my hand, gently but with certainty, and walks us into the living room, away from everyone else. "Sam's been through a lot, Beth."

"But what? Where has he been? What—"

"We'll talk about this later. Right now we have to go to this news conference. The police and sheriffs want us to speak to reporters, before the story leaks out on its own. They want us to give a few statements, for the media."

I'm about to ask another question—I have about a thousand—but he puts his hand on my shoulder. "Later. I promise."

And just like that we're out of the door and into Mom's car. Earl sits up front and drives, and Mom crawls in the back with Sam. She doesn't want to let go of him. I'm about to sit up front, but Sam holds the backseat door open. "Beth, come back here. Please?"

I really don't want to, but I look at Earl and he nods, so I crowd into the backseat, Sam in the middle. He clutches my hand, tightly, as Earl starts to drive, following the police car and the sedan to wherever it is we're headed.

No one says anything. Sam is trembling next to me. I grip his hand more tightly, like that might help. And it does, I think. I can feel his trembling wind down.

My mind goes back to one night when he was just a baby. God, fourteen years ago. This same shaking person next to me. I remember the night so clearly. I woke up, and I could hear him in his room, crying like crazy, worse than usual. I climbed out of my bed or whatever it was I slept in at that age. I wandered into his room, where Mom and Dad were trying to calm him. Mom paced back and forth and patted his back, while Dad looked on, smiling like it was all a ridiculous joke.

Mom must have said, "Beth, go back to bed." But I stood there, gawking. How could I sleep with all this shrieking?

Mom sat down on a chair in the corner of the room, with the crying Sam on her lap. I wanted to cup a hand over his mouth to make the noise stop. But instead, his tiny fingers closed on mine, and he looked up at me. I can see it, his ugly pinched face, the streaks of dark brown hair pasted on his little mushy head, those big brown eyes. He hiccupped into silence, squeezing my hand with his little fingers, his eyes looking into mine like he'd never seen me before and was mesmerized. And maybe before that moment he really hadn't truly seen me. Maybe, all of a sudden, he realized who I was. His sister.

"Will you look at that," Dad had said.

Whispering, as if worried she might break the spell, Mom said, "Beth's got the magic touch."

I felt a glow inside. Sam gurgled and held my hand till his eyes got heavy and his little head drifted back to Mom's shoulder. For the first time, I loved him.

But sitting here now in the car, holding Sam's hand, the tightness still in my chest, I feel something hovering about the air, something—I don't know? Something not quite right. Something that tempers the elation and happiness and the ecstatic shock we're all feeling. I think of those questions again, those questions that can't be ignored: Where has Sam been? What has happened to him? Three years. Three years of what?

The police car turns down a street and Earl follows, and I see that we're headed to Pine Forest Elementary. Where Sam went to school before all this happened. The parking lot is full of cars and news vans. It's crazy, but it dawns on me: Sam's reappearance is a huge story. Not just for my family, but also for everyone else.

I feel Sam's fingers tighten on mine, and I sense him turning to look at me. But I stare straight ahead. I can't look into his eyes. Those eyes that hold the secrets of where he's been for over three years. Of what he might have gone through. I just try to breathe. Because if I take slow breaths then I can probably keep the tight ache in my chest from erupting.

CHAPTER 2

The White Truck

Josh

Nick and I are practicing crosscourt forehands. Back and forth, back and forth, a nice rhythm. Everyone else on the team has left for the day, but we're still going at it.

"You two are workhorses," Coach Runyon said once, and by his tone and the big smile on his face I could tell that he appreciated our hard work. That day, I told Nick that we had to keep it up and push ourselves harder than the others. Nick and I, we're just freshmen, but there's a good chance we'll play varsity tennis this coming spring. We're pretty good. Not just for our age, but for any age. Our team lost a lot of seniors, and to be honest the older guys on the team aren't as solid. We really have a shot at this.

I'm supposed to go to a student council meeting at four. I'm vice president of my class. Homecoming's next week, and we have to decide on our parade float design, the nominations for homecoming court, stuff like that. After that, I'll go home and do my homework. I'm making all As so far, just like I did all through middle school. Everyone said high school was so tough, so different, but so far it's been a piece of cake.

Dad thinks I'm taking on too much. He teases me, says that it's okay if I relax now and then, but what can I say? I like to stay busy.

I guess I take after Mom in that way. She works long hours at a big firm in town—well, big for Tuscaloosa—doing bankruptcy law. She's never home early. She has to prove herself by putting in a lot of time. Just like Nick and I are doing on the court. Dad's a geology professor at the university, so his hours are more flexible. He's usually the one who makes dinner nowadays, and who picks me up in the afternoons.

So I'm surprised to see Mom's car drive up and pull into a parking spot alongside the courts. At first I think maybe it's someone else's car that just looks like hers. But then Mom gets out. I smack a forehand into the net. I drop my racket head and look over again. She waves. She's wearing shades, even though it's an overcast day.

"Hold on," I shout to Nick, who's staring over at her, too, maybe annoyed she messed up our rally. I cross two empty courts to get to the tall chain-link fence that separates the courts from the lot, and when I do, before I can even say hi and ask what she's doing here, she says, "You need to come with me."

"What is it?" I ask. It's not like Mom to just show up like

this, and the sunglasses are hiding her expression, so my heart starts going a million miles a minute. "Where's Dad?" I say.

"Dad's fine. Just grab your stuff and come to the car. I'll tell you then. Everything's okay."

"Okay," I say, feeling a little reassured, but still a little weirded out. I cross the courts again and grab my stuff. "I have to go," I yell at Nick, who's still standing on the baseline fingering his racket strings.

"What's up?" he asks. He starts walking over. Nick is my best friend. He's the reason I started playing tennis, to be honest.

"I don't know. My mom's being strange."

"Wait up," Nick calls as he gathers his things, but I head toward the gate without him. I see Mom watching me. She has her hands in her coat pockets, like she's cold. When I finally get to the car, I ask, "What is it?"

Mom takes her hands out of her pockets and removes her sunglasses. Her eyes are red. "I have some . . . good news," she says, but in a way that makes it seem like she has *bad* news.

Nick jogs up right behind me.

"Nick, you may as well know, too," she says. "Word's starting to spread."

"About what?" I ask.

She clears her throat, looks right at me. "They found Sam Walsh. He's home—he's alive."

For a second there's just the noise of cars whizzing by on Fifteenth Street. Just the sound of my own breathing.

"Whoa," Nick says, breaking the silence.

I just stare at her. At first it doesn't make sense. Sam? Who is Sam?

But I know.

"The police found him, in Anniston."

"Anniston?" Do I even know where that is? "He's alive?" I ask, but really I'm just repeating the words to make them real to myself. When I thought about Sam, he wasn't someone who was alive. But he wasn't someone who was dead, either. He was just gone. And, to be honest, I tried not to think about him at all.

"There's going to be a news conference at Pine Forest Elementary. Sam's going to be there, with his family. I want—I think we need to be there."

"Whoa," Nick says again.

"Nick, you should call your mother," Mom says.

He nods and starts digging in his bag for his cell. Nick was friends with Sam, too. In fact, he and Sam were best friends back in elementary school. It was only after Sam went away that Nick and I became close.

I look at Mom and she smiles at me, but it's a weird smile, like she's faking it to cover for some other feeling. I feel my heart start to beat faster and faster, how it does before a big match. Sam's back. Sam's *alive*. It's unbelievable.

I need to focus. Like when I'm losing a match and have to tell myself to just take it point by point, to not panic. "Should I change?" I ask Mom. I'm in my tennis clothes.

"Yes, okay," Mom says, nodding distractedly. "But hurry."

I jog through the side door of the gymnasium and into the empty locker room and start to change back into my regular clothes. If I keep my mind busy—if I focus on tying my shoes and buttoning my shirt—then I can trap out other things. Nick barges in.

"Dude, this is insane," he says. "I mean, I thought Sam was, like, dead. He's been missing for what—?"

"Three years," I say. Three years, three months. How many days?

"Holy shit. I mean, what happened to him?"

"How should *I* know?" I say. I stop tying my shoes and look up at him. "How should I know?"

"Hey, chill." He sits on a bench across from me, leans forward. "You okay?"

I nod again. I continue tying my shoe. "I'm fine," I say, speaking to the floor.

It was July. July 12. Mom was still in law school then, taking a course so she could finish that fall. She was always studying. Dad was teaching summer school, so he was on campus a lot.

Sam lived across the street with his mom, stepdad, and his sister. I guess Sam and I were what you would call friends. I don't think he really liked me much, honestly. But we were the same age. I'd known him since I was in first grade, and we were neighbors. During the summer, we'd ride our bikes around Pine Forest, or into the woods that butted up against our backyard, which had these well-worn trails and small mounds of dirt we could jump, though I never had the nerve to do anything too tricky, like shake my wheels about while flying through the air, which Sam did all the time.

"Pussy," Sam would always say when I refused to do any tricks. Then he would laugh, so I couldn't tell if he was being serious or if he was joking.

When it got really hot, Sam and I would stay inside and play video games or watch movies—usually at my house. I think he liked my house better because he fought with his sister a lot, and with his stepdad, who he called Earl but who I called Mr. Manderson. And his mom was tired and grumpy most of the time.

Mom and Dad liked Sam. He always put on his best face with them. Mom called him a charmer. But to me he was unpredictable. Nice one minute, mean the next.

That day in July, Sam was at my house and wanted to play this video game he'd heard about, but which I didn't own. What was it called? *Alien Invasion* or something dumb like that. I never really liked video games; I only ever played when Sam came over. So he thought we should go buy it—we could put in together, with our allowances. That sounded fine to me. I didn't really care.

The only problem was that Mom was studying and wouldn't drive us, and Sam's mom was at work.

I pressed Mom once more. "Please?"

"Honey, I have way too much to do. Besides, you don't need another video game. Play with the ones you have." Then she turned back to her big red legal books.

"We could bike to McFarland Mall," Sam said when we were back outside.

McFarland was the second-rate mall that was two or three miles down a busy road, but they had a decent video game store there. "That's too far."

"Not on our bikes."

"It's too hot. Besides, I'm not allowed to anyway."

"I'm not either. But so what? Do you always do what Mommy says?"

"Not always."

"Yeah you do," he said. "Goody Two-shoes."

"I am not," I said. I once stole a pack of Life Savers from a Publix. Sometimes I peed in the shower.

He smirked again, like he was going to challenge me. "Then let's go," he said. "Screw the rules."

I sighed. "Well, if we go, I need to get my money."

"Then get it. I'll go get mine. Meet you back out here in five minutes."

I went up to my room and grabbed my money from the

small top drawer in my dresser, enjoying the coolness of the house. Part of me didn't want to go back outside. I didn't want to ride to the mall. It's like I somehow knew it would be a disaster.

When I passed Mom on the way out, she was still totally wrapped up in her studying. I doubt she even heard me leave the house.

Back outside, I waited. *There's still time to back out*, I thought. Just then Sam rushed out of his house, hopped on his bike, and rode over. "Let's go."

In the car on the way to this news conference, I can't even remember the last time Mom and I talked about Sam. We'd moved away from Pine Forest a year after Sam went missing, and once we were gone it was like we forgot about anything that had happened there.

"Are they sure it's Sam?" I ask, still thinking it's all so unreal.

"What?" she says, like I've asked something dumb. "Of course they are."

"Where was he?" I ask.

Mom hears me, but she doesn't say anything for a few minutes. "He was in Anniston."

"You said that. But why?" I wait for more, but she doesn't offer anything. "Did he run away?" I know this isn't true, even when I ask it.

"No," she says. "He was living . . . he was with some man. We don't know much more than that. But he's okay." I see her furrow her brow, like she has doubts.

I start to feel a little queasy.

"We don't know what he's gone through," she says. "But none of that matters right now." Mom has one hand on the steering wheel, but with her free hand she reaches over and grabs mine. I let her, but I don't squeeze back. She stops at a red light.

Suddenly, I don't want to go to this news conference. I don't want to see Sam. I want to go back to when Nick and I were hitting tennis balls across the court, when the day and evening before me was plotted out, when there were no surprises. I turn and look at Mom. "I'm missing my student council meeting. Everyone will wonder where I'm at."

"It's okay. You can miss just this once."

The light is still red. Any minute it will turn green, and it will be a straight shot to the elementary school. That school I always hated. I unlock the door and unbuckle my seat belt. I step out of the car. Just before I slam the door, I hear Mom say, "Josh!"

I don't run. I just walk. I know this road. It's close to our old neighborhood, so I head back away from there. I walk and walk and then I hear gravel crunching, the sound of someone running behind me. I look back and see Mom.

"Josh!" Mom catches up and gets in front of me and grabs

me by the shoulders. "What are you doing?" She looks at me like she's pissed, but I see her eyes soften with alarm. She touches my cheek and wipes something away. "Oh, Joshie." I hate when she calls me that, and she knows it. But she pulls me tight against her, and my cheeks are wet against her shirt. I hadn't realized that I'd started crying.

"It's going to be okay," Mom says.

I pull back. I sniffle and wipe my nose with my sleeve. She's looking at me like I'm breaking her heart. Cars speed by and suddenly I'm embarrassed, exposed. "We're going to be late," I say.

"Are you sure you're up for it?"

"Yes," I say. I'd rather go home, or back to school. But a picture of Sam has been piecing together in my brain. Sam on that hot summer day, in his Superman T-shirt, cargo shorts, his brown hair wilted in the sun. And I know I have to see him to really believe he's back. That he's grown up, just like I have. That he's okay.

That day, Sam and I biked up the slight hill on the shaded side of the street, the side by the woods. Once we reached the top, the woods ended, and we burst into the sun, which was high in the sky, beating down on us.

We took a left onto Skyland Boulevard, a busy thruway from the west side of town to the east, broken in the middle by a grassy median. We rode our bikes on the left side shoulder, facing the oncoming traffic, as we'd always been told to do. We biked past the Toyota dealership, the entrance to a neighborhood called Eastlake, and then past Buddy's, a convenience store. Cars whizzed by. Sam sped ahead, and I shouted for him to wait up. I was getting tired already, and overheated. My shirt was sticking to my back. My forehead was dripping sweat. I had forgotten my hat. Up ahead, on the left, was the Department of Motor Vehicles, set well back from the road and fronted by a wide lawn. We still had a long way to go—more strip malls to pass, churches, even a cemetery. I knew all the landmarks well; we'd driven past them hundreds of times. But it all looked weird now, outside and up close. I kept pedaling, trying to catch up to Sam. Finally, I saw him slow down and circle back, probably annoyed at me for being a slowpoke.

Just then a bright red truck with a loud muffler sped toward us. I could see that there were a few guys wearing sunglasses and baseball caps sitting in the back of the truck. They drove by, and it was like time slowed, because I could see the two boys in the back—maybe college age, maybe older high school—sipping big plastic cups of soda. One flashed a grin and yelled "Faggot!" as they zoomed past. And then a cold explosion of liquid landed on my back. I was so surprised that I slammed on my brakes and then stuck my foot out to catch myself. But it wasn't enough. I fell to my side, the bike crashing on top of me.

There I was, in the dirt and gravel on the side of the road, covered in something wet. I tried to stand, but I had a burning scrape on my elbow and my leg. I saw an empty Chick-fil-A cup that had rolled to the side of the road.

I finally stood up, my heart racing. Up the road I saw the truck getting smaller and smaller, and then it was gone. I tried to brush the dirt from my legs and arms, but some was mixed in with the blood from my scrapes. I peeled my shirt back, briefly, before it stuck back again. I was a mess. I fought the urge to cry. Sam pedaled up, laughing.

I don't know why I expected sympathy.

"Wow, that was amazing!" he said. "They hit you like a bull's-eye!"

"It's not funny," I said.

"Are you okay?" he said, but he was still smiling.

"No," I said, hoping my voice didn't crack.

He snickered. "That cup must have been totally full of Coke. It looked like you got hit by a diarrhea water balloon."

I'd had enough of it. I hated him. I hated the world. I felt a kind of anger I'd never felt before.

"Fuck you," I said, feeling a perverse thrill saying those words. I picked up my bike, hopped on it, headed back toward home. I was still in pain, but that almost didn't matter anymore.

"Hey, where you going?" Sam called.

I didn't respond. I kept pedaling.

"Come on, don't go home! I'm sorry!"

I had my money in my pocket. He wouldn't be able to buy the video game without me. A short distance later, I heard him shout, "Pussy!"

I turned around, quickly, and yelled "Fuck you!" again.

They were the last words I spoke to Sam. I don't even know if he said anything back.

I kept pedaling as fast as I could. The trek was slightly uphill at that point. I started to feel sick. I had to stop and toss my bike down again. I bent over the side of the road and coughed and puked up a nasty puddle of clear liquid. My eyes were watery, and the sun continued to beat down on me.

At first I didn't notice the truck. I was too worried that more puke was coming. But then I snapped out of it and heard the purr of an engine nearby. I stood up and turned around and there it was, pulled halfway onto the shoulder, just a few feet away from me.

"You okay?"

I had to squint to see into the truck. It was a dusty white. Even though it wasn't dented or anything, it was old. You could tell. In the driver's seat was a heavy man, wearing sunglasses. He had a beard and messy brown hair. "You okay?" he asked again.

Don't talk to strangers. We'd all been told that since we were little kids. But that was dumb. You couldn't avoid it in real life. "Yeah," I said.

"I saw what those creeps did to you back there," he said, cocking his head.

I looked back down the road. Sam was nowhere in sight.

"You okay?" he said, for the third time. This time he took his shades off. Even from several feet away I could see one of his eyes was goofy—like it was focusing in a different direction than the other.

"I'm okay."

"Let me give you a ride home."

I stared at him.

"You can put your bike in the back. You live around here?"

My legs felt frozen. It was like one of those dreams—where someone approaches from a darkened hallway, coming right toward you, and you can't move and you can't speak or scream, and then you wake up. I woke up right then. I picked up my bike. I said, "No, thanks, I'm fine."

"You sure? It's no trouble." I heard a metallic click as he opened his door, and then a beeping noise.

I jumped onto my bike and shot off, speeding up the hill toward the road that would take me to Pine Forest. I glanced back a few times and saw he was still parked there, watching me, the door open. I pedaled faster. I finally turned onto the road, which sloped downhill, so I picked up speed. As I reached the part of the street that leveled out, I glanced back again and saw the white truck just turning onto the road. I looked ahead and figured he'd reach me before I could turn into the neighborhood, before I'd be anywhere close to home, so I steered my bike across the street into a driveway of one of the houses that wasn't really part of our neighborhood.

I had no idea who lived there. I tossed my bike down in the garage and banged on their kitchen door, banged and banged so hard I thought the glass panes might shatter. Through the panes of the door I saw that the kitchen was dark. Maybe no one was home. And just then I noticed that there were no cars in the garage. But there was a high wooden gate that led from the garage to the backyard, and I saw a dog sticking its nose through the wooden slats, sniffing and panting. I could see through the slats that it was a harmless sweet yellow Lab. Just as I heard the truck approach I reached and unlatched the wooden gate and went into the backyard where the dog jumped all over me excitedly.

"Hey, boy, hey," I whispered. "Shh. Calm down." I managed to both pet and calm the dog and peer through the slats at the same time. I saw the white truck drive past the house.

My heart pounded. I closed my eyes but tried to listen carefully for the sound of the truck, to see if it had stopped, or if it was turning around and coming back. The dog was still jumping on me, plastering me with licks and jabs of his wet nose. I turned and looked out at the backyard, and saw that the chain-link fence backed up to some woods that surrounded Pine Forest. I could climb that fence and escape that way if I had to, run through the woods, where I'd eventually reach one of the houses in our neighborhood. I looked to see if there were any sticks or weapons handy. I was making plans, my mind racing, my heart still beating like crazy.

I sat there for a few minutes. I opened my eyes and looked through the slats again, still listening carefully. The road led to a few other neighborhoods past ours, then dead-ended at a small lake. Maybe the truck would turn back. I had to be careful.

I continued petting the dog's head gently. I could have sat there all day doing that. But ten minutes had passed. I felt silly. The whole incident was probably nothing. Just some man who lived in one of the other neighborhoods, on his way home. I almost felt bad, for biking away like I did, but better safe than sorry.

I petted the Lab good-bye and nudged my way out of the gate. I walked to my bike and then peered out of the garage. The coast was clear. I rode home fast and parked my bike in the garage and walked to the front door. Before going in the house I stood there, remembering Mom was inside, still studying. I couldn't let her know anything had happened. I opened the door gently. Once inside, I peered out the little side windows. I thought Sam might ride up at any moment, ready to apologize.

But of course, he never did.

That afternoon is all kind of a blur to me now. Beth came over a few times, asking where Sam was, and Beth's mom did the same, and then everyone panicked because Sam still hadn't come back by the time it got dark out.

We all went over to Sam's house, to wait for the police. When they finally came, a man and a woman in dark official uniforms, their guns in holsters, their faces grim and serious—that's when I got scared. That's when I started to worry that something bad was happening. That something bad *had* happened.

I sat in their living room as I went over everything for what felt like the millionth time that day. I saw Beth hovering in the background. "And that's all, Josh?" the policewoman said, like she was trying to squeeze just a little more out of me. Like maybe she knew I was holding something back.

Now, I remember thinking. Now I should mention the man in the white truck. But to be honest, I thought it was unlikely that the two things—the man and Sam—were connected. I'd just overreacted, like a wuss. That guy was probably just trying to be nice, and I would get him in trouble. It was nothing. Besides, I'd never even looked at the truck's license plate. I couldn't even remember what make or model it was. My image of it—and the man himself—were fuzzy already, and getting fuzzier by the minute.

I said, "No, that's all. I've told you everything I remember."

When Mom pulls up to Pine Forest Elementary, the parking lot is packed. There are vans with satellite dishes taking up multiple parking spaces. I spot the local news logo on one, and also CNN, ABC, CBS, NBC, Fox.

"This is a circus," Mom says, circling the lot, finally finding a spot.

Is this a big news story? I guess I already know the answer. Kid missing for three years suddenly reappears, alive. Kid missing for three years, living only a few hours away all this time. It's crazy even if you don't know the boy in question. And if you *do* know him? If you were the last person to see him? It's unbelievable. Like a movie or something. But more than that. It's like I had stepped through a thin wall into another world, where fantastical things were possible. If Sam could come back alive, then maybe in this world I could fly. Maybe in this world I could twitch my nose and disappear.

"Josh? You ready to go in?"

I follow Mom into the gymnasium, where a huge crowd is gathered. The scene inside is noisy and festive, like everyone is there to welcome home a victorious sports team. Toward the front, underneath one of the basketball hoops, a long table is set up, as well as a podium. A bunch of folding chairs are out in front of this, most of the seats filled with people already, mainly adults. Who are these people? Why are they here? Do they even know Sam, or his parents?

Off to the side, reporters and people with cameras are all huddled together, roped off near a bunch of gym mats. I recognize a few of them from TV.

Mom and I stand in the back, behind all the chairs, so we have a clear view of the tables where Sam and his family are supposed to sit.

"You okay?" Mom says. "We can leave if you don't think—"

"I'm fine."

I'm not fine. I don't know what I am. Nervous, scared, excited, all of it mixed together. Still, I want to stay. I have to. I have to see him.

Finally, a sheriff or a policeman—some man wearing a uniform—comes out to the podium. The crowd immediately quiets down.

I watch, but I can't take in anything this man says. I'm waiting for Sam to appear. And then finally they're announced, the family, and out comes Mr. Manderson, and then Beth, followed by Mrs. Manderson, holding a boy's hand. Of course it's Sam. I know it. He's taller, lanky but with broad shoulders. His brown hair is shaggy, and from a distance it looks like he has piercings or something. He seems shy as the crowd starts to cheer, like we are all welcoming some reclusive rock star at a concert.

The family sits at the table in front of microphones that have been set up. Sam sits next to his mom and briefly leans his head on her shoulder, like a little kid would.

I stare at him, maybe hoping he'll notice me. He looks dazed, almost like he's not sure where he is.

Mrs. Manderson finally speaks into the microphone. "I always knew this day would come. I never gave up hope. I never stopped trying to find him. I never stopped praying."

I glance at Beth, sitting next to Sam. She's got her eyes focused down at the table, so I can't see her expression. She has to be happy, right?

"God has answered our prayers," Mrs. Manderson says, and the crowd murmurs in agreement. She looks at Sam fondly, and hugs him close before releasing him. Then she starts answering questions.

Right then Sam seems to come out of his daze and notice the crowd. He scans the room, like he's searching for someone.

Suddenly the gymnasium feels hot, too crowded. I look over at Mom, and she's riveted, her eyes glassy. I slowly back away through the crowd and once I clear the thickness of people I head for the doors. I push through them and see that it's dark out now, which is a relief for some reason.

Time hasn't stopped after all. The world's still turning. I stand there for a minute, picturing this new, older Sam. He didn't see me, I'm sure of that. But would he have recognized me? I've changed, too. Nick and I, we do push-ups and weights at the gym his dad belongs to. And I'm taller. I'm not the kid he used to know. Not the kid he could push around and laugh at.

"Josh?"

I turn and see Mom leaving the gym, walking toward me. "Honey, are you okay?"

I walk toward the car. "I want to go home," I say, not stopping.

When we get to the house, I just go to my room, and Mom lets me without sitting me down for a talk, thank God. I have homework to do. I turn my cell off. I know Nick has been texting. Max and Raj and Ty, too, all of my friends. I open my book bag and get to it, laying my folders and books and notes out on my bed, next to my desk, attacking everything in an orderly fashion. Spanish and biology quizzes tomorrow, so those are first. A set of algebra problems. A chapter in my Alabama history textbook. In English, we're reading *The Red Badge of Courage*, which is kind of boring, but I manage to get through about twenty pages before Mom knocks on the door. "Josh, dinner's ready," she says.

"I'm not really hungry," I reply, maybe a little too loudly.

She opens the door then, looks at me while I sit at my desk with my books. "Do you want to talk about it?" she says. "I know it's a lot to take in."

"I've still got a lot of homework." I turn back to my book, but I know she's staring at me, like she's trying to see if I'm okay or if I'm going to break down and cry or something.

"If you get hungry, come down and I'll fix you something. Or I could order you some pizza. Whatever you want."

"Okay," I say, really trying to focus on the words in the book. *The trees about the portal of the chapel moved soughingly in a soft wind.* Soughingly? I look to the door, and Mom's still there, and I smile at her and look back at the novel.

Finally, she closes the door. I listen, and I can hear faint voices downstairs. Mom and Dad, probably talking about me. Probably worried.

I shut the book. I sit there a minute. My phone is still off. Three years.

I wake up my laptop. Just a few minutes, then back to work. I go online and type in Sam's name and a ton of articles appear. I click on the first one and start reading, but there's not much information. He was found yesterday. The police knocked on an apartment door, looking for this man named Russell Lee Hunnicutt, and they found him. But they also found Sam. Sam was living there. When they asked, he told them he was Sam Walsh. "Can you take me home now?" he said.

My heart races as I scroll down the article. I need to see the man they arrested. The man he was living with. The man who took him.

And then there he is, near the end of the first article. I guess it's the mug shot after he was arrested. He's a big man, with messy brown hair, a not very well-trimmed beard. He's facing the camera, scowling. And those eyes. One of them looks off to the side. A lazy eye, that's what you call it. I remember now.

I just sit there and stare at him, hoping my own eyes are playing tricks on me. I blink and blink, but the picture stays the same.

It's the man in the white truck. I'm sure of it.

I slap my laptop closed and sit there. At first I think I'm going to be sick. I can't breathe. But then I count down from ten, like I do just before every match I play. *Ten nine eight seven six five four three two one.*

I open my eyes. *Everything is going to be okay.* That's what Mom said, wasn't it? Sam is home now. He's with his mom and his stepdad and Beth. He's back, probably sleeping in his old bed tonight, in his old bedroom in Pine Forest Estates. Sam's home and alive. *Everything is going to be okay.*

CHAPTER 3

Holding It Together

Beth

When Earl drives up to our house, news vans are lined up and down the street, like they followed us from the conference. Or maybe these are different trucks. People seem to be everywhere—in their own yards, watching what's going on at ours, and also surrounding our driveway in the street. Neighbors, well-wishers, but also reporters, TV people—the lights of their cameras blast in at us. Some neon-orange traffic cones are blocking our driveway, acting as a sort of barrier. Two cops see our car and move the cones aside. No one says anything as Earl eases the car into the driveway, but the crowd breaks into applause and cheers and I can hear things being shouted, like "Welcome home!" and "We love you!"

Earl pulls into the garage and kills the engine. Sam, sitting next to me, tightens his grip on my hand but doesn't say anything. He hasn't said a word since we left the news conference. Before we'd gone to face all the people and reporters, I'd excused myself and gone into the girls' locker room. I wanted to cry, to loosen the tightness that had been building in my chest, and I thought about going into a stall to do just that. Instead, I splashed cold water on my face in the sink. I knew I had to hold it together. And I did, sitting there calmly like a good daughter.

Earl unbuckles his seat belt and looks back at us and nods. I guess we all take this as a sign to get out of the car and deal with this craziness. The cheers and noise and shouting erupts all over again when we get out.

Mom grabs Sam's hand and walks toward the edge of the driveway, where the crowd is held back by a few policemen. Earl hovers close behind, but I stay where I am. I feel kind of light-headed, just seeing everyone crowded around like that.

Mrs. Sykes from next door is being held back by the cops, but she's waving and Earl nods to the police and they let her through. She's known both Sam and me since we were little kids, and used to babysit us a lot. She can't stop crying and hugging Mom, saying "It's a miracle, it's a miracle." Then she latches onto Sam, hugging him in what looks like a crushing embrace, even though he's taller and bigger than she is. "Baby," she says again and again. I look at the other people lingering and watching, with smiles on their faces and tears in their eyes. "Sam! Sam!" The police fend off the news reporters who are holding cameras and microphones. A few more neighbors are waving at us, beckoning to get through, and again Earl gives the go-ahead and a few are allowed to approach. That older couple whose kids have moved away, the Albertsons. Weird Mr. Davis, who has three loud Yorkshire terriers that he takes for walks while he smokes cigarettes. Mrs. Tomek and her ten-year-old son Ruben. The young couple, the ones who moved into the Kellers' old house—I forget their names. They don't even *know* Sam. All these people, they swarm around Mom and Sam, while Earl keeps watch. I back away toward the house, and no one notices, thankfully.

When I get inside the phone is ringing but I ignore it and just stand against the counter, glad to be away from the lights and noise. Just hours ago I was skipping class and doing homework and kissing a boy and now I'm at home and my dead brother is alive and it seems like the whole world is outside, grabbing at us, and it's just too much for me to process.

Water, I need water. I grab a glass and fill it at the sink and gulp so fast that I choke a little. I fill it again and guzzle more.

The phone finally stops ringing, but I can still hear the commotion outside. I don't look out the window. I just try to breathe normally. And it seems to work. The tightness in my chest eases even more. I'm safe at home.

After a few more minutes, Mom and Earl and Sam finally come inside. Mom sees me and comes over and hugs me. Sam just kind of stands there, unsure of what to do.

He's not used to his own house.

The phone in the kitchen—the landline Mom insisted we keep because that was the only number she knew Sam had memorized—starts ringing again. "I'll deal with this," Earl says, answering.

"You okay?" Mom asks Sam. Sam just flashes this weird cautious smile, the kind of smile you'd offer a stranger who held a door open for you.

He hadn't said a word at the news conference—he hadn't been allowed to. Mom did most of the talking, with Earl chiming in here and there, and then the sheriff and prosecutor and other people answering questions from the press.

I just sat there, silent. I kept stealing looks at Sam. But I couldn't look at him too long. I don't know why, but it made me uncomfortable, like he might catch me and see something on my face that would upset him.

"Come," Mom says now, grabbing Sam's hand. She leads him through the den, down the hallway.

"Here's your room," she says, as if Sam has never lived here.

Sam lets go of her hand and sits on his bed and looks around. Mom hasn't changed a thing in here since he vanished. The same baby blue paint on the walls, the same checkered bedspread on the bed. A stuffed elephant wearing a "Bama" T-shirt perched on his pillow. A few soccer trophies stacked on a shelf over his bed. Some framed photos—me and Sam, Sam and Mom, Sam standing in a field in his soccer uniform, a soccer ball perched under his foot—sit atop the dresser, along with a mason jar full of dusty coins.

Sometimes she would ignore the rest of the house, but every week, Mom would go in and vacuum and dust this room, even change the sheets, as if someone actually lived there. But I rarely set foot in here. It felt like a sacred space that shouldn't be disturbed.

Sam lies down on the bed, in a tucked position. "It's good to be home," he says, as if he's only been away for a few weeks. Then he closes his eyes. He hasn't said much, but I can still tell there is something different about the way he speaks. Of course he has a deeper voice now, but that's not what I mean. It's like everything he says is practiced and careful.

Earl calls for Mom from the kitchen. She turns and looks down the hall, but then back at Sam. She rubs her eyes, like she's worried she's hallucinating. Earl shouts again.

Mom sighs. "Will you stay with him?" she asks me. "I need to see what he wants. Can you do that for me?"

"Yeah," I say.

She pauses, glances over at Sam one more time. I can tell she probably doesn't ever want him out of her sight again. But she walks out of the room, leaving the door cracked a smidge. I sit on the floor by the door and lean against the wall, tucking my knees under my arms. Sam's eyes are still closed, but I know he isn't asleep. I scrutinize him, like maybe if I stare hard enough I can start to see the boy he was three years ago.

This boy—he's different. But not just his appearance. That bratty kid is nowhere to be seen. The boy in front of me is quiet, shy. Maybe a little afraid. The Sam I knew loved horror movies. He wasn't afraid of the dark. I feel a lump in my throat and I swallow.

I know some man had Sam. In Anniston. I don't know much more than that. Everyone was very deliberate at the conference, and didn't talk about anything that specific. It was all happiness and excitement and God answering our prayers and miracles.

Finally, Sam opens his eyes. "Beth?"

"Yeah?"

"I'm really here. It's not a dream?"

He sounds so afraid, so unsure of things. That lump in my throat, I feel like it might choke me, so I swallow again, and another time, before I am ready to respond. "It's not a dream," I say. "You're really home."

He smiles, just a slight smirk. My heart leaps. *There* is Sam. There he is! But then he closes his eyes, and the old Sam is gone.

I can hear Mom and Earl down the hall, their voices on the phone. I know my friends are probably trying to reach me. Other classmates, too. And Donal. Donal who kissed me earlier, which now feels like a hundred years ago. My phone is likely clogging up with texts, my Facebook wall exploding with messages from friends and even strangers. But I just sit there, watching Sam, hoping we can hold everyone and everything off for a little bit longer. I want to live in this quiet bubble.

A little later, Mom comes back to Sam's room. She whispers, "Is he asleep?"

Sam opens his eyes and looks right at her. "No," he says. She goes to the bed and crawls behind him and clutches him, and he closes his eyes and leans back into her. I keep waiting for Mom to cry, but she just strokes his hair, her eyes closed, that contented smile on her face. Mom smiling is such an odd sight that she looks weird, almost crazy.

I leave them and go to my room and shut the door. It's only eight or so, not bedtime, but I feel so tired from everything that has happened. Like I could sleep for days.

I wake with a start, not sure how long I've been out. I look at my clock and see that it's a little after midnight. But I'm not sleepy at all now. I have a feeling I've missed something important.

I get off my bed and open my bedroom door. I look down the hall and see light coming from the kitchen. In the other direction, Sam's bedroom door is shut, but a strip of light still glows under the door. I think about knocking, but then I hear Mom's voice. I creep closer but I can't really make out what she's saying. Then I smell cigarette smoke from the other direction. I walk to the kitchen and there's Earl sitting at the table. He's got a cigarette lit and has a glass of brown liquid in front of him. Mom had said no smoking in the house, especially since she'd quit last year. Normally, the smell of smoke bothers me. But Earl deserves whatever he wants.

I sit down and he smiles at me. He looks so tired, his normally thick reddish-blond hair limp, little bags under his eyes, his usually well-trimmed beard a little scruffy. He's always looked so robust to me, but tonight he seems flattened.

"You should be in bed," he says.

"I fell asleep for a bit. But now I'm not tired."

"That makes two of us."

"Mom's still in there with him," I say.

Earl nods, takes a drag from his cigarette, exhales. "He can't sleep. He didn't want her to leave him."

On TV, people always say "I need a drink" after a rough day, so I reach and take a sip of Earl's and he doesn't stop me. It burns going down, but I like it. I look at him and he shakes his head. I crack a slight smile. We sit there in silence for a bit, enjoying the peace. I guess the news vans are long gone, or else shut down for the night.

"Your father called," Earl says.

I try not to look surprised, but I am. I'd almost forgotten about him. After the divorce, when I was nine, he'd moved all the way to Ohio, where my grandparents—his parents—lived. He visited once each summer, for three years running, but that stopped—he always had an excuse. He called at Christmas and sent birthday cards with measly checks inside and swore he wanted us to visit him in Columbus, but no real invitation ever came.

"He wanted to speak to Sam, but your mother wouldn't let him. Not yet."

"Oh," I say, not wanting to ask the question that comes next, but asking anyway: "Did he ask to speak to me?"

Earl looks down at his drink. "I don't know." He looks like he's about to say something else, but he knows I don't want to hear any crap.

"Whatever. I don't care," I say.

I do care about Earl, though. He's been in my life for seven years now. And for the last three years, more of a dad than my supposed real father. When he fell in love with my mom, she came with two kids he had to deal with. Then one kid vanished, and his wife turned into a different sort of woman than the one he married—distraught, bitter, sad, obsessed.

That left me.

That's why Earl and I got so close, I guess. Before Sam

disappeared, we didn't get along that well. But with Sam gone, when Mom kind of shut down, it was me and Earl, working together, trying to keep everything from falling apart. Mom worked all day, and then she'd come home and glue herself to the computer, or else make phone calls, and so Earl and I would cook dinner sometimes—nothing fancy, nothing like Mom could cook, but it got food on the table. When the house got messy, Earl and I would pick up the slack and vacuum, mop the kitchen, change sheets, scrub the bathrooms, do the laundry, all the stuff Mom used to do on autopilot. When she had one of her crying spells, we'd both sit next to her and just hold her till she calmed down. When she had one of her bad patches, where all she could do was lie in bed, either crying or half-sleeping, Earl and I would just sit and watch the TV on low volume, ready to go to her if she called out. Or I'd do my homework at the kitchen table while he read a book in his recliner till he started snoring and I'd tap his feet with my pencil and he'd wake.

I take another sip of the drink and, again, he doesn't stop me. He's staring at his cigarette now. What must he be thinking? Is he happy, or scared? Is he thinking about what our lives will be like now? Sam is back. And maybe Mom is back—back to who she was before Sam went away. What does that mean for us? As if reading my thoughts, Earl reaches his hand across the table. I take it in mine. He doesn't answer the questions in my head. He doesn't speak. And neither do I. The silence is nice, so we just sit there, safe in the present moment.

During the first few weeks after Sam had vanished, I had to sit at home and wait for any important phone calls while neighbors hovered about—Mrs. Sykes, the Kellers, others, depending on the day. Aunt Shelley came for a week, too, before she had to get back to Nashville, feeling helpless. Mom and Earl, went out driving, looking around. The police were looking, too, of course. But Mom took matters into her own hands. "I have to do something," she told me. "I can't just sit and wait." She organized a search of the woods, even though that's not where Sam was last seen, and other places, too. Mr. and Mrs. Keller, everyone in the neighborhood, Mom's boss and other coworkers, the guys on Earl's construction crew—everyone tried to help. They scoured any snatches of forest along Skyland. They knocked on doors and posted signs. They went on the news, making appeals for anyone to come forward if they'd seen Sam. Surely, on that busy road, someone had seen *something*. Sam's picture—his fifth-grade school portrait, where he's wearing a blue-and-red-striped polo and his impish, winning grin—was published in the newspaper each day for weeks. Mom and Earl were on the phone constantly—with the police, sheriffs, FBI. I never could understand who was in charge of what. There were leads, tons of them, but they all proved to be false. It seems that people thought that every eleven-year-old kid in the state of Alabama might just be Sam. In those first weeks, looking for Sam consumed every waking moment of our lives.

A lot of the time I was at home alone, waiting, sitting around. I felt bad if I read a book, or watched TV. Any mental space not devoted to Sam felt like a betrayal. Like I was a bad sister. A bad daughter. Just a bad person all around.

I thought back to that day and wondered what I could have done differently. I should have put my foot down— *No, Sam, you can't go.* Or I should have gone with him and Josh. Maybe I should have tattled on him as soon as Mom got home. No, I should have called her the minute he left the house. Over and over in my mind, there was always something I could have done—one little thing—and Sam would still be with us. And sometimes I got angry. I wanted to run over to Josh's house and grab him and slap him, ask him why he left my brother like that. And then I'd get mad at Sam, for being so dumb. *You brat*, I would think, *you always had to get your way. If you'd just have obeyed the rules for once, we'd all be fine. You'd be here still.* Sometimes, I'd cry myself to sleep, hating Josh and hating Sam and then hating myself most of all.

At the end of August, our despair about Sam reached a fever pitch. The blistering heat didn't help. Going outside, it felt like God was mocking us. *Oh, your brother's missing? How about some sunburn and heatstroke to go along with that?* I started taking long cold showers, and that way the sound of the water could stifle my sobs.

One night, I heard Mom on the phone, speaking loudly like she was upset, or more upset than usual. I cracked my door open so I could hear. For a terrifying moment I thought she had some news about Sam.

"No, don't come," I heard her say. "I told you a million times these past few weeks, it wouldn't do any good."

I knew then that she was talking to my dad. Not just by what she said, but from the contempt in her voice.

"Don't take that tone with me. I know you blame me, but—no, but . . ." I hadn't seen him in two years. I hadn't wanted to. Part of me hated him. He'd left us. He'd chosen to be away from us. Why should I miss him? But right then, for some reason, it hit me: I *did* miss him. I was desperate for him. I crept down the hall. Mom paced about on the cordless, her back to me.

"It would just be a distraction. . . . No, she doesn't need you, you'd just—"

"Mom!"

She spun around. She cupped the mouthpiece and said, "Go back to bed."

"I wanna speak to Dad."

"It's late. You can speak with him tomorrow."

"Dad!" I shouted, something inside me erupting. "Daddy, come home!" Daddy—had I ever called him that? I ran up to Mom and tried to snatch the phone away, but she dodged me.

"Beth, stop it!"

I kept shouting "Daddy!" I clawed for the phone, and she looked at me like I was crazy. And I guess I *was* crazy. We all were by then. Tears on my cheeks, my eyes cloudy, I started hyperventilating. And suddenly Earl was there and had his arms around me and was walking me back to my room. "I want my daddy," I said through my sobs, like a pathetic little girl.

"Shhh," Earl said.

Earl told me to focus on breathing. In and out, in and out. And I don't know why, but I think that's when it really and truly hit me that Sam was gone forever. But more than that: That's when I first thought that he was probably dead. I couldn't fool myself any longer. Something horrible had happened to him and he was never coming back.

Suddenly, the ache I felt was almost too much to bear. It was hard to breathe and I felt the hysterics creeping back like a sneeze you can't stop. All I had left was a mother who blamed and hated me, and a father who hadn't bothered to see me in years, and a stepfather who wasn't even related to me so why should he care either, even though right then he was holding me in his arms, trying to calm me.

Eventually Earl left me to sleep, and I did, for more hours than I had in weeks. When I woke up the next day—how can I describe it? I felt different. Like I'd had a bad fever that broke and I'd sweated out all the sickness. Somehow, I knew I had no use for drama and tears anymore. None of it would do any good. None of it would bring Sam back. It was time to face a life without him. I was sick of being sad, sick of crying, sick of feeling guilty. Sick of wondering where he was.

He was dead. I knew it.

I felt armored then. The worst had already happened, hadn't it? I could handle anything. Nothing, nobody could hurt me now.

Someone is shaking me. "Wake up, honey." I'm groggy and confused but I open my eyes and of course it's Mom. I see her smiling face, and then I remember that Sam is home. Warm relief floods through my body, and I can't help but smile back up at her.

"It's a lovely morning, isn't it?" Mom says. I look toward the window and see the sun pushing on the closed blinds. "I mean, it's lovely because Sam's here."

"Yes," I say.

"I know we didn't have much time to take it all in yesterday."

That's an understatement. I say, "I still can't believe it."

"Believe it," she says, brushing my hair aside, gazing at me like I'm still her little girl. She hasn't acted this way in years, even when Sam was here. It's like I've woken up to an entirely different life.

"I want to talk to you about a few things. About what happened to Sam."

My stomach lurches. With just a few words, all that good feeling floats away, and I feel a chill go up my back. "Okay."

"We don't know everything yet. And we're not going to ask Sam about it."

At the news conference, I'd listened but didn't take everything in. I guess I was still in shock, and the words in the air just sounded like white noise. But I do remember that Sam had been found at some man's apartment, just about two or three hours away.

Mom continues: "He'll tell us everything in due time, when he's ready. The thing—the important thing for now is to not push it. We need to give him time to readjust. Dr. Rao said that—"

"Do I have to go back to see her?" I ask. Dr. Rao is this psychologist they sent me to a few months after Sam disappeared. I didn't see the point of it, so I stopped going after a few months.

"No. I mean, not right now. But you can if you want to."

"I don't want to."

"That's okay. But I called her—I just, I needed to talk to

someone we knew, not some social worker who doesn't really know us or Sam. She said that it's going to take Sam time to open up. That he's probably experiencing post-traumatic stress, or shock, or something like that. So we can't push him too hard or too fast, okay? And we can't let him see us upset. We need to be strong for Sam."

"Okay."

"Good. I just wanted to make sure we're all on the same page."

I hear the phone ringing, and then the doorbell.

"I better get out there. Get up and eat some breakfast."

I nod, but before she leaves the room, I ask, "What *did* happen to him?"

Her face kind of tenses and her smile falls off, but then she pastes it back on again. "The important thing is he's home, safe and sound. Let's focus on that for now. Okay?" Mom stands there, watching me with a weird smile, waiting for me to agree. All I can do is nod, because I know she doesn't want me to ask any more questions.

After she leaves I lock my door and then turn on my laptop and go online. Mom knows something, or a lot of things, and she's not telling me any of it. But it's easy to find a ton of articles—on the *Tuscaloosa News* site, but also in all the national news websites, too.

Most of the stories all say the same things. The man who abducted Sam is named Russell Lee Hunnicutt. Judging by his mug shot he's a scowling fat guy with brown hair and a gross beard and a funny eye. He lived in a one-bedroom apartment in Anniston, Alabama. He worked as a manager at a BBQ restaurant, also sometimes answered phones on the night shift at a funeral home (I'm not kidding). He didn't have a criminal record. He wasn't a registered sex offender. When I read those words, I shiver like a blast of cool air has blown through my room. Maybe I should stop.

But I have to continue.

This man had two older brothers, who lived in Georgia. His parents lived in Georgia, too. It doesn't sound like they were a close family—they hadn't seen him in years. All of his coworkers at the BBQ place said he was quiet, a hard worker, though sometimes a stickler. They are all *shocked* that he was harboring a fourteen-year-old boy in his apartment. Almost all the articles say something like "There's still so much authorities don't know."

It makes no sense to me. I shake my head. How could a man keep a kid like this without anyone knowing?

It's a stroke of luck that Sam was finally discovered. Or maybe it was just that Hunnicutt finally screwed up. The day before Sam was found, he tried to snatch a ten-year-old kid named Brandon in Gadsden, Alabama—maybe a half hour from Anniston. This kid realized something fishy was going on and started screaming, and Hunnicutt sped off in a panic. But this kid snapped a picture of the truck with his phone, and when he reported what had happened to the police, they enhanced the picture, traced the license plate number, and found Hunnicutt. When the police got to his apartment in Anniston, Hunnicutt answered the door and surrendered without a fight. But the police were surprised to see someone else there, sitting quietly, watching them. The police asked this kid who he was, and he said, "Sam Walsh."

One of the cops recognized that name. "The Sam Walsh who'd been missing for over three years?" he asked.

"Yes, sir." He also said, "Are you going to take me home now?"

I close my laptop. I've read enough. I sit there and clutch myself, and slowly the cold trembling in my body winds down.

I leave my room, wobbly and light-headed, like I've just left a dark theater after seeing a terrifying movie. I head to the kitchen. Mom and Earl are in the living room, talking with some man dressed like he's ready for church—slacks, a nice shirt, a tie. He's older than Mom and Earl, with receding brownish-gray hair.

"They'll pay," he says, "but they want an exclusive."

Right then someone knocks on the kitchen door. It's Mrs. Sykes, so I let her in. Beyond her, on the streets, I still see a few news vans, but most of the crowd has died down. Mrs. Sykes comes in holding a bulging Belk's shopping bag. Mom

76

comes out of the living room and greets her with a hug.

Mrs. Sykes says, "How are we this precious morning?"

"It's a bit hectic, but we're still floating on air," Mom says.

"I can only imagine." She pats me on the shoulder and smiles. "Well, I don't want to keep you long, I just brought over these clothes that I collected from the neighbors last night—you know, clothes that might fit Sam."

Mom opens the bag and looks in without saying anything, but soon she starts tearing up and Mrs. Sykes hugs her, and they hold on like that for what seems like forever. At first I don't know why this is making Mom so emotional, but then I get it: Sam doesn't have any clothes that fit him anymore. Only a closet full of clothes for an eleven-year-old boy.

"Thank you so much," Mom says. "You're an angel."

"I'll take these to Sam," I say. "Okay?" Maybe it will feel more normal now, seeing him in the daytime.

"Thanks, honey," Mom says.

I knock on Sam's door. "Come in," he says faintly.

Inside, he's standing by his dresser, wearing the clothes he'd been wearing the day before. Maybe he slept in them. Even in the dim light I can see his piercings. I want to ask him about them, but then I remember what Mom said about not asking questions. They look a little ridiculous, because even though Sam is older, his face is still boyish and innocent-looking.

"The neighbors brought some clothes." I set the sack down on the neatly made bed.

"Thanks," he says, offering that polite, timid smile.

Even from a few feet away, I can smell his body odor—musky, the way the guys on the soccer team smell after a long practice. I wonder why Mom or Earl haven't made him shower, and then I feel bad for even thinking that. He's home now. It doesn't matter.

Sam just stands there, unsure of what to do, so I pick up the bag and dump the contents onto the bed. "I don't know if you'll want to wear any of it," I say, surveying the pile. I grab some jeans that look sort of acid-washed. "I mean, these are tragic."

He looks at me, then at the jeans, and lets out a little laugh. To my surprise, I laugh, too. Sam comes over and starts picking through the pile with me. Some of it's fine, but there are some other horrors, like a neon tank top and some pleated red shorts. I try to push back the thought that I don't know what kinds of things Sam wears because I don't know who he is anymore. I don't know his style, what he likes, what he hates—I don't know anything. I see his knapsack, sitting by his bed—the knapsack he brought with him from Anniston. What's in it? I want to know, but I know I can't ask him. Instead I just hold up a collared shirt with light blue vertical stripes. "This might look good on you."

"You think?" he says, staring at it like it's some strange

costume. He picks it up and then walks to the small mirror above the dresser.

"Yeah, it looks great."

He stands there for a bit, looking at himself. Then he walks to the window and peers out the blinds.

I keep going through the clothes, organizing things in piles—ugly shirts, decent shirts, hideous pants, acceptable pants, and then things that can't be classified, like a pair of boxer shorts with pineapples on them. Sam just keeps standing there, clutching the shirt, staring outside.

Finally, Mom comes in. "Look at all these clothes," she says. Sam still holds his gaze out the window. Is there something out there to see?

To me, she whispers, "Can you come talk?"

I nod. "We'll be back in a minute, okay, hon?" she says to Sam.

She takes me to the den and we sit. I can hear Earl, still in the living room with that man, who has a really loud voice. "Sure, you can wait, sure. But there will be fewer opportunities the more time passes. People have short memories," I hear him say.

"Who is that?" I ask.

"That's what I want to discuss. His name's Bud Walker. He's a, well, like a lawyer. I mean, he *is* a lawyer, but he also helps people deal with stuff. Like the media and interviews, that sort of thing. We're getting a lot of interview requests—

it's overwhelming. He fields requests, handles details, acts as our spokesperson, stuff like that. People want to know Sam's story. Our story."

"Why?" I ask.

"I guess because it's . . . It's a story that will give people hope."

"Is that what that man says?"

"It's what everyone says," she says, bringing her hand up to my cheek and smiling. I can't get used to this touchy-feely Mom. "Producers from TV shows have been calling." She puts her hand back down. "And that's what I wanted to tell you. We're going to New York in a few days. All of us."

"Seriously?" I ask, feeling a twinge of excitement. "Like, to be on *Good Morning America* or something?"

"Well, we're deciding on the offers right now."

"Wow," I say. "What does Sam think?"

She looks at me, then down at the floor, like she's embarrassed or something. "He wants to do it—we wouldn't do it otherwise. He says he wants to help other kids."

I have a ton more questions, but Mom keeps going: "Honey, this is a hard decision. Part of me just wants to move on and keep things private. And we will do that. But, they're . . . well, they're offering money. Good money. And we can use that, to pay for Sam's college."

College? Sam's fourteen and he's been gone for years and she's thinking about *college*? Whenever I brought up college, she always told me that my only option was the University of Alabama. It was all we could afford, and I'd still have to get a job. But she never pushed me about college, like my friends' parents seemed to do. She was too busy always thinking about Sam. And now that Sam is back, not much has changed.

"And your college, too," she adds, because I must have made a face. "Okay," I say, wondering if it's an empty promise.

"You should start packing," she says, patting me on the knee before she joins Earl and Mr. Walker.

I walk back to Sam's room. He's still peering out the window.

"What are you looking at?" I ask.

He drops the blinds quickly, like I startled him. After a few seconds he says, "They moved?"

"Who? The Kellers? Oh yeah, like, a few years ago. Across town."

"Does he . . . does Josh go to school with you?"

"Yeah," I say. "I see him, but we don't really talk." He's on the tennis team—I see him almost every day as I walk to soccer practice. He's not as tall as Sam is, but he's not all shy and wimpy like he used to be.

Sam walks to the bed, picks up a T-shirt from the decent pile and holds it up. It's gray with long dark blue sleeves. "I like that one," I say. He drops it and looks over at me and then surprises me by reaching in for a hug. After a few seconds, I pull back.

He's smiling at me, but it's still the polite smile you'd give to someone you barely knew. He seems so fragile. He's shy around us—which makes sense I guess. "Sam, are you sure you want to . . . to go on TV?"

He shrugs. "Mom says people want to know my story."

"But what do you want?"

"I . . . I . . ."

But then Mom comes in. "You find any good stuff?" she says, gesturing to the clothes. It's clear that only some of it is suitable. He'll have to buy new things. New things for his new life.

It all happens so fast. Sam's back for a blip of time, and all of a sudden we're packing our bags for New York.

Mom and Earl have agreed on Helen Winters. She always gets the "big" interviews, apparently. She's "classy and respectful," Mom said, which is probably what Bud Walker told her. "She's been in the business for years. She's interviewed presidents, world leaders, everyone." The big-time producers are flying us up, first class, and putting us up in a fancy hotel.

I have my suitcase on my bed when Mom comes in. "Don't pack too much. We're just going for a few nights."

"Okay," I say, glancing at the clothes in my closet and not seeing anything that looks remotely cool or hip enough for New York City.

"I know I don't need to say this," she says, "but this isn't a pleasure trip. It's work."

"We can't even go up the Empire State Building, or see a show?" I ask, feeling like a brat for even thinking it.

"We'll go back one day, I promise," Mom says.

Later, after Bud Walker leaves, we all scarf down some of the food that the neighbors have been bringing over. Then Sam goes to bed and I go to my room. I look at my phone, which is still turned off. I put it in my desk drawer. After a while I get thirsty and want some water so I head to kitchen. But I stop before I get there. I can hear Mom and Earl.

"This is the right decision, isn't it?" she says, sounding uncertain. "I mean, it's for Sam's future. For our future."

"I think so," Earl says. "Plus, maybe we'll inspire other families with missing kids—inspire them to not give up."

"You're right," Mom says. "We'll do it, we'll get it over with, and then we can just get on with our lives."

Get on with our lives. I want to laugh, or scream, something. Because it's like Mom thinks our lives are like some TV show that got interrupted, like when something big happens and the news cuts in and once they're done, the announcer says, "We now return to regular programming."

Sam was gone and now he's back. We now return to regular life.

A driver wearing a suit is waiting for us at the airport in New York. He helps us with our bags and ushers us all into a big black SUV. As the driver speeds through traffic, Mr.

Walker goes over the schedule again, but I don't really listen. I just want to take in the sights. I guess we're not really in the city yet, but on the outskirts. Still, everything is so alive. Rows and rows of brick buildings, streets crammed with parked cars, giant billboards that announce new movies and TV shows, taxis zooming by, people headed toward a zillion possible destinations.

The driver veers off onto yet another freeway and soon, up ahead, we can see the city in the distance, ablaze with so many lights—the Empire State Building, and all these other gigantic ones that I don't know the names of. It all looks so imposing and exciting.

"Tomorrow's going to be a long day," Mr. Walker says, ignoring our surroundings. Maybe he's been here a lot.

"We'll try and get a good night's sleep," Mom says.

I look over at Sam, but he's staring out the window, gobbling up the views like I am. It must be even more overwhelming for him.

The driver slows down through a tollbooth and then we're in a tunnel and then, just as suddenly, we're in the city. We're all quiet as the SUV creeps through traffic. I've seen New York a lot on TV, but it's still kind of weird actually seeing it all up close. So many types of people—women dolled up and in high heels, scraggly men shuffling along in dirty coats, cyclists snaking through traffic. Restaurants and shops everywhere— nothing closed, even though it's a little after nine o'clock.

The SUV finally pulls up to our hotel. It's on a street lined with trees and fancy apartment buildings. It's not far from Central Park, the driver tells us.

When we get out, bellhops in dark-green uniforms spring out to help us with our bags. It's kind of embarrassing, especially since we don't have much with us. The inside of the hotel lobby is shiny, full of marble and brass. Mom sits in one of the lobby's chairs and waits while Earl and Mr. Walker deal with check-in. Sam stands next to Mom, looking shell-shocked.

But I'm energized and excited. I stand there hoping someone famous will come out of the elevators, because this seems like a place where celebrities might stay. But I look at Sam and feel a pang of guilt for thinking—even briefly—that I'm just a normal tourist. We're not here for fun. We don't even really get to leave the hotel, since we're doing the interview here. According to Mr. Walker, when privacy and security are important, Helen Winters conducts interviews in the penthouse suite. He explained this to us at the airport this afternoon, before we took off, when I had mentioned it would be so cool being near Times Square, where the network's studio was. I think he got a little pleasure out of dashing my hopes. But then he added, "She interviewed the Pope at the hotel. And Britney Spears once." He sounded like we should be grateful, like that would make up for the past three years.

"We're all set," Mr. Walker says now, walking up with Earl. "You guys are in Suite eight-o-seven. Now, one of the producers wants to meet with us over breakfast, so be downstairs at the restaurant at eight. And then the makeup and wardrobe people are coming at ten, to get you dressed and ready. And then Ms. Winters will arrive around noon. I imagine the interview will start soon after that, after she chats with you guys for a little bit. For dinner tonight, help yourself to room service." My heart sinks. I was hoping we could venture out—go to a real restaurant and see more of the city up close. But no. We have to stay holed up. We could be anywhere in the world, really, it wouldn't matter.

The suite is huge at least, with a big main room decked out with polished furniture and a couch, a big flat-screen TV mounted in the wall, and large windows that look out onto the street, flanked by heavy dark green drapes. Then, on each side, there are two rooms with huge king-size beds, each with its own bathroom. The idea was for Earl and Sam to share a room, and for me and Mom to share one, but Mom has slept in Sam's room each night since he's been back, so I'm not sure what will happen.

"Okay, let's unpack," Earl says.

But I sit on the couch and flip on the TV. Sam sits next to me.

"Beth," Mom says.

"I'll unpack in a minute," I say. "Can't we just relax?"

"This isn't a trip for relaxing," she says, her tone grumpy and tired, the way I'm used to her sounding.

Sam stands and grabs his duffel bag—one he borrowed from Earl—carrying it into one of the rooms.

I turn back to the TV but it's just commercials. I'm about to change the channel when suddenly there's a picture of Sam. Sam as a little kid, and Sam now—a still from the news conference. A voice says, "This week, an exclusive—" I switch it off. I look over at where Mom was but luckily she's now in one of the bedrooms. Earl too. I stand and walk to the window, look down at the street as cars and taxis whiz by. A woman walks by on the sidewalk in a puffy coat. I think, if that woman watches the interview, she'll know who we are, she'll know all the horrible truths about our lives. She'll think, what an incredible story, and then flip the channel and get on with her life. I think how amazing that is, and how unfair.

The format for the show is simple: The whole family will appear on camera in a group interview. Then just Mom and Earl. And then we're done.

Just as Mr. Walker said, the TV network sends over hair and makeup people that morning after we eat breakfast. They invade our suite like they're long-lost relatives, familiar and aggressive. There are two people for each of us, carrying makeup cases and wheeling in racks of clothes.

Sam's up first. But before they do anything, Mom makes him take his piercings out.

"I can put them back in after, right?" he asks, sounding almost panicked. It's the first time I've seen him show this much emotion, and my heart sputters from the surprise of it.

"We'll see," she says. But I know she doesn't want to see those piercings ever again.

Slowly, carefully, Sam takes the piercings out and places them on the table. I can tell Mom wants to brush them into the garbage, but she rummages in her purse and empties an Advil bottle. "We'll keep them in here for now, okay?" He nods, touching his lip, looking pained.

I wish Sam would look over at me, so that I could smile and reassure him. But he doesn't meet my eye.

Next they start to work on Sam's hair, trimming it down to the normal length for a preppy young boy. Instantly, Sam seems transformed, closer to how he looked when he was a kid, the way I always remembered him.

"That looks cute," I say.

He looks at himself in the mirror in a mournful way, touching his head, but then he smiles. It's a fake smile. A smile to signal he gets it. He has to look different.

Eventually two young women—Sheila and LaVonne—whisk me away to the bedroom. Sheila's in charge of the clothes and she holds up countless pants and blouse combos, then skirts, and thankfully we settle on something that doesn't make me gag—a charcoal-gray skirt, white blouse, with a maroon sweater on top. Preppier than I'd like, but dressing up once won't kill me. LaVonne gets to work on my makeup and hair. "You're a natural beauty, so we won't glob it on you, okay, hon?" she says. I nod, feeling myself blush.

While LaVonne does her thing, I close my eyes. It feels nice to be pampered, though when she says, "Take a look," I open my eyes and look in the mirror and I don't look all that different. My cheeks are a little flusher, and the eyeliner highlights the brown of my eyes a bit more than usual, and my lips are pinker and fuller, but in a natural way. My light brown hair has been trimmed to make it a little more even—less all over the place, the way it can get. But I can recognize myself. And I start to think, with a little embarrassment, I should spend more time on my appearance from now on.

"What do you think?" LaVonne says.

"Not bad," I say, smiling at myself, then at her. Then I add, "Thank you," and she pats me on the shoulder. I wish Chita and the girls could see me now. They would probably tease the hell out of me. And Donal would—no. I can't think about him right now. I have enough confusion in my life; I don't need more.

I go out to the main room and everyone is dressed up. Mom's wearing a blue skirt suit and Earl's in a coat and tie.

Sam's in khakis and a blue button-down, looking nothing like he did a few hours ago. We look like the perfect family, headed to church.

A chubby guy with a clipboard barges in. "You guys ready?"

I look at Mom, and she looks at Sam, and Sam just stares down at his feet. I guess we're all sort of shocked that this moment is here. It's Earl who says, "Yes, sir." We follow the clipboard guy and some other people up the elevator to the penthouse. The elevators open onto a smaller room, like a foyer. The clipboard guy leads us down the hall and into a huge room crowded with equipment and people. Glaring lights are set up around a setoff area with a chair and a big couch.

"Ah, here's Ms. Winters," I hear someone say.

A woman strides down the hall. She's shorter than I thought. She's wearing a plum-colored dress suit, with a blue silk scarf tied around neck. Her fake blond hair is poofed impeccably. She's got tons of makeup on, you can tell. Up close she looks stitched together, like she's made of cracked porcelain and if you pushed your thumb into her skin she might break into pieces. She smiles at all of us, clearly a smile she's used to busting out on cue.

"Thank you all for coming up here. I'm so honored to meet you." Then she zooms in on Sam. "Young man, you're an inspiration to us all." She takes his hand and pats it and then clasps both hands on top of his. "You're very brave to share your story."

"Thank you, ma'am," he says, looking at her old, small hands.

She laughs. "So brave, and so polite!" And then, she lets go of his hands, turns and calls out "Are we ready?" to no one in particular. We all take our places on the couch, waiting for cameras to roll. Mom, then Sam, me, then Earl. The lights shine at us like hot little suns. A makeup artist comes over and powder puffs our faces. My heart starts pounding, and I have to remind myself that we're doing a good thing, that this is for college, that we're giving hope to other families. *Calm down.* As if he can sense my nervousness, Earl pats me on the knee. I give him my left hand and he squeezes it.

Helen Winters takes her seat and shuffles her notes. Someone comes and touches up her hair, and I can see some tech guys adjusting the lights, a few other people hovering off to the side, including a guy with an earpiece. She's unfazed, sitting there, and after a bit she looks over at us, giving us a reassuring smile.

Sam reaches and grabs my hand, and Mom takes his free hand, and now we're all linked, like a family chain. And though I'm still freaked about the idea of being on TV, I'm a little calmer knowing we're all in this together.

The guy with the earpiece counts down from five, then says, "Rolling!"

Ms. Winters directs her first questions at Sam. The questions are obvious: *How do you feel being back home? What was it like seeing your family again after all these years? Tell me about the moment when you first saw your mom's face.*

And Sam offers up his answers. *It feels great. It was amazing, incredible.*

Then there's a pause. Ms. Winters, who had been smiling gently, furrows her brows, moving from pleasant to serious. "Sam, how did you survive those three years? What got you through each day?"

He doesn't say anything right away, but when he does his voice is nervous, spoken in that oddly clipped way that I noticed earlier. "I just never gave up hope."

Ms. Winters looks like she's about to ask a follow-up, but Sam keeps going. "I mean, at times I thought about giving up hope. But I kept thinking. Of Mom, and my sister. And my stepdad. My dad. My aunt and my friends. I knew they were searching for me. I knew they weren't giving up. So I knew I couldn't give up, either."

"And how has it been since you've been back?"

"I mean . . . It's only been a few days. But I'm so happy. I'm so . . . happy." I turn and look at him, and he's smiling. But something about it is weird. It's not at all how he used to smile. It hits me that he's only telling her what she wants to hear. What we all want to hear. That's he's just fine and dandy.

Sam is lying to all of us.

My stomach tightens. Why would he lie? To protect us from something? A prickle of coldness moves through my body.

"Do you feel like a different person than when you last saw your family?"

He closes his mouth and nods right away. "I feel like I've grown up a lot over the years."

She nods, then frowns again. "Do you think, after all this, that you'll ever have a normal life?"

His hand tightens in mine. "Sure. I hope so. That's what I want. A normal life."

That would be a good place to end, but Ms. Winters looks at me, and my heart starts to thud. She asks me predictable, dull questions, and I try not to stammer. My voice sounds scared and breathless—the way it does when I have to give class presentations. I wish I were back at school, with my classmates and friends, not here, under the lights, soon to be watched by millions of people. Ms. Winters gets that serious face she gave to Sam, and I brace myself.

"Beth, it must have been hard, these past three years."

"Yes, ma'am," I say, glancing over briefly at Mom, who's giving me a reassuring smile.

"Did *you* ever give up hope?"

My mouth goes dry and tight. "Uh, well."

I can feel the force of Mom's eyes on me, like she's trying

to tell me something telepathically. And Sam—his hand is still tight in mine.

"No, ma'am," I say. "I never gave up hope."

"You always thought Sam was alive?"

My gut twists. I can't tell the truth—not on national TV. I nod. "Yes, ma'am. I knew he was alive. I knew he'd come home." I turn and smile at Sam, and he rests his head on my shoulder for a second. A perfect, tear-jerking moment.

Right then a director guy yells, "Okay, let's stop here!" A few of the lights dim and my relief is instant. Ms. Winters comes over to us on the couch. "That was very brave," she says. "You're a brave young man."

Sam nods, bashful.

"And you too, young lady," she says, but it seems like she's giving me this skeptical look, like she can see right through the lies I just told. Still, she smiles, like she understands why I did it.

"I'm going to talk to your parents alone now, okay?" she asks, as if we have any say about it.

Mom and Earl hug Sam and me, and then one of the producers motions for us to head toward the door, where Mr. Walker is standing. "Can I stay and watch?" I ask. Mr. Walker looks over at Mom and Earl, and the room pauses. "Please?"

Earl mutters something to Mom that I can't hear.

Mr. Walker, in his booming voice, says, "I can watch Sam."

Mom nods. "You can stay."

"Okay then," Mr. Walker says. "I'll take Sam back to the suite for a snack. Would you like that?"

Sam walks over to him, silent.

I'm not sure how much time has passed today. It seems like minutes, could be hours—who knows? After some more touch-ups, they start filming again. I stand in the back of the room, out of the reach of the lights.

Ms. Winters gets right down to it. "Sam was with this man, Russell Lee Hunnicutt, for over three years. During those years, do you have any idea what he went through?"

Mom: "Well, yes, we have some idea, from the police and sheriffs and social workers and county prosecutors. But Sam hasn't talked about it. We're just giving him time. When he wants to talk about it, he will."

Ms. Winters nods, but her face is still the picture of seriousness. "I'm just going to go ahead and ask it. Was Sam sexually abused?"

The room feels suddenly stuffy, stuffier than when I was under the lights. Sweat pools on my forehead, and I wipe it with my sleeve.

There's silence, before Mom says, "Yes."

The word lands like a punch and I feel myself teeter where I'm standing. I lean against an armchair that has been pulled aside from the main set. My stomach churns like I might get sick.

Ms. Winters: "Was Sam tortured?"

Earl: "We don't know that yet."

Mom: "We don't know specifics." She sniffles, starting to cry.

Earl: "There's more than one kind of torture. There's physical torture, then there's mental torture."

"Was he brainwashed?" she asks. "By some accounts, Sam had opportunities to escape. He had some freedoms." She cocks her head.

He did?

Mom wipes her eyes and takes a breath. She doesn't look sad now—she seems kind of pissed, as if Ms. Winters is accusing Sam of something.

It's too hot in here. I think I might puke. I can't take it anymore.

I leave the room. I move down the hallway, and push the button for the elevator a few times before it comes. I take it all the way down to the lobby and then race through and out the door. Once I take in the cool air, I feel like I can breathe a little easier.

I head toward the park, past an apartment building with a doorman out front, his hands cupped behind his back. When I get to Fifth Avenue, Central Park is across the street. When the signal changes, I cross, searching for an entrance, careful to remember the way I came so I don't get lost. When I find a way in I walk along a path lined with iron benches. On a patch of lawn in the shade of some trees, a few squirrels scurry about, seemingly unconcerned about the people just feet from them. There are a ton of people out—bikers, joggers, a few women pushing strollers. People who are leading carefree, wonderful, glamorous New York lives. I walk along the path, trying to pretend that I'm one of them, a New Yorker just out for a stroll.

But soon I slow down. Because I know I'm not like these other people. And what I heard earlier in the hotel—I can't forget it. Those words land on me again like a slap. "Yes," Mom had said. Sam had been abused. And I can see her stricken face again, and my heart lurches. I can't pretend that this horrible thing hasn't happened to Sam. To my family.

As I walk, I feel an ache in my chest, pounding like it wants to get out. I have to keep moving. If I move, maybe I can stop these feelings from erupting.

There's a huge gray rock ahead, and I walk along it and come to another path, which leads down to a pond. Up through the trees I can see slivers of the skyscrapers that surround the park, and then down a slope, I can see the greenish waters of a pond, people sitting on benches, some standing on the sidewalk along the pond's shore.

Then I see Sam, with a few other boys. *Sam.* They're gazing out at the pond and throwing rocks, laughing. I want to call out, but Sam turns his face and I see it's not him at all, but some other kid, a kid with dark hair, close to Sam's age.

This kid is laughing now. He shoves one of his buddies, and his friend shoves him back, jokingly, and they start running, chasing each other up the path. Normal teenage boys.

Torture. Many kinds of torture. Abuse. Sexual abuse.

Three years. *Three years.*

I turn around and practically jog back up the little hill. I'm almost to the exit when I stop. I lean my back against the stone wall surrounding the park and hold myself there, close my eyes. But all I can see is Sam, and when I see Sam all I can think about are the things that happened to him.

No, I think, my chest tightening. My muscles are rubbery. I sit down, my back against the wall, pulling my knees toward me. I take a deep breath, and that's a mistake because it just makes me split open and I just let go, sobbing hysterically, maybe almost screaming, my head between my legs, tears falling to the ground. I must look psychotic, but it feels so good to let it all out. *Sam, Sam. My little brother. I'm so sorry. I was supposed to watch you.* I'm glad he can't see me like this, falling to pieces. *We need to be strong for Sam*, Mom had said. But in my head I'm screaming, *I don't know how to be strong!*

Eventually, through my sobs, I hear someone speaking to me.

"You okay? Hey there, it's okay."

I squint and look up through my drowning eyes, and I see a woman. She's got a headband and a jacket on, and she's looking at me with concern. I wipe my eyes, feeling jolted from my breakdown or whatever you would call it. I stand up, unsteady, and see a man behind her, wearing a baseball cap and running clothes. He's tall. Two joggers. A couple, I guess. In their twenties maybe.

"You okay?" the woman repeats.

My crying dies down, and I catch my breath, nodding. The tightness in my chest is gone. "Uh-huh." I've forgotten how stuffed your nose gets when you cry, and more than anything right now I want a tissue.

"You sure? Can we help you?"

God, I think, I *wish* you could help me. "I'm lost," I say.

"You're not from here?"

I shake my head and say, "No, I'm visiting. With my family. With my brother."

"Okay, sweetie. Where you staying? Near the park? We can help you find your way back."

I tell her the name of the hotel. "Okay, well, let's get you back there." She takes my hand and we start walking, the boyfriend or husband up ahead a little, fiddling with his phone, maybe searching for the address. He keeps glancing back, like he's afraid he might lose us.

"When I first moved here from Michigan, I got lost all the time," the girl tells me. "Where are you from?"

I'm still sniffling, wiping my eyes. "Tuscaloosa, Alabama," I say.

"Roll tide," the guy says, smiling back at me. "I went to

LSU," he says. "I'm from New Orleans."

"What brought you to New York?" the girl asks. "To see the sights, catch some shows?"

Because my brother was abducted and then he came back to us and now everyone wants to know our incredible and awful story. We're about to be semi-famous, at least for a little bit, for something really horrible.

But I don't tell her any of this. "Yeah, to see the sights," I say instead.

Finally, we reach the block of the hotel. "I see it up ahead."

"We can walk you," the girl says.

"That's okay," I say.

"If you're sure," she says.

"Thank you," I say. I think the tears are going to start rolling again, so I give her a quick wave and turn to walk to the hotel. A few seconds later, I look back once, quickly, and they're still both there, watching me. That's when the tears start again, an onslaught. I stop on the sidewalk. I'm not ready to go back inside. Then I see Mom come out, still in her fancy interview suit. She glances down the street, looking for me, maybe pissed or scared.

And then she spots me, and I know I have to walk toward her. I have to keep moving, no matter what's going to happen to me. No matter what's going to happen to us.

CHAPTER 4

Connected

Josh

It's Thursday night of homecoming week. I'm shoving red tissue paper into the chicken wire that covers the base of the parade float that my classmates have been building. We've set up shop in a gymnasium that the Alberta First Methodist Church doesn't use anymore. It has this big freight entrance where we can drag the entire float out when we're finished. The big doors are open now, and cool air blows in from outside. Some people are working, some are just standing around socializing, and a few are walking around giving orders. To be honest, I'm sort of in a haze. If I focus on just shoving the tissue paper into the wire, then at least it will look like I'm busy and maybe no one will bother me.

Tomorrow is the homecoming parade, so we have to finish the float tonight. Since I'm class vice president, I'll get to ride on it through the streets of downtown Tuscaloosa, with people on the sidewalks waving and hollering. Then there's the football game tomorrow night, followed by the dance right after. We were supposed to be working on the float each night, but we were really just talking about it and goofing off, so now we're in a last-minute rush. I know I should be enjoying all of this. Normally I would. And I'm trying to. But it's been hard.

Right now everyone is focused on the other parts of the float—the falcon (our mascot), which will be perched on top of a bobcat (the mascot of our rivals), and a giant football and then a goalpost. These constructions are spread out all over the gym, surrounded by small groups of my classmates trying to make it all come together. The float's base—a long flat wooden structure, also surrounded with chicken wire—is the easy part, and for most of the night I've been the only one working on it. But I see Becca, our class president, walking over, bringing Hunter and Declan with her. I step away, like I'm trying to get a better look at it from afar.

Nick is around here somewhere. We haven't talked much today, which is kind of weird. Even at tennis practice he was quiet. I do see Madison Jones—my date for the game and the dance tomorrow—working on the bobcat. Everyone calls her Madison Jones or Madison J., because there are about seven Madisons in our class. She's pretty, I guess, and nice, though she kind of talks too much. She's on the track team. I think she likes me as more than a friend. She glances over at me and smiles while she holds a stack of yellow tissue paper, and I quickly look back at the base of the float.

"Hey," Becca calls out. "We need to spell out 'Freshman' on both sides of the base, don't you think?" She's really the one who's handled all of this, rounding up people in the class to help, pushing the ideas through, giving us constant pep talks. Her boyfriend, Hunter, is on the football team, and he's here mainly just to lend his football-star presence, wearing his stupid jersey to remind us that he's more special than everyone else. And there's Declan, too, who's not on the football team but who hangs out with a lot of the players, and so he thinks he's supercool.

"What do you think, Josh?" Becca asks. She's got her dark hair up in a ponytail.

I walk over to them. "Yeah," I say. "That makes sense."

"I think the lettering should be white," she says, "on a red background." She's always so decisive, which is why she's a good president.

I grab a stack of white tissue. "I'll start with the *F*. Fresh-*man* or fresh*men*?"

"Fresh*men*," Becca says.

Hunter and Declan edge closer, watching us.

"Did you guys see that kid on TV?" Declan asks.

I start to work, ruffling the tissue, hoping to make noise to drown out the conversation. All day, people have been talking about the interview with Sam and his family, which aired last night.

"What kid?" Becca asks.

"That interview. That kid Sam Walsh."

"Oh, *that* kid. The whole story is so insane," Becca says. She's squatting near me, marking out where the other letters should go.

I don't chime in. I focus on making the *F* fat and even. But yeah, of course I watched the interview. We all did. At first Dad didn't want to let me. But Mom said, "Honey, we can't shield him from this." Besides, anything I wanted to know about the case was all over the Internet.

Sam was only on for a little while, and he didn't say much. He looked preppy in khakis and a button-down shirt. His scraggly hair, his piercings—all that was gone. I stared and tried to remember the Sam I knew. But it was like I was watching someone different altogether.

"My dad says that man probably raped him, like, all the time," Declan says.

"Gross," Hunter says.

"And he stayed there with him," Declan continues. "He stayed all those years. He's got to be a fag."

"Declan," Becca says, in a scolding tone.

I feel my face flush, and I turn away so they can't see me.

"Just saying," Declan says. "There's something fucked up about him. You could tell just by the way he looked."

"Well, wouldn't *you* be messed up after going through something like that?" Becca says, sounding annoyed.

"No. I'd have kicked that sicko's ass," Declan says. "I'd have kicked his ass and gotten out of there."

"Damn right," Hunter says.

"Let's not talk about it," Becca says. I can't tell if she finds it distasteful, or if she just wants to focus on the work at hand, but I'm glad she's trying to change the subject.

"But think about it. He was, like, settled in there. Why would he have stayed unless he was enjoying it? He didn't—"

"Shut up," I say, louder than I mean to. I continue shoving the tissue paper into the slots, not missing a beat. "Just shut up," I say again.

"Chill out, man," Declan says.

"Yeah, what's your problem?" Hunter asks.

I don't respond. A few moments pass in silence. But I know it can't last.

"His sister's on the soccer team with me. Beth Walsh?" Becca says.

I almost chime in that I know her. That we were neighbors. That I was there when it all happened. But I don't.

"She never talked about it—about her brother," Becca says. "I only found out from some of the other girls. She's pretty quiet."

"I just hope that freak brother of hers doesn't come to *our* school," Declan says.

"He'll probably be homeschooled," Becca says. "After all he's been through."

"Besides being abused and stuff, I bet it was cool to just sit at home and watch TV and play video games all day," Declan says, laughing.

"Stop," Becca says.

"Dude, not funny," Hunter says, probably just trying to please Becca.

"What? I'm just saying."

I drop the tissue and sit there for a minute.

"You okay?" Becca asks. That question I'm sick of being asked.

I stand up and look over at Declan. "He was my friend," I say.

Declan just gives me a confused look and says, "What?"

He's dumb as a box of rocks. Not worth it. I just start walking toward the exit. I can hear Becca call out to me, but I don't stop.

Outside, there's a side parking lot, separated from the church's main lot, but it's mostly empty since no one here can drive. We're all stuck until our parents or older siblings show up to get us. It's dark out, but because of the nearby streetlights I see Nick at the edge of the lot, hands in the pockets of his hoodie, talking to this girl Sarah. Sarah is his homecoming date. She's new to town and is on the tennis team. I guess I knew he kind of liked her, but he'd always been shy about talking to her until recently. I hesitate for a moment, but then I walk toward them.

"Oh hey," Nick says, seeing me approach. "How's the float going?"

"Fine," I say.

"Hi," Sarah says. She's petite, with glossy shoulder-length blond hair. Nick calls her California, because she moved here from San Diego.

"Can I talk to you?" I say, looking at Nick.

"Okay," he says, sounding hesitant.

"I'll see you inside," Sarah says, walking off.

"What's up?" he asks. I can tell he's miffed that I broke up this great romantic chat they were having. He flips his hood down and pushes his hair out of his eyes. He needs a haircut. I see him watching Sarah walk away.

"They were talking about him. About Sam."

He looks back at me, like he's aware of me for the first time. "So?"

"Declan called him a freak. He called him a fag."

"So? Declan's a tool. Just ignore him."

"It's not true."

"What's not true?" He looks toward the gym again, then back at me.

"What they're saying about him." I want Nick to agree, to say something, but he's just quiet. "Nick?" I ask.

"Why do you want to bring up all that?" Nick looks down at his sneakers, kicks a piece of broken glass away, then looks back at me, fiddling with his hair again.

"I don't know. Because we were friends with him? I mean—"

"I don't want to talk about him, okay? He's back and I'm happy for his family. But that's the end of it."

That's the end of it.

For Nick maybe. But he didn't see the man in the truck. He didn't keep that from the police. He's not the one who biked away, leaving Sam all by himself.

A breeze starts up, and leaves blow across the parking lot, making a papery scraping sound along the concrete.

"You're gonna stay till we finish the float aren't you?" Nick says.

"Yeah, I'll stay." I'm sure Nick wants to be here so he can flirt with Sarah. He hasn't done any actual work all night.

From the direction of the gym, I hear a few people laughing, everyone excited and delirious from the long week. For a brief moment I try to picture Sam with us. In a flash, I think of a different world where Sam never went away, where nothing happened to him, and he's with us now, he's in there, helping build the falcon. He's laughing, maybe even flirting with the girl who's his homecoming date. Yeah, I can almost see him. But I don't see myself. Where would I be?

"Let's go," Nick says.

As we walk toward the gym, the image of Sam fades away. When we enter the chaos inside, I head back to the float and grab some tissue paper and carry on.

===

The next night, Mom drives me to pick up Madison for the homecoming game. She only lives a few streets over. Sometimes I see her run by our house on one of her jogs. She always looks up at my window.

"You look so handsome," Mom says.

I hate when she does that—tells me I'm handsome or smart or special, like she thinks I need a boost of confidence. I'm dressed up in a blazer and a tie. I hold a corsage for Madison in a plastic case on my lap.

I want this night to be over with. Two weeks ago it seemed like the biggest event in my life. Now, I just think it's dumb.

Madison's parents answer the door and greet me, and then Madison steps outside and hugs me. She's in a sleeveless baby blue dress, and she has a pink shawl. Her parents come out, too, waving to Mom in the car. She gets out to join the festivities.

I hand the corsage to Madison.

"How sweet," she says, hugging me again. Thank God Mrs. Jones takes the corsage and helps me pin it on.

Mom and Mr. and Mrs. Jones all smile and make small talk while Madison forces us to pose for a few selfies. "Don't we look cute?" she says, showing me one, and I'm so glad she didn't throw the word couple in there. And no, we don't look cute. Or I don't. I actually look kind of tired. I haven't really been sleeping all that well, to be honest.

Mom drives us to the stadium, both of us sitting in the backseat, like we're being chauffeured. Madison talks and talks and I sit there and try and pay attention, but for some reason I feel—well, anxious.

"Josh?" Mom says from the front seat.

"Huh?"

"Madison asked you a question."

"Oh, sorry."

She smiles at me, though I can tell she feels sort of deflated. Most guys would be hanging on every word she said. "I asked if you thought we'd win the game? The Bobcats are undefeated. Aren't we supposed to play *bad* teams at homecoming? It's so annoying."

"I don't know," I say. "I'm sure we'll win." I smile at her, trying to make an effort.

Traffic is heavy near the stadium, but Mom insists on getting us as close as possible. I get out and walk around the car and open the door for Madison, like a gentleman. Mom unrolls her window. "You guys have fun. I'll pick you up at eleven thirty."

"Thanks, Mrs. Keller!"

Up ahead, I see Nick and Sarah. They're holding hands, so as we walk toward them I grab Madison's, even if my heart's not in it.

We all bunch up at the side of the entrance, the crowds swirling around us. A few more guys show up with their dates—Max and Hilary, Raj and Madison Hinkle, Ty and Aisha—and then we all go in together, heading toward the stands. The bright green of the football field seems to shine under the heavy lights. The band members are all gathered in the end zone for now, before they take their spot in the stands. Blaring horns and trumpets and drums, loud and sort of obnoxious, trying to get the crowd jazzed up. But the crowd doesn't seem to need the band to get excited—there's already a charge in the air. I try to let the energy boost me. But I still feel weird. Not myself.

I follow along, Madison clutching my sweaty hand. We have to sit in the upper rows, the unofficial designated spot for freshmen, and when we start to climb the stands to our seats, I look to my right. In the very first row I see them— Mr. and Mrs. Manderson, and in between the two of them, Sam.

I almost don't recognize him. He could be any of my classmates. He *should* be my classmate. He's just sitting there, wearing jeans and a red jacket that seems too small on him, hands at his side, watching the cheerleaders, or staring at something on the field. What is he doing here?

Madison keeps walking and my hand slips from hers. She looks back and I say, "Hold on." Then I step toward Mr. Manderson, sitting at the aisle seat. "Hello," I say.

It's Mrs. Manderson who recognizes me. "Oh, Josh. Hello!" She stands and moves in to hug me. "Look at you, all grown up and handsome." She sounds so happy and excited and it's weird because I remember she always seemed grumpy. "Say hi to Sam," she says, stepping aside and motioning to him.

"Hi," I say. My heart pounds. It's like the noisy crowd around me has gone silent and they're all watching this reunion unfold.

"Hey, Josh," Sam says after what seems like minutes but was really just a second or two. He smiles at me in a weird way—like he's truly happy to see me. *Fuck you*—the last two words I spoke to him. I feel shy all of a sudden and have to look away. But I force myself to look back and he's still smiling at me, almost eagerly now. "It's good to see you," I say, knowing that sounds stupid.

He nods quickly, nervously. "You too."

Right then there is a burst of applause as the football players storm the field, crashing through one of those paper banners that the cheerleaders have decorated. We all look to the field and start clapping and cheering, grateful for the interruption.

I can sense Madison waiting impatiently a few steps up. Above all the yells, I say, "Well, I better go find my seat."

"Okay, sweetie. Enjoy the game," Mrs. Manderson says.

I look at Sam. He opens his mouth like he wants to say something, but he doesn't.

Madison grabs my hand and practically yanks me up the

stairs, where we squeeze our way down an upper row, to sit by Nick and Sarah. Max and Hilary are farther down, and Raj and Madison H. and Ty and Aisha are one row up, right behind us. It's packed and everyone's standing and hollering.

Nick says, "What are they doing here?"

"I don't know."

"What did you say to him?" Nick says. I see him gaze toward where Sam sits.

"Just hi."

"Remember what a jerk he was to you in school?" Nick says.

Right then there's a big play and the crowd goes crazy, and so I don't bother responding to Nick.

I'm careful not to look down there, where Sam sits. But when Central scores a touchdown, and everyone goes nuts, I sneak a glimpse, thinking it's safe. I mean, they're far down, and Sam probably doesn't know where I'm sitting. I see Sam clapping along with everyone else.

Raj leans down to me and whispers, "It's so funny we're both dating Madisons," and I don't correct him because he's smiling, and in such a good mood.

I peek back at where Sam's sitting, and right then I see him glance up my way, as if he could sense me looking at him. He knows where I'm sitting. He must have watched me walk up the steps.

I snap my eyes away, back to the field, trying to look like I'm focused only on the game. But I'm glad Sam saw me, surrounded by friends, with a date. I bet that's a surprise to him. I'm not that Josh he could push around. I feel a flash of pride, but it doesn't last long. Soon a kind of shame prickles my skin. Sam's down there with just his parents, and I'm up here with everyone else in the freshman class, with all these friends, and I know that's not the way it should be.

At some point, Madison clutches my hand and says, "You okay?" But just then the Bobcats fumble and I scream and cheer along with everyone else. I look at Nick, and we give each other a high five, and everything feels normal again.

A few weeks after Sam had vanished, after days of being shut up in the air-conditioned house, Mom came to my room.

"Okay, no more of this sitting around. I've enrolled you in tennis camp."

"Tennis camp?" I envisioned a campfire and tents and wondered how in the world tennis fit into that.

"It's for two weeks, at the University courts. It'll get you out of the house."

"But I've never played. I don't even have a racket."

"We'll go buy one today. Some physical activity will be good for you."

"But I won't know anyone there."

"Mrs. Lanzano said Nick signed up."

I'd known Nick since first grade, just like Sam. They'd been best friends. Nick had always been nice to me, but we didn't hang out or even talk. Even if Nick had wanted me as a friend, I always felt like Sam stood in the way of that. At school, Sam didn't need me anymore, and he was always finding ways of blocking me from his small circle—the athletic kids. So hearing that Nick would be at this tennis camp didn't give me much comfort.

"I don't know."

"It's all settled." Mom sounded like she was angry with me, like she'd reached the last straw about something. "Put your shoes on, we're going shopping for a racket."

In the car she drove faster than usual. She even cursed under her breath when she had to stop at a red light.

"Mom, what's wrong?"

"What?" she said, snapping to my attention.

"Did I do something wrong? Is that why you're sending me to camp?"

Her eyes softened. "Oh, no, honey. No, it's nothing like that. It's just that . . . these past few weeks have been tough. For all of us. Just sitting around the house, waiting for news. I think we're all going a little crazy. And when Mrs. Lanzano told me about the tennis camp for beginners, I thought it would be something for you to do, that's all." Mrs. Lanzano was a lawyer, and Mom had done some clerking for her firm, so they were becoming friends.

"Okay," I said.

And so a few days later Mom dropped me off at the tennis courts at the University. It was August then, even hotter than July. There were about fifteen other kids there, and we all stood around holding our rackets, awkwardly as beginners do, while two guys in their twenties, assistant coaches on the University team, taught us the basics: feeding us ball after ball, showing us the proper way to hit a forehand, then a backhand, on to volleys, then the serve.

On that first day, Nick and I didn't say much to each other. I hadn't seen him since the end of school. He seemed taller. He had dark hair and these heavy eyebrows, olive skin. He sort of intimidated me. One of those kids—like Sam—who exuded confidence, who was good at sports, who got a lot of attention from girls. I just blended into the group and focused on the tasks at hand. Afterward, the two coaches took us aside—just Nick and me—and told us that we were both naturals. That we had great hand-eye coordination, which was a shock to me because I'd never been good at any sport—not soccer, not basketball, not football, not even T-ball. But tennis felt like something I might master. There was a satisfaction, a challenge, about manipulating that little ball around a box with clearly defined boundaries. And I enjoyed the distraction. For the first time in weeks, I hadn't thought about Sam all day.

The next day, Nick asked if I wanted to come over some-time and play video games after camp. I didn't really like video games, but I wanted to hang out with Nick—to spend as much time as possible away from home. Away from the sight of Sam's house.

Nick's family had recently moved to the other side of town—the side of town where we eventually moved, too. That day I'd brought an extra change of clothes. Once changed, we plopped in front of the couch and fired up the video game. I forget what the game was, but I was horrible at it. Instead of ridiculing me, or laughing, as Sam would have done, Nick tried to show me the tricks, explaining things patiently.

"You'll get the hang of it," he said.

When we reached a good stopping place (the game seemed to have no end point), Nick got us some Cokes and a bag of Doritos. We sat back down on the couch and ate and watched TV.

Out of nowhere, Nick said, "Do you think Sam is dead?"

"I don't know," I said after chewing a mouthful of Doritos, wiping the red dust on my shirt. My belly started churning. I wasn't too crazy about having to think about Sam. Espe-cially when associated with the word *dead*.

"I think he is," Nick said.

"I was with him, the day he went missing. I was the last person to see him—" I stopped myself before saying the word *alive*.

"You were?" Nick looked at me. "For real?"

"Yeah." I could tell Nick found this fascinating, the way he fixed his total attention at me. I felt like I had prestige, being so connected to such a melodramatic story. I told him an abbreviated version, changing some of the details—like not mentioning the soda being tossed at me, the name that was called out, instead saying I just fell off my bike. I told him how Sam laughed at me. I felt a twinge of guilt, saying it—like now that he had vanished, like now that maybe something bad had happened to him, I should just forget that he had ever been a jerk.

"Wow," Nick said. "I mean, did the police interview you, since you were the last one to see him?"

"Yeah, they interviewed me a bunch."

A moment of silence, as if Nick were taking all this in. I expected him to keep asking questions, but instead he said, "Can I tell you something?"

"Sure."

"I don't like him much. I mean, I didn't like him period, or whatever."

"I thought you were best friends."

"Maybe *he* thought so. I don't know. There were times when he was fun and cool, you know? But sometimes he was just, I don't know . . . He could be mean. And he was a liar."

"He *could* be mean."

"He stole a baseball of mine. A signed one that I got at a Braves' game."

"He did?" I tried to recall if I'd ever seen a baseball in his room, if he'd ever shown that off, but I couldn't remember anything.

"Yeah, totally. He swore that he didn't steal it, but I know he did. Plus, he took money from my wallet once. A twenty-dollar bill. Can you believe that?"

"That's horrible."

"That kid could be a real asshole," Nick said.

"Yeah," I said, but already I felt guilty. Sam was gone, unable to defend himself.

"He always said you were lame."

"He did?"

Nick nodded. "Yeah, but forget it, man. Hey, you want to go to the University pool tomorrow after tennis? My parents have a membership."

"Yeah," I said. "That would be fun."

"Cool." Nick flipped the video game back on from where we'd paused it. But before we got going, Nick said, "I mean, I hope Sam's *not* dead. Don't get me wrong. But I don't miss him. I'm kind of glad he's gone. But don't tell anyone, okay?"

Over the next few days we continued with the tennis camp, then hung out afterward. Even after camp officially ended, we met up to practice, and we kept hanging out at his house. By the end of the summer, just before we started sixth grade, I guess we were on our way to being best friends. To be honest, I hadn't had many friends before that, not real friends anyway. That September, I felt like I was a new person. Like Sam had never existed. It got easier and easier to forget about him.

The afternoon after the Homecoming game, I'm up in my room doing homework when Mom knocks on the door. "Come in," I say.

"So," she says. Her face looks weird—nervous, like she has bad news. "Diane Manderson just called. Sam's mom." She pauses, waiting for me to say something, but I just stare at her. "The local news is doing some kind of follow-up story, now that Sam is settled back home. They want Sam to be around old friends, family—that sort of thing. She asked if we would come. She said Sam specifically asked if you could come."

I stare at her for a minute. "Really?" I think back to last night, the way Sam had stared in that funny way—like he was desperate for something from me.

"If you're not comfortable going, I can tell her—"

"I'll go," I say.

Mom looks a little surprised. "Okay," she says, sounding uncertain. She comes over and pats my back as I sit at my desk. "You're a good boy," she says before she leaves.

I'm not sure why I agreed to go so quickly. I guess, in a weird way, I want to see him up close, to talk to him. It's curiosity more than anything.

We drive over the next day after lunch. It's sunny out, but chilly and windy. I haven't been back to Pine Forest since we moved away. When we drive up, the houses, the yards—they all look smaller, shabbier, like after we left things just fell apart. Dad parks along the curb. There's already a Channel 4 news truck parked there, and a few other cars. I wonder who else is coming. Surely Nick was invited, but I haven't heard anything from him. He's probably doing something with Sarah. At the dance, I saw them making out in a corner before one of the chaperones broke them up. All I did with Madison was give her a hug good night.

Inside, everyone is gathered in the living room—Mrs. Manderson; Beth; that lady Mrs. Sykes from next door; a tall baldish man and a woman with a bob of gray hair and their little girl, who looks to be about eight or nine; Mrs. Tomek, from a few doors down, and her son, Ruben, who's like ten or something now. And then there's Sam, sitting on the couch—the only one sitting—looking like his mind is miles away.

"So glad you could make it," Mrs. Manderson says, coming over to hug Mom and Dad. Again, she's all smiley, like a totally new person, not the grouch I remember. Her hair is grayer now. She always seemed so much younger than Mom and Dad, but now they all seem the same age.

"Glad to be here," Mom says. I see her glance over at Sam. She walks to him and he snaps to attention, stands and greets her with a hug, and then he shakes Dad's hand. It's all formal but friendly, slightly uncomfortable. I mean, what do you say in this situation? Welcome back from your imprisonment? So glad you're not dead?

Sam walks over to me, his hands in his pockets. This time he's not smiling. "Hey, Josh. I'm glad you could come over," he says, like reading from a script. His eyes look dewy and red, like maybe he'd been crying just before we got here.

"Me too," I say, wondering why he looks sad. Like, isn't he happy to be home? I thought he'd be smiling nonstop.

I get introduced then to the other people. The baldish man is their lawyer, Mr. Walker, and he's here with his wife and daughter. I say hello to Mrs. Sykes, to the Tomeks. I look over at Beth. She's quiet, staring off like she finds this whole situation mortifying.

"Guys," Mr. Walker says, "the film crew wants us to be outside, sort of acting normal."

Acting normal. I hear Beth let out a quick laugh that sounds like "huh."

"Maybe the kids can kick the soccer ball around?" Mr. Walker suggests.

Mrs. Manderson looks over at Sam. "Is that okay, honey?"

He just nods. "I'll get the ball in my room."

"I have it in my room," Beth says. "I'll get it."

We all go outside. The front yard is large and triangular, on the corner lot, with an oak tree that provides shade to just a small part of the yard. Ruben and Sam head onto the grass with the ball. I know I'm expected to join in, but I hate soccer. Over by the driveway I see the news reporter, in a black skirt and white shirt, her hair all shellacked, and she heads over with her microphone, while a scruffy guy fiddles around with his camera.

Beth stands next to me on the porch. She says, "This is a joke."

I don't say anything back. I watch as Ruben kicks the ball to Sam. The ball sails past him and for a second he just watches it, like he's confused about what he's supposed to do, but then he breaks into a run and goes for it.

"We don't even really know that man, Mr. Walker. I'd never met his wife and daughter until today. They just wanted people here. Mom asked all of Sam's old friends to come over for this. Nick. Max. Some others. And not a single one of them would come. They all had excuses." We both watch as Sam kicks the ball right to Ruben, a smooth grounder. I think about Sam's eyes, how sad they looked earlier. But now, running around, he seems happy. I can see him smiling as he chases the ball.

"I'm here," I say.

I step off the porch and walk out onto the lawn to join them. Everyone else just stands aside and watches us like we're doing something fascinating. Sam has the ball and kicks it over to me, and I'm able to stop it and kick it back to him. I don't think I look too spastic, but who knows. It's better than standing around. And honestly, after a while it starts to seem natural, the three of us aimlessly kicking the ball, like we're totally unaware that this is being filmed for some sort of "feel good" story on the local news.

The cameraman eventually sets his camera down—I guess he has all the footage he needs. Even though he's stopped filming, we keep kicking the ball. Beth is still staring from the porch. Even from this distance, I can see that she's frowning. The adults are all talking to one another, and Mr. Walker and Sam's mom are dealing with the TV people. Ruben's mother calls him over, tells him it's time to go home. So then it's just the two of us. Sam dribbles the ball over to me.

"We can stop if you want," he says. His hair is pasted to his forehead and a film of sweat coats his face.

I'm sweaty, too, and a little winded, so I say, "Okay."

We both look toward the house, toward the reporter, who's now interviewing Mrs. Manderson as the cameraman films.

"I haven't played in so long."

"You can't tell," I say. You should try out for the team, I want to say, but I don't. I don't know if Sam will even come back to school.

We're silent for a few seconds, just standing there, then Sam says, "I knew you'd come."

I turn and meet his eyes. He looks down at the soccer ball, then back up. He says, "We're connected, you and me."

I glance at Beth. She's watching her mother, who's still talking to the camera. Beth and I are connected, too, I guess. We all are—by that day, all those years ago. "Yeah," I finally say.

Sam drops the soccer ball and dribbles away. He's kind of gangly, but still there's a grace in the way he moves around the yard. He kicks the ball up and then bounces it on his head a few times, before it rolls off into the grass.

Sam's okay, I think. *Anyone who can do that is fine.* He heads back my way. He doesn't say a word, but he comes to a stop right next to me. He's a little too close. I can hear his breathing. I feel like he's about to say something else, so I steal the ball from Sam and start dribbling away from the adults, away from Sam, toward the farther reaches of the yard, past the oak tree, almost to the curb. I hear Sam chasing after me, laughing, and he finally steals the ball back, snatching it from my feet so that I almost trip. But I catch myself and stop, and he turns around after running a bit and stares over at me. He looks triumphant and happy, smiling wide, his face flush, his chest heaving, just a normal boy having fun with his friend. Maybe his only friend in the world.

We're connected, you and me. It only dawns on me just then that this wasn't a question. It was a fact.

CHAPTER 5
The Famous Beth Walsh

Beth

Instead of parking in the student lot in back of school, I park in one of the lots near the athletic fields. It's a longer walk, but I don't care. It's my first day back since Sam returned. After New York, I told Mom I didn't feel well. I fake-sicked my way through Homecoming week. But I knew I'd have to go back eventually, and so here I am now, walking through the front doors.

I plan to head right to my locker and then homeroom, but the assistant vice principal, Mr. Bishop, carries his walkie-talkie at his side and walks up to me and tells me it's so good to see me. Welcome back.

He's never said a word to me before.

"Okay, thanks," I say.

And then it's my classmates—a bunch I don't even know that well—smiling at me, saying hello, they are so happy for me and my family, what a miracle. Two juniors fist-bump me. *We saw you on TV, omigod, what was it like meeting Helen Winters?*

I clear through the crowd and beeline up the stairs to my locker, keeping my eyes on the floor. But when I get there, my locker's insane. It looks like a shrine. There's stuff taped to the door—envelopes, scrawled messages on Post-its and notebook paper. There's more stuff on the floor surrounding the locker—a few stuffed animals, some gift bags, candy bars, even a tiny bundle of wilted flowers. What on earth.

Chita's standing by my locker. She usually greets me with some sarcastic remark, like, "Another day in paradise." But today she has this weird smile on her face. "We waited for you in the parking lot," she says gently, like she's talking to a shy kid.

"I parked somewhere else today." I don't want to explain why.

She reaches in and hugs me, which is *not* how we greet each other normally. It's weird, and unsettling, and I just want her to act normal. I look back at my locker and say, "What *is* all this?"

"All your best friends in the world," she says, clearing her throat, "welcoming you back." There's sarcasm in her voice, and she sounds like herself finally.

I keep staring at all that stuff. I know I'm supposed to be grateful, but really I feel like I'm under attack.

"I can help you with it, if you want?" she says. She bends down and picks up a stuffed animal frog and brings it up close to my face. *"Ribbit."*

I start turning the locker combination.

"So, why didn't you call me? Why didn't you return any of my messages?" She sounds weird again, needy and sad. "Ainsley and Darla, too," she continues. "Nobody heard from you. We were worried."

I pull the locker open. Some more notes have been shoved through the slots, but otherwise it's how I left it that afternoon before I snuck off with Donal, which feels like it happened years ago.

"Sorry," I say.

"You don't have to be sorry," she says, but I can tell she still wants an explanation. She pats me on the shoulder and keeps her hand there.

I put a few books in my backpack, grab the notes and shove them in there, too. "Things have been kinda busy," I say, with maybe a little too much edge in my voice. "With my brother coming back and all."

"I know. But we want to be here for you. You can talk to us."

I can't explain it to her. At home, I was always aware that Sam was missing. My mom's obsession with finding him, and her bouts of sadness all filled the air and smothered me. School was so separate; it was like a refuge from all of that. I hardly ever talked about that part of my life with my friends, and they never asked. But now it's all been dumped out in the open, just like all this stuff by my locker.

"Sorry," I say again. By now more people are pouring through the halls and everyone is staring at me or saying hi. I wish I could just hide.

Then Ainsley and Darla walk up, and they both take turns hugging me. *Great*, I think. And then Chita has to get one more hug in, too.

"We missed you," Darla says.

"How's it feel to be back?" Ainsley says.

"Weird," I say, but what I really want to say is *Terrible*. "Why is everyone being so nice to me?"

"You're famous now," Ainsley says, and I can't tell if she's kidding or not.

"You're gonna need an extra bag for this stuff," Darla says, eyeing the display.

Chita's just staring at me, like she's trying to read my mind. Over the years, I'd have these spells, where things at home were especially bad—when Mom entered what I started to call a Black Hole—and it always seemed like Chita knew. She'd crack jokes or talk about something ridiculous that we could make fun of together to distract me right when I needed it most. But she never made me talk about any of it.

Darla and Ainsley help me shove the gifts and stuff in my backpack, or at least the stuff that will fit, and the rest we shove into my locker.

The warning bell for homeroom rings.

"How's your ankle?" Chita asks as we walk down the hall.

"Fine. It's fine."

"Will you be able to practice?" Ainsley says.

"I think so," I say.

We all reach the spot in the hall where we usually veer our separate ways. They all want to hug me again, so I let them. I know they all mean well, but it feels strange some-how. "See you at lunch," Chita says.

"Sure," I say, already walking away.

Sam had been gone about six weeks when it was time for me to start my freshman year. I was so relieved to escape from the endless days of waiting, Mom's crying and Earl consol-ing her, me hiding in my room, everyone jumping out of their skin when the phone rang.

Relieved and also kind of excited. Excited to start high school. Excited to see my best friend Grace again. Mom thought Grace was too prissy ("Miss Teen USA," she al-ways called her), and that she "put on airs," whatever that meant. I remember Sam sort of had a crush on her, because he turned bashful and quiet when Grace came over. We'd been tight all through middle school and I figured we'd pick up where we left off.

But I hadn't seen her for weeks. She'd called and texted, after Sam went missing, but I couldn't bring myself to respond. The last time I heard from her, she texted me reminding me about cheerleading practice, which was going to be held a few weeks before school started. "You *have* to do this with me," she said in the message—and it's true, that had been our plan all along. We'd spent so many days that summer practicing in Grace's big backyard. But the thought of asking Mom or even Earl to take away one minute of their search for Sam so I could try out for *cheerleading*—well, I couldn't do it. I never sent Grace anything back.

When the first day arrived, I wasn't really prepared. Mom hadn't taken me shopping for any new clothes. I only had a few supplies—ink pens and pencils and notebooks left over from the year before. Back then I didn't have a laptop. All we had was the one desktop computer, "for the family," which sat on the small desk in the corner of the den. Mom was using it constantly, sending out e-mails and checking missing persons reports and message boards.

On that first day, I got dressed, making do with my old clothes, and I made my own breakfast—Cheerios and a cut-up banana. I packed my book bag and grabbed a print-out of the class schedule the school had e-mailed a few weeks earlier.

Mom dressed for work. She'd gone back by then. She had to—we needed money coming in. I told her I could take the bus to school, but she said no way. I don't think she wanted me walking anywhere by myself. In this new world, no one was safe.

Sam should have been starting sixth grade that day at the middle school. That morning, while waiting for Mom, I'd seen Josh and his dad drive off.

Mom let me off at the curb in front. I was jumping out the door when she said, "Have a good first day, okay? Earl will pick you up at three thirty. At that parking lot over by the soccer fields?" I nodded and slammed the door. I walked toward the school and paused. I suddenly felt sick to my stomach. I turned and saw Mom, still staring at me. She wouldn't leave till she saw me go through those doors. So I did.

The hallways were brightly lit and crazy with people everywhere. I found my locker and then started to head to my homeroom. I was nervous, but the sick feeling in my stomach started to ease. I realized as I walked through the halls that it felt good to be around other people, not trapped in the house. But soon enough I noticed everyone looking at me funny. Sad glances before they would quickly turn away. I saw two girls whisper as I walked by. A teacher passed me and smiled—a pity smile.

Once I found my homeroom, I was faced with it all over again—the stares, the whispering. And the teacher, when she called my name, gave me an overly sympathetic smile and said, "Hello, dear" in a way that made it sound like I had some terminal disease.

Beth Walsh. The girl with the missing brother. The dead

brother. Somehow everyone knew. But I didn't understand why I was being singled out this way. I wasn't the one who'd disappeared. I was still here. I was moving on with my life.

Or I was trying to.

At lunch in the huge cafeteria, I looked for Grace. I hadn't seen her all day—somehow we hadn't had any classes together. When I finally spotted her, she was sitting with some girls who I knew had also tried out for cheerleading. Popular girls. We'd sort of been drifting into their orbit that spring before school ended. We'd always claimed to despise them, until they started being friendlier to us, and then they were so nice, so great, so cool.

I walked over. The table was full, and there Grace was, in the middle of all those girls. Grace looked different—too tan, and wearing this sparkly eyeliner. Finally, she saw me. "Hi, Beth, how *are* you?" she said, smiling at me like I was a wet kitten—a cute but sad thing. Then all the other girls smiled, too, in almost exactly the same way.

I can't remember what I said, but I must have mumbled something. I expected Grace to maybe get up and hug me. To acknowledge what I'd been through but also acknowledge she was my best friend. But all she could do was stare at me with pity. Finally, she said, "I made the squad, can you believe it?" She looked around at the others as if asking for help, then back at me, still with that dumb smile. My own best friend, treating me the way a stranger would.

"That's great," I said. I looked and saw one empty seat. I moved toward it but some girl put her hand down and said, "Sorry, we're saving that for someone."

"Oh, okay," I said. I didn't even look back at Grace. I just walked away, to the other side of the room.

There were no completely empty tables, but there was a mostly empty one, so I sat there. At the other end, a few guys had staked their spots. A set of twins. A black kid. A really blond kid. And then a guy with red hair. He was the one who looked over—even sitting I could see he was tall and gangly, clearly a freshman like me, with ears that stuck out like they were too large for his head. I could tell he wanted to talk to me or something, to try and be friendly or whatever. But I looked down at my food. He finally ignored me and carried on with his conversation with his friends—stupid boy stuff, which I mostly tuned out. For the rest of the lunch period I ate in silence and waited for the bell to ring.

The redheaded guy was Donal Murphy, and he was in my next class—biology. He was Irish—like, *really* Irish, with the accent and all. What the hell was he doing in Tuscaloosa, I wondered. Turned out his father was an econ professor at the University, but I found that out later. All through class I tried not to look at him, although I knew he kept stealing looks at me.

Finally, when that first day of school ended, I grabbed my

things from my locker and waited for Earl by the parking lot near the soccer field. Off behind me, I saw the soccer teams practicing. Or maybe it was tryouts, I didn't know. I'd never played except when they made us in gym. Sam had played soccer from a young age. He'd been a star player, and I'd usually gone to his games.

Suddenly a ball rolled past me, headed toward the parking lot. I raced toward it and caught it with my foot before it could enter. I turned and dribbled the ball a little, looking for who it belonged to. Up ahead, some girl was running toward me. When she got closer she slowed down and stopped, giving me the once-over.

I kicked the ball to her. "Hey. You trying out?" She had black hair, cut short like a boy's, and olive skin. She wore crimson-colored knee-high socks, matching knee pads, white shorts, and a Central Falcons Soccer T-shirt. And on her wrist was a rainbow bracelet that looked homemade.

"Nope," I said.

"Maybe you should," she said. "Those were some good moves."

"Yeah, right," I said.

"They were. You should *see* some of those girls trying out," she said, rolling her eyes. "But for real. This week we have open tryouts. I'm helping Coach Bailey with the drills and stuff. Coach Bailey loves me—I've got some pull. Come."

"My brother played," I said, dodging her.

"He on the boys' team?"

"No," I said. I almost added, he's too young. But I stopped myself. This girl had no idea who I was, I realized. I liked that.

"I'm Conchita, but everyone calls me Chita," she said.

"Beth," I said.

"Well, Beth, I still think you should try out."

I had some trouble imagining that my mom would let me leave the house for anything other than school. "I can't today."

"Tomorrow then."

"Maybe."

She just stood there, sort of smiling at me. I saw she had dirt on her cheek, like she'd rolled around on the ground. But she didn't seem to care. "I've never seen you before," I said.

"I used to go to Holy Spirit. But their team sucks. I wanted to play on a good team—well, a better team, anyway. A team that has a chance at State." She picked the ball up and bounced it on her head a few times, while crossing her eyes and sticking her tongue out.

I let out a little laugh. My first laugh in weeks, probably. Earl's truck pulled up and I saw him wave. "Well, my ride's here," I said, with a stab of regret. This was the first real conversation—the first conversation not centered on Sam—I'd had with anyone in weeks.

"Come by tomorrow. I'll be waiting for you. Right here."

"We'll see," I said, smiling.

That afternoon, after Earl went back to the construction site and while Mom was still at work, I went into Sam's room and paused, feeling like I was in some sacred space that shouldn't be disturbed. I wanted to be out of there, so I quickly found his soccer ball in his closet and left. I went to the backyard and kicked the ball into the fence like I was trying to score a goal, dribbled the ball till I was tired and sweaty. I wasn't so bad at it, I realized. After, I went back in the house and put the soccer ball in my closet. It wasn't like Sam was here to use it.

The next day, after the bell rang, I changed into my gym clothes in one of the bathroom stalls, avoiding the locker rooms so I wouldn't have to deal with anyone. Then I walked to where I'd waited yesterday. I'd told Earl I had to stay late for a Yearbook staff meeting. But on my way to the field, my stomach started feeling knotted. I thought I might chicken out. Hadn't some of these girls played competitively for years? Despite what Chita said, how did I know if I was any good? I might fall on my face and risk humiliation. The idea seemed crazier and crazier.

But Chita was waiting for me, like she promised. "I knew you'd come," she said, sounding triumphant.

I kept a stone face. "Listen. Will this take up a lot of time after school?" I didn't tell her it was because I hated being home.

Chita smiled. "This will keep you plenty busy. I can promise you that."

"Then let's go," I said, walking toward where the coach stood.

Chita trotted alongside me, and when I glanced over at one point I could see her grinning a mile wide. Darla was there that day, too, the only black girl in the whole group, and Ainsley, with streaks of blue in her hair, so tall that she seemed more like a basketball player. Across the way, the boys' soccer players had gathered for *their* tryouts. And I saw some of the guys from lunch, including Donal, sitting in the grass stretching. He saw me and waved like a spaz. I'd sat at his lunch table again earlier that day, and ignored all of them, and then ignored Donal in biology class, too. I could have ignored him again right there, but I waved back. The sun was on my skin, and the breeze blew my hair around. I felt excited and hopeful again. For the first time in weeks, I was happy.

When I enter the cafeteria for lunch, Grace Cutler comes right up to me, like she was camped out waiting. "Beth!" she says, beaming, like she's still my best girlfriend, three years later.

"Oh, hi," I say.

It's not like we haven't seen each other since freshman year. Since she went her way—cheerleading and all that—

and I went mine, we have had plenty of classes together. But usually we both acted like strangers.

"I just want to tell you how happy I am for you—for your family. It's just so amazing," she says.

"Thanks," I say. Grace is still blond and pretty, but she doesn't wear too much makeup like she did freshman year. From what I know, she doesn't have a boyfriend. But she has that confidence about her, from knowing other girls—not me, but some—admire her, look up to her. Envy her.

"You must be so happy!" She's still beaming, flashing big teeth that are so white she must use those whitening strips. Maybe I look blank or confused, because she continues: "I mean, obviously you're happy. But it's just—it's just so wonderful."

"Yes, it is," is all I can manage to say.

Right then a few of Grace's friends come and hover around us. I know these girls, but I've never really talked to any of them before.

"Come sit with us," Grace says. "Can you?"

I look toward my usual table but don't see Chita or anyone else. We've sat at the same table together every year of high school. I guess Grace sees me hesitate.

"Please," she says, sounding like she did years ago, when she begged me to try out with her. "It's been too long," she says.

"Okay, sure," I say, because how can I say no?

"Good," she says, sounding almost relieved.

You don't switch lunch tables. You just don't. But my feet keep walking along with Grace and her squad. I sit down at their table and it's like they've always had this seat open for me, saving it for when I was ready. I feel jumbled when they all talk to me at once.

"You were so calm and collected on TV," this girl named Margo says. Then another girl says, "You looked really pretty."

"You have to tell us *everything* about it," Grace adds, flipping her hair aside, like I'm some boy she's flirting with. It's nice, I realize, that Grace is talking to me like no time has passed.

"It was crazy," I say, surprised that they're all looking at me like I have something important to say. "They had people to do our makeup and hair, and tons of clothes to choose from." I go on and on about it, and they all sit there like what I'm telling them is the most electrifying thing they've ever heard in their lives.

"I grew up with Beth," Grace says to the group. "I knew Sam when he was little. I think he had a crush on me."

"He did." I laugh, remembering suddenly those times when she slept over and Sam would bug us.

"I mean, seeing him on TV, I can't believe how much he's grown up. It's just such a miracle he's back," Grace says, clasping her hands in front of her chest.

"Omigod, tell us about Helen Winters," this girl Aimee says. She's a cheerleader. They all are, I realize.

"She's really old. Like, grandmother old," I say, which gets a few laughs. Right then I see Chita enter the cafeteria, heading to our usual table. I look back at the girls before me. "But she was very nice to us. They put us up in this fancy hotel, like near Central Park. A lot of celebs stay there."

"Omigod, did you see anyone famous?" Margo asks.

"Well, we were there just for a little while, so I didn't see anyone. But they told me, like, Selena Gomez and Ryan Gosling and a bunch of other people stay there all the time."

"So cool!"

I glance over to my old table, and I see Chita staring over at me, confused. Darla sits down and I see Chita say something to her as she watches me. I turn back to the cheerleaders. Margo's speaking now, talking about *her* trip to New York, how they saw so-and-so on the street, but I'm not really listening to the words. I'm just nodding, smiling, trying to act like I belong.

"What sights did you see?" Aimee asks. "And what shows?"

"Did you shop?" Margo asks.

"Well, it was a quick trip. But Mom says we'll go back."

"Your mom is so nice," Grace says.

My mom, nice?

"Come with me to get some food?" she asks. "I'm starving."

"Sure," I say, following her to the food line. It's like I've gone back in time to freshman year, and this is the first day, and this is how things should have gone.

We stop at the salad bar and before we load our plates, Grace looks at me, suddenly serious. "This is nice," she says. "Talking to you."

"Yeah," I say.

"I feel . . ." she starts to say, then stops. "It's just . . . It's been too long."

"Yeah," I say, the hardness I'd felt for Grace melting away inside, like whatever happened between us, all those years ago, doesn't matter anymore.

Once we get our food, I sit back down at the table with Grace, careful to avoid looking at Chita and the girls. I mean, is it so bad that I want to re-establish an old friendship? It doesn't mean I'm abandoning them. I just think back to something Mom said, on the plane coming home from New York, when Earl and Sam were dozing off in the row in front of us. "When we get back home, we'll make a fresh start. A new beginning."

Mom made it sound so easy. But maybe she had a point. Because that's what I'm doing now, I think. Making a new beginning for myself.

===

When the bell rings for the last period of the day, I walk out to the soccer field, dressed in my normal clothes. I'm going to chat with Coach, to see if she thinks I can work out with the team. My ankle feels better, and it might be nice to just be outside, so I can clear my head and not think about Sam or anything. On my way, Donal jogs up to me. He's already in his cleats.

"Hey, Beth," he says, slowing down to match my pace.

"Hey." I feel my face flush a little and look away. The last time I was this close to him, we were kissing.

"I'm glad you're back," he says. His accent has faded over the years, but it's still there, so *glad* sounds like *glod*, and *back* like *bock*. "I was worried about you. I left you some messages."

"Yeah, things have been sort of crazy."

"I bet. I mean, your brother, Sam. Your brother! That's so incredible. I just wanted to . . . To tell you I'm happy for you."

"Thanks," I say. I'd never talked to Donal about Sam, but he must have known about it—everyone did at some point. Then they filed it away and it didn't matter. I was just Beth to them. But not anymore. Now everyone is so concerned. Everyone wants hugs. It's like they all want me to break down so they can comfort me.

"We missed you at lunch today."

"I was there."

"Yeah, I saw you. With Grace and those girls."

"So?" I stop walking. "What about it?"

He stops and holds up his hands. "Nothing."

I start walking again.

"You okay?" he asks.

"I'm *fine*," I say, so sick of having to tell everyone that. We're almost at the field. I can tell he wants to ask me something else but is holding back.

"So, that day at my house?" he says, sounding hesitant, looking off toward the field. He swallows, his Adam's apple poking out sharply.

"The day I found out about Sam?" I say. I was a different person then. A different Beth.

"I . . . Uh. Never mind," he says.

At the field, Donal gives me a quick wave bye and jogs off to join the guys' team. When she sees me, Coach Bailey hugs me, and so do the others, and it's just like when I arrived at school, all these emotional demands that I don't want to deal with. We should be stretching, cutting up, talking shit, like we always do before practice. I was thinking it would be nice to be back out there, but now I realize things will be weird here, too. That it's going to be weird everywhere, maybe.

Coach says, "How's that ankle?"

"Doctor says I need more rest," I tell her, shaking it for effect.

"Okay," she says, patting me on the back, and I flinch and she gives me a funny face, like I've hurt her feelings. "Well, okay, we won't rush things."

Chita looks over and holds out her hands, like she's asking, *What gives?*

I look away and take my seat in the bleachers and take out my phone. I already see a text from Grace: **"Glad UR Back. XXOO."**

When I get home from school, Mom's making cookies. She hasn't done this in ages. "How was school?" she asks, smiling like she's Mom of the Year. I'm not used to her being home till well after five, but she's taken a leave of absence at work—to be there for Sam "during the transition."

"Fine," I say.

Let me state the obvious: Home is different now that Sam is back. Sure, I guess it's a happier place. Or Mom is happier, and so is Earl. But that initial euphoria has worn off. Now it's like Sam is an awkward guest that we're all being overly polite to. So far he's quiet, and doesn't say much unless prompted. He has that slight, cautious smile on his face a lot, and sometimes a spaced-out look, like maybe he's lost in his own unknowable memories. Something must be wrong with me, because I feel uneasy around him. A normal person would want to spend every second with him, to make up for lost time. Wouldn't they?

"I bet it was good to see all your friends," Mom says.

"Yeah," I say. I'm too tired to tell her about all the attention I got, or about Grace, or about all the presents that are hidden in my backpack, weighing me down.

Mom says, "I took Sam to see his counselor today. The man that Dr. Rao recommended. Dr. Saylor." Sam's seeing this doctor so someone can assess his psychological condition and monitor his progress. I don't know how much this doctor tells Mom and Earl—or how much Sam tells the doctor. As a family, the policy is that we're still not asking him about those three years. It's up to Sam to tell us when or if he's ready, Mom says. And, according to Mom, he's not ready yet. And that's fine by me.

He's also getting a tutor, to see how far behind he is in school.

"Where is he?" I ask.

"He's on the back patio, drawing. He draws now, did you know that?"

I shake my head. Yet another fact that makes him seem like a stranger.

"You should see his stuff. He's very good. Go out and say hello."

"I've got a lot of homework to catch up on," I say.

"Beth," Mom says. She stops spooning the dough onto the pan and looks at me. She's not frowning or anything, but I know it's an admonishment. "Can you go say hello?

I know he'd like that. And it would mean a lot to me."

"Okay," I say.

Outside on the back patio, Sam's sitting at the rickety iron table, his sketch pad resting in front of him. He's holding a pencil in his hand, nibbling on the eraser. He looks up at me when I walk over.

"What are you drawing?" I sit down on one of the cold iron chairs.

"I'm just thinking."

I look out toward the corner of the yard. We had a swing set there once, but Earl ripped it up a few years ago and planted a few shrubs. I used to push Sam in it, when he was a little kid. "Higher," he'd say, "higher."

"Mom says you're on the soccer team," he says.

"Yeah. I'm on the team. Midfielder."

"That's so cool," he says. He stares off, twirls his pencil. I look over at his sketch pad, and it's blank. He sees me taking a look. "Yeah, I haven't figured out what to draw yet. But I can show you some of my other drawings. If you want?"

"Sure," I say.

"I'll be right back."

I watch him head into the house, then look at the blank sketch pad resting on the table. Sam used to hate sitting still. He never even really liked crayons as a kid, except to write stuff on his bedroom wall. He didn't seem to have an artistic bone in his body.

Now he's back, carrying this older-looking sketch pad with a worn red cover. I can see that loose-leaf pages are stuffed into it when he sets it down. He starts flipping through the pages, but I can't see anything.

"I left a lot of my drawings there."

There.

"But here's one I did, sort of scenic."

He hands it over. It's this pencil drawing of some mountains seen from a distance. It's really good—detailed and precise. He hands over some others. Still lifes, I guess you call them, of random stuff, like a cup of coffee, a tape dispenser, a bowl of fruit. There's a great one of a cat hunched up on what looks like a picnic table, another of a courtyard with a bicycle on the ground. I'm kind of shocked at how good it all is. I mean, I'm no art critic, but I know I couldn't do anything like this.

"These are great, Sam. Really."

He shakes his head. "They're so-so."

"No, they're good." I want to ask how he learned to do this, but I don't.

He pulls out another. He studies it, hesitates.

"Can I see?"

"It's terrible."

"I doubt it. Let me?"

He turns the picture around and right away I see that it's a self-portrait, in what looks like colored pencil, of when he was a little younger. It's not bad, just a little weird. Like the eyes and nose and ears are slightly bigger than they should be, the coloring a little too bright. But it's unmistakably Sam.

"I love it," I say, even though I don't. It's kind of creepy.

"You can have it."

I take it.

"I tried to draw pictures of what I thought you'd look like. I did, like, hundreds of bad, stupid drawings, but I left—I mean I threw most of them away. They sucked. They didn't look a thing like you."

Something in my chest starts to ache, thinking of him trying to draw me, in that place. And then my mind goes where I don't want it to: *Abuse. Torture.* All the things he went through that I can't—won't—imagine. I swallow and say, "It's okay. You can draw me anytime."

He picks up his fresh sketch pad and perches it on his knee, propped so I can't see. He starts moving the pencil around, darting his eyes up to me, back to the pad, back and forth. He goes on for a few minutes. On the outside, he looks so normal. No scars that I can see, his hands smooth and strong, his face clear of blemishes. No trace that anything happened to him. I feel my throat tightening.

"I really need to get to my homework," I finally say, hoping I don't sound funny.

He rests his pencil. "Oh, okay."

"I've just got so much to do, being out of school for so long." Once I say it, I feel stupid—Sam has been out of school for way longer than me.

"It's okay. I understand." I stand and start walking back to the house. "Don't forget this," he says.

I turn back and he's holding up the self-portrait. "Oh yeah. Thanks."

Back in my room, I set the picture on my desk. Younger Sam looks up at me. What had he already been through when he drew this, in that awful place? *No. Don't think about that stuff. We're not talking about all of that.* I open the bottom drawer of my desk, where I keep old school papers and stuff. I take all of that out, put the picture on the bottom of the drawer, and then pile everything back in, and shut it.

Every morning, I park by the athletic fields, away from the main lot where most of the seniors and juniors park. And every morning, Chita and Darla and Ainsley wait for me at my locker, undeterred.

"How are you today?" one of them will ask. Or, "You doing okay? How's Sam?"

And always, I say, "I'm fine." And, "He's okay," as if I know. But what I want to say is, "Can we go back to a few weeks ago? Let's talk about normal things. Please don't make me think about my brother." They all look at me like I might crack apart. When we separate before homeroom, they all hug me. We never used to do that.

At lunch every day that week, I sit with Grace and those girls—not with the soccer gang. It's not what I intended to do, but each day Grace is waiting for me and takes me to the table like I'm in need of an escort. After that first day, no one really brings up Sam or New York. It's almost like I'm part of their group. I know I'm not. But at least they don't treat me like a fragile flower, like someone they want to heal with hugs.

On Thursday, Grace mentions a Halloween party out at someone's lake house. "It's anti-costume theme. No dressing up allowed. Can you come?"

A party, with these girls and their crowd—football players and meatheads—doesn't sound like my scene. Grace sees the hesitation in my face. "Please?" she says.

I'm too caught off guard to think of an excuse. "Okay," I say.

"It will be a blast. I promise."

When I go to my locker at the end of the day, Chita is there.

"Why are you doing this?" she asks. Her voice sounds raw. She's leaning against another person's locker, like she's exhausted.

I open my locker and unload some books. I feel so tired, right then. Tired of the concern. Tired of the attention. "Doing what?" I finally say, but I know what.

"You always hated those bitches."

I cringe at that word. "They're not . . . bitches," I say. "They're actually nice. And Grace and I go way back, actually. Did you know that? She was my best friend in middle school."

Chita squints at me like I've said something crazy. "But you've hardly spoken to her for three years," she says. "Or she's hardly spoken to you."

I look into my locker and fiddle with a few things, kind of hoping Chita will just walk away.

"Beth," she says.

I finally turn to her. "What?" It sounds sharper than I mean it to.

"Something's wrong," she says. "Does it have to do with Sam being—"

"Can you just stop?" I ask. I slam my locker shut.

"Wow," she mutters, and then walks away.

And I know I should yell at her to stop and come back.

I should, but I don't.

At dinner that night, Mom asks, "How's Chita? How are the girls?"

Shame floods through me, and I get that tired feeling again, like my arms and legs weigh a ton. I look up and force a smile. "They're fine," I say, and she doesn't push me.

Sam's sitting there, methodically eating his food, looking

from Mom to Earl as they talk. Before he got back, we usually sat on the couch for dinner, in front of the TV, my plate on the coffee table, not talking.

"Can I go to a party tomorrow night?" I ask.

"A Halloween party?" Mom asks. "With the girls?"

"No. With Grace."

"Grace Cutler?" Mom asks, sounding surprised.

"Yeah. We're hanging out again."

"That's great," Mom says, not sounding like she means it.

"Where is this party?" Earl asks.

"Somewhere across the river. One of her friend's houses. It's small, not many people. No costumes, thank God. Grace will pick me up."

"As long as you're home by eleven."

"Okay."

A few minutes pass as everyone keeps eating.

"We met Sam's tutor today," Mom says, breaking the silence. "Her name's Lane. A nice young woman. She used to teach at Hillcrest but left to be a mom. But now that her kids are in school, she's gone into tutoring."

"Did you like her?" Earl asks Sam.

"Yeah, she was nice. She was pretty."

Earl laughs and Mom smiles. I guess they think this is cute. Or maybe they're relieved that Sam thinks a woman is pretty, just like a normal teenage boy.

"Listen, I wanted to talk to you both about something,"

Mom says, changing the subject. Her tone is serious. "I've been speaking—" She pauses and looks over at Earl, and he nods, like he's giving her permission. "I've been speaking with Hank—with your father. He wants to come see you."

"Sam," I say without thinking. "He wants to see Sam."

"He wants to see you, too," Mom says.

I just look down at my plate and eat some more even though now I'm not hungry.

"We thought maybe your father could come down for a day or two over Thanksgiving weekend, next month."

"I don't care," I say. "Whatever." I grab my plate and bring it to the kitchen. Normally Mom would yell and tell me to excuse myself first, but not tonight.

I go to my room and shut the door. I grab my phone. I type a text to Chita—Sorry about earlier—but I don't send it. I delete it and then lay on my bed and just stare at the ceiling. When a text chimes, I grab my phone and see it's from Donal: How are you?

I set it down. I don't reply. Even though I want to tell him that I feel terrible. Confused. I start crying, just a little, and the tears leak out and I cup my hand over my mouth and I hope that Mom doesn't knock because I don't want her to see me like this. I don't want *anyone* to see me like this. I'm supposed to be happy now, aren't I? So why have I turned into such a mess?

===

Grace picks me up Friday at eight. Aimee and Margo are in the car, too. "Cute house," Margo says from the passenger seat. Both Aimee and Margo live in big houses in Forest Lake, so I know "cute" means small.

"I hate it," I say, which makes Aimee laugh. She has this kind of annoying laugh, like a whiny hiccup. "We might move," I say, which is a lie. "We got some money from doing the TV interview."

No one seems impressed by that, and I feel my face color. *Relax*, I think.

"What's the address of this party again?" Grace asks, typing into her GPS.

"It's out on Lake Tuscaloosa," Margo says.

"I know," Grace says. "I need *the address*."

Aimee calls it out, her eyes never leaving her phone.

"Whose house is this?" I ask.

"Tark Culpepper."

"Tark Culpepper?" I say. Tark is a name?

"He goes to the Academy," Margo says. "But some of his friends go to Central. You know, like Mitchell Lumpkin? And Chase Warren?"

"Yeah," I say, though those names mean nothing to me.

"So, are you dating Donal Murphy?" Aimee asks.

"The Irish dude?" Margo asks.

"No," I say. "We're just friends." Which is true. Right?

"Someone said you were," Aimee says.

"Nope," I say, wondering who said that. Did Donal tell the other guys about the day at his house? My face reddens.

"He's a cutie. You should go for that," Aimee says.

"Speaking of, Tark is a total hottie," Margo says. "Grace and I are totally going to fight each other over him."

"We are not," Grace says, laughing. "He's all yours."

"Well, sorry to burst your bubbles, but I heard Simone and Tark hooked up," Aimee says. "At Harrison's homecoming party."

"Ugh, Simone," Margo says. "Figures."

They keep talking, throwing out names of more people I don't know—Leslie, Jed, Harrison, Cecily. These girls have an easy rapport with one another. But I feel tongue-tied. I can't follow what or who they're talking about. *What am I doing here*, I think. But it's too late to back out.

We finally pull up to where the party is—a big brick house with a circular drive, with tons of tall pine trees everywhere, like we're in a magical forest.

The party inside is packed, and there are some faces I recognize, but mostly faces I don't. I shield myself behind the girls as they make their way through the crowd. They stop and talk to the other partygoers, but I just stand there awkwardly, like an afterthought. I see people heading to one of the back rooms—the kitchen—so I break off and make my way there. In the kitchen I see a keg and bottles of liquor set out. A guy pours vodka into a plastic cup with ice, then pours orange juice, and stirs it with a long spoon. "Want one?" he asks, noticing me. I nod and he hands me the drink. "Thanks," I say, but he's too busy mixing another one for himself to acknowledge me.

I walk from room to room, not stopping. Stopping means standing there and looking like I don't belong.

My drink is strong, but the orange juice makes it taste bearable. I start to feel calmer. Grace walks up behind me. "Hey! Where'd you go?" she says. She's flushed, grinning, with some guy in tow. He's got insanely green eyes and carefully combed dark brown hair. He's so chiseled he almost looks like a cartoon character. "This is Tark," Grace says.

"So you're the famous Beth Walsh." I can't tell if he's being jokey or flirty or something else. He reaches out his hand and I shake it. He holds on a bit longer than I'm used to.

"I'm not famous," I say, twitching inside at the reference to Sam. I take another quick sip of my drink.

"Uh, yeah, you are," he says. "Your story's like something out of a movie."

"A movie. Totally," Grace says. "Beth, who would play you?"

"So, how's your brother doing?" Tark asks, ignoring Grace.

I have no idea. "He's okay."

"That's great. That's really awesome," he says, smiling

like he's posing for a yearbook photo. "Hey, come meet some of my friends," he says, grabbing my hand and tugging me to a side room, where some of his private-school friends are holding court. I shoot Grace a look, but she's smiling, like this is what she had in mind all along, parading around her "famous" friend.

"Hey, guys, this is Beth. Beth Walsh. Her brother is the kid that vanished and then came back."

"Omigod," some girl says, bounding up from her seat. She's in a shimmery cocktail dress, like she's at some fashion show instead of a dumb high school kegger. "I saw you on TV!"

"Who?" some guy sitting on the couch asks. His hair is long and looks dirty and he probably thinks he looks cool.

"The girl whose brother went missing," she says, sounding impatient.

"We were just talking about how Beth's life could be made into a movie," Tark says.

"Oh, totally," the girl says. "Or maybe a miniseries!"

I shake my drink cup around. "I think I need another," I say, and then I turn around and walk away. I know I'm being rude, but I can't stand there anymore. I make my way back to the kitchen and try to pour myself the same drink that guy made me, but it tastes way worse than before.

When I turn around, Tark's behind me. "Did we scare you off?" he asks.

"No," I lie. "I just needed a drink."

"Come," he says, "I'll show you the lake." I follow him, and as we walk through the crowd I spot Aimee from a distance, and when she sees me with Tark, she sticks her tongue out and smiles.

Outside, the night air is cool. Tark leads me across the deck, past more clumps of people, down some steps, and then along a slight dirt path that weaves through a bunch of trees. Once we clear the trees we are on a wooden boat dock, the lake spreading out before us, gentle ripples visible in the moonlight.

"It's pretty," I say, walking to the dock's edge. I take another sip. And another. The dock creaks as he moves closer to me, closer, till I can smell his cologne.

"*You're* pretty," he says, putting his hand on my back, cupping himself behind me.

I want to like this. I want to want this. I want to feel like this is a world I could walk around in—parties, drinking, hot guys. But this whole night is wrong. When Tark starts to nuzzle his mouth on my neck, I step to the side, and walk to the other side of the dock.

"Um, okay?" he says. Maybe I'm the first girl who hasn't swooned and fallen into his arms.

"Listen, it's nothing personal." My voice sounds wobbly. "You're only giving me the time of day because you think I'm some celebrity. The girl with the brother who came back from the dead. The famous Beth Walsh."

He stands there, across from me, and turns to face the water, maybe to look at the moon—at anything besides me. I've ruined the moment he had in mind. But I don't care.

"You know, when I first started at Central, everyone knew who I was. The girl with the missing brother. But I made some friends, and they didn't care about that. They just knew me as Beth." I think of Chita and Darla and Ainsley and wonder what they're doing, if they're all hanging out, and I feel a jolt of remorse at how I've been acting. "And then everyone at school forgot about all that stuff. They just knew me as Beth, too. The girl on the soccer team. No one special." I take another sip of my drink. "But all that's changed again. Now I'm Beth whose brother miraculously reappeared. Beth from national TV. Beth whose life could be a movie. But that's bullshit, because I'm still just Beth. I just want to be Beth." I laugh to myself, because who is that? Who the hell am I? I don't really know anymore. I laugh again, and even in the faint moonlight I see Tark look back at me like I'm a lunatic.

I have to get away. I leave the dock and rush back up the slope to the house, back to the kitchen. I make myself another drink. I stand there for a bit, sort of in a trance, feeling like I'm not fully present in my body. Someone nudges me to get to the booze, so I walk to the main room and I see Tark talking with Margo in a corner, probably telling her what a weirdo I am. I shuffle back down the hall and bump into someone and spill my drink, splashing a little on the floor. "Sorry," I say, keeping my head down.

"Beth?"

I look up, hearing the accent. "What are you doing here?" Donal asks.

"What are *you* doing here?"

"Just here with the twins."

I see Jake and Jackson across the room, their matching dark flops of hair. "Oh God," I moan, my stomach rumbling all of a sudden. I hand him my drink and barrel my way through people.

Bathroom. Must find bathroom. There's a line when I get there, so instead I rush out the front door, push past a few people just arriving, onto the lawn, where I bend over and retch and then puke. I'm not sure how long this goes on. Everyone in the party must be peering through the windows, laughing.

"Beth?"

I jolt up. It's Donal, thank God.

"You okay?"

"Can you take me home?" I ask.

"Yeah. Of course." We walk down the street to his Jeep. He opens the passenger door for me, and I get in. "You sure you're okay?" he asks.

"Just take me home." And he does. And it's like he knows not to talk to me, because we're quiet most of the way, until we get closer to my house.

"I don't know what I was doing there," I say. "I made a fool of myself."

"I doubt that," he says. He pulls into my neighborhood. I click my phone and see it's almost eleven, just in time for my curfew. I hope Mom and Earl are asleep. I don't want them to see me like this.

"How's your ankle?" Donal asks.

For a second I wonder what he's talking about, and then I remember. "Okay, I guess."

"It seems like you're walking normal now. You going to be back on the field soon? Maybe we could kick the ball around?" He gives me a quick glance, probably hoping I'll nod my head in agreement.

"Bowl?" I ask.

"Ball," he says. "*Ball.*" He smiles, shakes his head. "You making fun of me?" he says, exaggerating his accent. He grins, hoping I'll laugh, and normally I would. But my brain is soupy. "I don't know," I say. "I may quit."

"You will not," Donal says. "I'm afraid I won't allow it."

I almost smile. His damn accent still gets to me. Even after all these years. Is that what makes him seem different than the other guys, or is it something else?

He pulls up to my house and stops the car. We sit there

and I can tell he wants to reach over and kiss me, like he did that day at his house. There's a charge in the air of the car, and I can sense him hoping for some sign—the same kind of sign I must have given off that day.

But I have nothing to give tonight. I open my door and get out. He gets out, too, and comes around to my side of the car. But he doesn't try to touch me. He stands there, his hands in his jeans pockets, respectful.

"Thanks for the ride. For getting me out of there."

"Any time," he says.

I start walking to the kitchen door, careful with my feet.

"Beth?" he says loudly.

I stop and turn back to him.

"Can you text me when you wake up tomorrow, so I know you're okay?"

It's dark out but I can still see him clearly because of his car's headlights. He looks solid, tall and strong—not slouchy and awkward like so many of the guys in my class. His endearingly big ears fit his face better. I know a lot of girls have a crush on him. But he's looking at me like I'm the only thing in the world he can see. I want to warn him away. I want to say, *Don't bother with me.* Instead I say, "Okay," before walking on.

I step inside and shut the door and lean back against it and close my eyes. A few seconds later, I hear the Jeep speed away. I open my eyes. The light above the stove provides a slight glow in the darkness. I creep into the den. The TV is off. The lights are off. I'm relieved but also ready to just collapse. I'm heading to my room when I notice something out of the corner of my eye.

Someone is on the couch, sitting in the dark. I can see the faintest suggestion of a body. "Hello?" I whisper, my heart suddenly pounding.

"Hi, Beth." Sam's voice cuts through the darkness.

"What are you doing?" I say, just above a murmur.

"Just sitting here," he says quietly, as if that's a normal thing to be doing—like watching TV, or reading a book. Just sitting in the dark.

I tiptoe to one of the armchairs across from the couch. I still have my jacket on but I sit down. Sam flicks on the little side lamp. He's in his jeans and a flannel shirt unbuttoned over a tee, wearing his shoes, like he was on his way out somewhere. Dressed the way he was when he returned, except his hair is trimmed. Those piercings are gone. I still can't get used to teenage Sam.

"How was the party?"

"Awful," I say. I shudder thinking about all of it—Tark and those kids and puking my brains out. The famous Beth Walsh. "What are you doing out here?"

He doesn't answer right away. He's just sort of looking off to the side as if he's searching for a response. "Sometimes I can't sleep."

Goose bumps bloom on my skin. "I can't sleep some-times, too," I say.

He flashes his eyes at me, like he's just noticing I'm here. "It's so quiet here," he says. "I'm used to . . . I'm not used to it being so quiet. That's funny, isn't it?" He looks off into space again, smiling that slight smile of his. "Sometimes I wake up, and I realize all over again that I'm home, not at Rusty's. And I'm so happy . . . too happy to go back to sleep. Like I . . ."

But he hesitates, and his face goes blank, like a switch has been flipped. Do I look panicked? That name—*Rusty*. Wasn't his name Russell? I feel my stomach rumble. Maybe I didn't puke all the booze out. Or maybe I did. *Rusty*. A nickname. I can tell Sam is about to add something else, something I don't want to hear, so I say, "I'm so tired."

Sam doesn't respond at first. I close my eyes, like that can protect me. Finally, he mumbles, "Don't tell Mom you saw me tonight, out here. I don't want her to worry."

"All she does is worry," I say, opening my eyes again.

Sam cracks a slight smile. After all these years, he still knows what our mother is like.

I feel a stab of closeness to him then, not fear. And I almost open my mouth and say, *Sam, it's okay, you can tell me about what happened.*

But no words come.

No words come because I don't want to know.

And it's like he can read this on my face because he says, "Good night, Beth," and he flicks the light off and then we're back in the dark.

I don't say anything. I just feel my way toward my room. I undress and crawl into bed. I'm not tired, despite what I said. And I thought my buzz was gone, but I guess it isn't because when I lie down my head starts spinning. I close my eyes and almost enjoy it, like I'm a kid again on a merry-go-round. Round and round I go, without a care in the world.

CHAPTER 6
Lickety-Split

Josh

After tennis practice on Monday, I wait for Dad to pick me up. I'm not in the best mood, and I wasn't hitting well today. "You're gonna have days like this," Coach Runyon said. "Don't be so hard on yourself." This was after I'd slammed my racket on the ground. When I picked my racket up, a lot of the guys stared over at me, because I never really show emotion on the court.

Nick usually waits with me after practice, but he's off talking with Sarah. I try not to look over at them, but I can't help it. Nick has his hands in his track pants pockets and is swaying back and forth, while Sarah smiles up at him adoringly. I think he could be saying anything and she'd still look that way. Girls have always had crushes on Nick, but before Sarah came along it's like he didn't notice or care. I hear Sarah laugh and then Nick laugh back at her, and I feel like bashing my racket on the ground again.

Dad's late. I look over toward the soccer field. My friend Raj is on the team, junior varsity, and I see him huddled in a group, talking to the coach. The huddle breaks and he runs out with his teammates onto the field.

Sam would probably be on that team. Maybe one day he will be, when he comes back to school. If he comes back.

Stop it. Stop thinking about him.

"Josh!" Nick says, walking up to me with his tennis stuff and backpack. In the distance I see Sarah getting into a car. "You still waiting on your dad?"

"Yeah," I say. I want to ask, *How's Sarah?* in a mocking way. But I keep quiet. I look at his hair, which keeps getting longer and longer. "You need a haircut," I say.

"What?" He runs a hand through it. "No way, man. Sarah wants me to grow it out." He grins big, thinking I will, too. I roll my eyes. Raj actually *cut* his hair, because Madison H. said she liked it short. Since when did my friends start acting like they don't have minds of their own?

Just then, Nick's mom pulls up. She rolls down the window and waves at me. "You need a ride, Josh?"

"No thanks, my dad's coming soon," I say.

Nick looks at me. "Later, bud," he says, tousling his hair like he's giving me the finger.

Dad finally pulls up after a few more minutes.

"Sorry, kiddo," he says when I hop in. I don't say anything back, just give an annoyed look, but he's oblivious.

Dad has NPR on, as always. A lady with a soothing voice is interviewing some man. He's talking about the brain, and junk food, something that has to do with science and chemicals and cravings and how companies know how to exploit the taste buds. I like that science can explain almost everything.

"How was practice?" Dad says when a commercial comes on.

Shitty, I want to say. "Okay."

"And how was school?"

Dad knows I hate this question. "Okay."

"Okay then. Everything is okay," Dad says with a chuckle. I feel his eyes on me, but I just look at the scenery out the window. It's not like we have big conversations all the time, but today I'm just not in the mood to say much.

The commercial ends, and the NPR lady comes back on and says stay tuned for local news. After another commercial, the local host is on. I'm really only half-listening, but suddenly I hear the name Russell Hunnicutt, then Sam Walsh.

"In a Calhoun County courtroom today, Hunnicutt pleaded guilty to seventy-three charges, including kidnapping, sexual abuse, attempted murder, and child—" And right then Dad changes the channel.

"Hey! I want to hear that," I say.

"Josh," Dad says.

"What? Dad, turn it back," I say.

Instead, he flicks the radio off completely.

"What's the big deal?" I ask.

"I just didn't want hearing that stuff to upset you."

"I'm not a kid. It's all over the news anyway. It's not like I don't know anything."

"I understand," he says. "It's just. Well, some of it's pretty serious. Stuff you shouldn't have to think or worry about." *At your age*, he refrains from saying but I know that's what he means.

We cross Woolsey Finnell Bridge, the water of the Black Warrior River muddy and cresting high on the banks since it rained last night. "How can there be seventy-three charges?" I ask.

"I don't know. It's very upsetting." But I can tell he does know, he's just not telling me. And *attempted murder?*

At home, I think of going online and digging around. But I just look at my laptop, like it's some mysterious box I'm too scared to open. The easiest thing is to just get my home-work done.

Later, once Mom is home, I hear the two of them fixing dinner in the kitchen. I creep downstairs. Usually what they talk about is super boring—Mom's job, Dad's research and students and faculty crap. But today they're talking about Sam.

"Well, it's a blessing," Mom says.

"I guess you're right," Dad says. "Sam won't have to tes-tify at a trial. He won't have to relive any of that stuff."

I walk back upstairs and shut myself in my room. I still have homework to do. But when I sit down at my desk I just stare at my textbooks.

I'll take a break. That won't kill me.

I think about getting out the Box. The Box is where I keep all this stuff that I don't want anyone to see. My *Archie* comic books. A few copies of *Sports Illustrated* that I saved because of the pictures inside—pictures of some of my favorite male tennis players in action. There was also my rock collection that I'd built up for years with Dad's help. My *Star Wars* action figures that I used to line up on a shelf above my bed. My old stuffed bear that I stupidly named Teddy. I started the Box a few years ago, after the first time Nick came into my room and walked around, noticing all this stuff (but not the magazines, those I always stashed in my desk). "What's this?" he'd asked, smirking, holding up Teddy by his leg. When he saw the *Star Wars* figures, he'd said something like, "Nerd heaven." He wasn't mean about it, really. But I knew, after that, I had to get rid of that stuff, or hide it. I mean, I was in sixth grade—time to grow up.

There's also a paper file in the Box, too, with one news clipping I saved from the weeks after Sam vanished. The paper did a story about how the neighborhood was coping or something like that. A photographer came and took some pictures, and I was in one. It was just a view up the street toward the house where Beth and her mom and stepdad lived, but in the far right corner of the picture you could see a figure in our driveway, just standing there and looking where the camera was directed. A kid. Me.

I get down on my knees and slide the Box out and take the lid off. It smells a little musty inside, but there's all that stuff. Poor Teddy, stuck in there.

I hear Mom yell my name for dinner.

I grab the folder and flip it open and there's the clip, slightly yellowed, with the picture to illustrate the story. "Weeks Later, Pine Forest Residents Still Hopeful for Boy's Return." And there I am, on that August day. What was I doing? Staring at Sam's house, like I expected him to come outside like he always did when I was in my yard? I remember how if I took my bike out and rode around, it was only a matter of minutes before Sam came out, too, like he was watching and waiting. He wasn't that nice, but he seemed to want to spend time with me.

"Josh, dinner!" I hear Mom yell again.

I close the folder and shove the Box back under the bed.

A few nights later, when I'm studying in my room, the phone rings. It's always weird when the house phone rings. Usually it's just telemarketers or the school or my aunt Helen, who lives in New Mexico and refuses to get a cell.

A bit later, when I head downstairs to the kitchen, Mom

and Dad are facing each other while leaning against the counters. They look upset.

"What's up?" I say.

Mom looks at Dad, as if cuing him to speak. "Sam's step-dad called. He—they—invited us to the Alabama game on Saturday. They were given tickets and have two extras. He said Sam wanted to see if you would come."

"Oh," I said.

"I didn't give him a definite answer. I just said I'd have to see if you had anything planned. I didn't want to—"

"We can go," I say.

"I thought maybe you had plans with Nick or Raj or those guys."

"No."

"I thought you didn't like football," Mom says.

Big eye roll. You can't not like football here—she should know that. "No, I like it fine. And it would be rude to say no, wouldn't it?"

"Well, we could come up with some excuse," Dad says. I see him look at Mom, like he's hoping she'll help him think of something.

"No, let's go," I say.

And Mom crosses her arms over her chest and gazes at me like she's baffled.

"What?" I say.

"You don't have to do this," she says.

"Do what?"

"Kiddo, it's wonderful that Sam is home," Dad says. "But I think—well, he's been through a lot. He's adjusting."

"You don't owe him anything," Mom says.

"Are you saying we can't be friends?"

"No, that's not what we're saying," Dad says.

"It's just . . . Well, Sam's not the same person he was when you were friends back in Pine Forest," Mom says.

"I know that." What they don't get is that I'm not the same person, either. "I want to go. Can you call his stepdad and tell him yes?"

"Sure," Dad says. He smiles then, like he feels bad for having put up any resistance.

I open the door to the back deck and walk outside, even though I'm barefoot and it's turned kind of chilly. In one corner of our backyard there is a swing set that we've yet to get rid of, left over from the people who lived here before us. Dad says he might plant a garden there. But he hasn't yet. We've lived here a few years, but it's like we still haven't fully settled in. Right then I think: What if we had moved here years earlier? Like, four years earlier.

Then that day would never have happened.

I start feeling pissed at Mom and Dad, for not taking me away from Pine Forest sooner. I hear someone step outside.

"You have a good heart," Mom says, sidling up next to me.

I nod but don't say anything.

"I just worry sometimes," she says.

Like I don't know that, I think to myself. It's what parents do. But my parents especially. Maybe because of what happened with Sam. For weeks that summer they asked if I wanted to see a therapist. And even after they stopped hounding me about it, when school started, I knew they still worried about how everything was affecting me. I guess I had some bad dreams, but I stopped telling them about them because I saw it freaked them out. They got a little better after we moved, but not completely. Whenever they asked me "How're you doing?" it wasn't a tossed-off phrase. I could see on their faces that they thought I was fragile. And that's how they were looking at me tonight—how they've been looking at me since Sam came back. "Don't worry," I finally say to her, even if I know it's useless to try and convince them I'm fine.

Mom puts her arm around my shoulder. *You don't owe him anything.*

But she's wrong. I do.

"They're here," Dad announces, yanking open the front door. Through the window I can see Mr. Manderson's big dark green truck parked at the curb. I guess we'd both been anxious, dressed and ready to go for almost half an hour. We're taking one car, Dad's Jeep, because he has a spot in the faculty garage.

It's sunny out but chilly. I'm wearing a jacket over a maroon polo—trying to look like a legit Bama fan, I guess. Sam's in jeans and a blue jacket, unzipped, a red button-down shirt visible underneath. We all meet halfway down the front walk. Dad and Mr. Manderson shake hands and make small talk while Sam and I just stand there. I haven't seen him since that day we kicked the soccer ball around.

"This should be fun," Dad says, smiling in an encouraging way.

"Yeah. We should whip Ole Miss," Mr. Manderson says.

Dad and Mr. Manderson sit in the front seat, Sam and I in the back.

"We have good seats," Sam says, taking out the tickets from his jacket pocket, displaying them like a hand of playing cards. "The athletic director sent them over to us. Just out of the blue. People keep sending me gifts and stuff. People I've never met in my life. From all over—not just Tuscaloosa. It's weird. Mom turns most of it down now. She says it's gotten out of hand. But she let us keep the football tickets."

"Must be kind of cool to get all that stuff," I respond, realizing that's a stupid thing to say.

"I dunno. People just feel bad for me, I guess."

Why would people do that, I wonder, send stuff to a complete stranger. Like gifts can make everything better.

After fighting through the game-day traffic, Dad finds his

way to the garage and weaves his way up to his spot. When we get out of the garage, we're surrounded by waves and waves of people wearing red and crimson heading to the stadium. Dad and Mr. Manderson sort of hem us in next to them so we all don't get lost. Mr. Manderson especially—he always has one hand on Sam.

At the stadium this old man scans our tickets and we pass through the gates, climb the stairs, and find our seats. Mr. Manderson and Dad go in first, then Sam and me. Sam's right—they're good seats. Right on the 50-yard line, about ten rows up.

"You ever been to a game before?" I ask, trying to get some small talk going.

He looks at me and kind of smiles, squints like I'm stupid. "You don't remember?"

"What?"

"You and your dad took me to a few games. We were ten, maybe? That was the year Bama wasn't too good so tickets weren't as hard to get."

I remember going to games with my parents, or with just my dad. I think Sam must have us confused with some other people. Still, I go along with it. I say, "Oh yeah."

"You always got popcorn and I got Cracker Jacks," he says.

I feel kind of sad then, that he has to make up memories.

A woman in the row in front of us with a sweatshirt on turns and smiles up at us. Every few minutes or so she keeps looking back, like she knows us. She's older, but trying to look younger with too-tight jeans and hair dyed a shade of purple-red. When she turns around for the fourth time, she says, her eyes landing right on Sam, "You're him."

Sam just purses his lips and looks at her, doesn't acknowledge what she's just said. And maybe he doesn't know what she means, but I do.

"You a big Alabama fan?" she says, breaking the awkward silence. Her voice is husky—she probably smokes. She looks at my father, then at Mr. Manderson—but they're talking to each other, not paying attention.

"Yes, ma'am," Sam finally says.

"It must be so wonderful to be home," the woman says.

I know she means well, but I can sense Sam squirming. "Yes, it is," he finally says.

The lady smiles, satisfied with herself. "I was just saying the other day that—"

"We're just here for the game, like everyone else," I say, cutting her off. Maybe I sound rude because the woman wipes that stupid smile off her face and gives me a confused look.

I shake my head at her—real quick, so it's not obvious.

She gets the hint. She smiles in an exaggerated way and says, "Well, you boys enjoy the game." She faces forward and starts whispering to the man she's with.

Sam's watching the field, taking it all in—the crowd, the

hoopla, the cheerleaders, all the people still milling about.

"It's weird," Sam says a few minutes later.

"What is?" I ask.

"Being recognized."

Right then the Rebels storm the field, and people in the small Ole Miss section across the field start cheering, but I hear some boos, too. Then Bama takes the field and the cheers that erupt drown out everything else.

When things calm down a few minutes later, Sam leans over and says, "But Mom says I'll be old news soon." He smiles to himself while looking out at the field again.

The referees are conferring with some of the players. The crowd still roars around us. The two bands are playing, at opposite ends of the field.

"I hope she's right," Sam says, speaking louder now.

Dad and Mr. Manderson go to the concession and bring back Cokes and hot dogs for me and Sam, and beers for themselves. After that, we settle in to watch the game. It's easy not to have to talk. The action is steady, the noise constant. Bama fumbles early and the crowd groans, but soon they get the ball back. Alabama goes up 28–0 by the end of the first half.

"So you play tennis now," Sam says as we wait for the game to start back up.

"Yeah," I say.

"Mom says you're pretty good. She says you were written up in the paper, for winning some tournaments."

I'd forgotten about those articles. "I'm okay."

"It looks kind of fun. Will you show me how to play sometime?"

I look over, thinking he's joking. For some reason, it seems weird that he'd want to learn how to play a sport from me. "Sure," I say.

"I know it's hard and all. I'll probably be terrible."

"You can't be any worse than I am at soccer."

He laughs at this, and it's weird because I get a jolt of the old Sam, and it's a mix of good and bad—good because I haven't heard him laugh at all, bad because I'm reminded of how Sam used to laugh at me.

"You're not terrible," he says. "The other day you kicked the ball around pretty good."

"Yeah, right," I say, and he laughs again, smiles, bumps his knee against mine. I turn to look out at the field, because for some reason I'm blushing. And to be honest, I'm actually having a good time, and it makes my stomach start to churn, like the hot dog I ate earlier is making me sick.

"Maybe next weekend?" he says. His eyes are hopeful.

"Sure," I say. "That sounds good."

Later that night, long after the game is over, we're home resting on the couch, watching a movie on Netflix while munching microwave popcorn. Mom pauses the movie to go pee. It's just me and Dad.

"Did we take Sam to football games before? Years ago?" I ask.

Dad grabs a handful of popcorn. "Yeah, remember? I think a few times. They weren't good games. We played Western Kentucky or Kent State."

"I don't remember," I say.

"Really?" he asks.

Mom comes back then and we restart the movie. But I can't focus. I try to recall any details of those games. I have a hazy image of Sam and me, high-fiving each other when Bama scored. And Sam wanting more and more of my popcorn, and then him accidentally knocking over my Coke and saying he was sorry so many times I finally had to tell him to shut up. And how when we got home, he seemed sad to leave us, to have to go back to his house, and how I felt a little sorry for him.

But maybe none of that's true.

I spent three years burying any thoughts of him. Except for the day he vanished, all my other memories of Sam, good and bad, are as fuzzy as those dreams you try to remember when you wake up in the morning.

"You have fun at the game this weekend?" Nick asks. We're waiting for our rides after practice, as usual.

"Yeah," I say. "We went with Sam and his stepdad."

"Seriously?" Nick says.

"He invited us. I mean, his stepdad invited us. They got free tickets."

"So you *went*?"

"Dad didn't want to be rude and say no," I lie.

"I would have said no," Nick says.

"Why?"

"I don't want to be around . . . all that. No way I'm hanging out with that kid."

I don't say anything, because I'm a little annoyed. What does he know?

"I mean, does he talk about it? About what happened?" Nick says.

"Nope," I say, which is the truth.

Nick looks over at me then. Like he can't figure me out. Like I'm a stranger. His hair is still too long. It's starting to look dumb, like he thinks he's a rock star or something. "I don't get it," he says.

"What?"

"I don't get why you hang out with him."

I look away and start fiddling with the zipper on my tennis bag. When I look back at him, he's still eyeing me, waiting. "I was there that day," I say. *Connected*, I think.

"Yeah, I know. You've told me that a million times. So what?"

"But I never told . . ." And then I stop. The first year, after Sam was gone, while Nick and I started playing tennis, while we started becoming friends, there were moments when I wanted to tell him everything. About how Beth and I let hours go by before we told anyone where Sam and I actually had ridden our bikes. About the man in the white truck. I would always start forming the words in my head. I would practice and then I'd say, "Nick?" And he'd look at me, totally unsuspecting, and then I would chicken out.

Like right now.

"Never told me what?"

"Nothing," I say.

There *was* one night when I told Nick the full story. It was a sleepover, at his house, just the two of us. I remember it being cold out, so this was many months after Sam had vanished, like January or February. We had tried to play tennis outdoors that afternoon, but our hands and ears got cold so we went back to his house and drank hot chocolate and watched TV. Later, we were both in sleeping bags, in the family den, watching a movie. His parents were asleep. Outside, I could see the trees blowing in the cold wind. The movie wasn't too loud, but loud enough. I looked over at Nick and his eyes were closed.

"Nick?" I said in a whisper. Then, in a normal voice, "Nick." He stirred, slightly, but his eyes stayed shut. I lay there, wide awake, and watched till the movie ended. Then I turned the TV off.

"Nick?" I asked again. Nothing.

I looked out the living room window. A car drove by, the lights flashing against the wall of the room. Then silence, except for the sound of the trees rustling. After a few minutes I had an eerie feeling that someone was watching me, that someone was out there, about to peep in the window. I waited and watched, my heart thudding, and then Sam appeared, cupping his eyes against the glass. I wanted to scream but nothing came out, and then I woke up with a jolt. I don't know when I'd fallen asleep, but when I woke I could hear Nick snoring.

I didn't want to fall back asleep, so I started talking quietly. "That day, Nick," I said, "this man in a white truck came after me. After I'd left Sam. After we had our fight." I looked over at Nick again. Still asleep. "He came after me and said he'd give me a ride home, and I knew something was off. So I said no and rode my bike home, and—he followed me."

I looked at the window again. My heart pounded, like I was actually back on that day, in the hot sun along that road. "I hid in someone's backyard. He drove by, he didn't see me, and he didn't stop. And I went home and I just waited for Sam to come back."

I looked over at Nick again, hoping his eyes were open, but sort of relieved that he was still asleep. "But he didn't come back. And then I thought about the man in the truck. Like maybe there was a connection. But I didn't say anything. I mean, the more I thought about it, the more I thought maybe it was just some adult trying to be nice. I didn't want to get some innocent person in trouble, you know? So I didn't say anything about that. It seemed like it didn't matter." I let a minute pass, almost lulled to sleep by Nick's rhythmic breathing noises. My heart was slowing down. "Do you think I did something wrong?"

He didn't say anything back. But I felt better then, because it was like his silence was all the approval I needed.

It rains on Saturday, all day. I feel like I'm trapped in my room. I'm standing at the window as the rain falls outside, when Mom knocks on the door.

"Phone for you," she says.

I take the cordless from her and she shuts my door. I think it might be Nick, though he never calls the landline, or calls at all—only texts.

"Hello?"

"Hi, Josh?"

I recognize the clipped, cautious voice. "Oh, hi, Sam." My heart beats faster, but I'm not sure why.

"Do you think you might still want to play tennis tomorrow? Like we talked about last weekend?"

I look out the window again. "It's raining."

"But not tomorrow. It's going to stop soon. Tomorrow's supposed to be nice."

"Oh," I say.

"It's okay if you don't want to," he says.

"No," I say. "I mean, yeah, sure, I can play."

"Okay, good."

We make a plan to meet at the public courts at Bowers Park, at two.

"You can use one of my rackets," I say.

"It's okay. I have one. A sporting goods store donated a bunch of stuff to us."

"Okay," I say. "See you tomorrow."

Later, when I tell Mom and Dad at dinner, they're quiet at first. Dad finally says, "That's so nice of you." And then he looks at Mom and I'm not a fool, I can see it. They're worried.

"I want to be his friend," I say. And I mean it. I actually do.

Just like Sam said, the next day is really nice—clear skies, warm temperatures. A beautiful day in the middle of November.

When Dad and I drive up, Sam's standing beside his mother's car with his racket hanging limply at his side. "We'll come get you at four."

"Yep," I say. I get out and walk over to Sam while Dad waves to Mrs. Manderson and then drives off. Sam's dressed all wrong—neon-yellow running shoes instead of proper tennis shoes—and he's wearing those mesh basketball shorts that don't have pockets. You really should have pockets in tennis, to hold the balls. But I guess it doesn't matter.

Mrs. Manderson sits in the driver's seat with sunglasses on. "You boys have fun, okay?"

"Sure," I say. We walk to the court and I unpack my tennis bag. "Let me see that." I grab Sam's racket. It's not a bad one—an older Dunlop model, nice and light. No telling what tension they strung the racket at. I realize all the stuff that matters to me—grip size, racket-string tension, racket-head size—doesn't mean anything to Sam.

I see Sam looking over at his mom's car. She's still parked in the lot, watching us. He frowns. "Just a second." He walks over and leans down into her window. They talk for a few minutes, before she finally drives off. Sam gets back and says, "Okay, ready to play?"

We start hitting and because Sam's a total beginner it's not much of a challenge for me, but that's not the point. The point is for me to help Sam, so after we hit for a bit I cross the net and show him a few things—like how to hold the racket better, and how he needs to swing through with his stroke and swivel his hips and step toward the ball. I'm just used to doing this stuff now, so I'm not a great teacher. But once we start hitting again, it seems to come naturally for Sam. It's not graceful, his form is kind of bad, but he starts connecting on shots and playing decently. Which is kind of annoying. Honestly, some guys are always good at any sport. Sam was sort of like that as a kid, from what I remember.

At one point, Sam sprays a ball over the fence and I run to get it. When I get back, he's sitting against the back fence, in the shade of some tall shrubs that grow outside. We're the only ones out here now. It's peaceful.

"This is fun," Sam says. "But tiring. I really feel it in my legs."

"Yeah," I say. I look at his legs then, which are muscular, a fuzz of dark hair tracing down his calves. "If you keep playing, you might be pretty good one day." He's so close I can smell the sweat on him. It's kind of gross, but also not.

"So you started playing that summer, huh?"

"Yeah," I say. *That summer.* He said those words calmly, like he didn't mean anything, but I feel that squirmy chill you get when someone confronts you.

"With Nick, right? Mom told me he plays, too."

"Yeah," I say.

"I saw you with him at that Homecoming game." Again, he says this like he's just stating a fact.

"Yeah," I say, feeling embarrassed all of a sudden, though I'm not sure why.

We're both quiet for a bit. Sam seems different now, free from the watchfulness of his family. Calmer. Looser. Like he feels comfortable asking me more questions—questions I don't want to answer.

"Nick doesn't want to have anything to do with me," Sam says.

I want to try and say something—to deny it, to defend

Nick, to make Sam feel better. But he's right. And then I can't believe it—I look at Sam and tears are falling from his eyes. I'm frozen, unsure what to do. But he sniffles and wipes his eyes and takes a deep breath, and then another one. "I'm sorry," he says.

"It's okay," I say. I think of the other day, at Sam's house, how his eyes looked sad.

"Sometimes things hit me. Like, bam, I start crying. Or I shake. It's like I can't control my own body."

I nod. "I know the feeling." Like right now, my belly is doing little flips. I fiddle with my racket's strings, hoping that will calm me down, because it does during my matches. But it doesn't now.

"That day," he says.

That day. There's only one day. I sit there, my back pressed into the chain-link fence, bracing myself. I grip the frame of my racket tight.

"My bike got a flat tire," he says.

I could stop him right now. It's like when you find out that someone talked about you behind your back. You don't want to know what they said. But you *have* to know.

"I got a flat tire," he says again calmly. No more tears. "Right near the cemetery. I fell off the bike when it happened. It was like a blowout. I was like: It serves me right. After what happened to you."

Three years later, I can still feel the cold of the soda

exploding on my back. I can still feel the pebbles digging into my knees. I can still hear *Faggot!* And Sam's laugh.

"I never made it to the mall. I had to turn back around and walk. It was so hot. Remember that?"

"Yeah," I say. Where was I when Sam was walking, I wonder? At home yet? I must have been. In my room, enjoying the AC. Or maybe in the bathroom, washing up my scrapes. Safe.

"I walked with the bike along the road. Sweating. Getting thirsty. There was hardly any shade. So I try and go as fast as I can, but it's like I never make any headway. I finally get to that street that intersects Skyland. The one where if you turn left it goes down a hill, past the Nissan dealership. I forget the name. Anyway, I see there's a lot of shade down there. All these big pine trees. I just need a moment out of the sun. So I walk my bike off Skyland, to where the trees are. I just stand on the side of the road in the shade."

He pauses and then takes a swig from his water bottle. I watch his Adam's apple as he gulps, then look away. I drop my racket beside me, because my hands hurt from gripping it so tightly.

"My therapist says I can talk to him about all this stuff. But . . . it's weird, telling stuff to a stranger, you know? I can't talk to my parents about it. They just want . . . They just want to . . . to forget it. Especially Mom. I can't talk to Beth, either."

"Why not?" I say.

"I don't know. I want to. But I think she's scared of me.

The way she looks at me. The other night, she . . . Never mind." He looks away.

"You can tell me stuff," I say. And I mean it. But I also hope he doesn't want to tell me anything else.

He still stares off. "Thanks."

A breeze blows through, causing one of the tennis balls to roll away a little. The shrubs rustle behind me, a soothing sound. But then Sam starts speaking again: "I was standing in the shade and then this white truck comes down the street."

My heart flutters. It's like I was just walking along peacefully and then suddenly I tripped.

"This truck slows down and pulls up next to me. It's Rusty. I mean, I didn't know it was Rusty then. But it was him. He says, 'Hey, kid, you okay?'"

The same thing happened to me, I almost say, but I don't. I can't.

"At first I didn't say anything, but he kept looking at me so I told him I was fine, just hot."

"Then what you doing out here in this heat, Superman?"

"My bike got a flat."

"That's too bad. You need a lift?"

"Nah, I'm okay."

"You sure? I can put your bike in my truck bed, get you home lickety-split."

Sam pauses and I look up at him and he's smiling in a weird way—the way you'd smile at something stupid.

"That phrase, 'lickety-split.' My dad used to say that. That's weird, isn't it? But I remember him saying that and it calmed me down. And I was so hot and tired. So I said okay. He puts my bike in the back, and I get in the passenger seat. I tell him I live in Pine Forest Estates, just up the road a bit, I'll show him. 'Buckle up,' he says, smiling at me. I guess right about then I knew he was weird. Right when I clicked that seat belt, it's like I knew. And I could have unclicked right then, before he drove off, I could have jumped out and run off and ditched my bike. But he started the car and I froze."

A little gust of wind blows across us again and I close my eyes. For a second I wish Sam would say that he yanked the door open then. That he ran. But I know that this isn't the way the story goes.

"Anyway, I tell him to take a left but he goes right. I said, 'No, I live the other way. You should turn around.'"

"'I know where you live,' he said."

"'You do?' I asked, but he just drove on. Looked over and smiled at me again. But not a friendly smile, you know? 'Roll your window up,' he said."

"I rolled it up. I thought he was going to turn on the AC but he didn't. 'You're going the wrong way,' I said again. He didn't say anything at first. It all happened so fast." Sam pauses.

I open my eyes then. I think he's going to stop. My heart's still pounding, because I know the worst is still to come.

Sam's still leaning back, his hands pushed against the cement, really close to mine. I could slide my hand over and touch his, and comfort him, but I don't. Boys don't do that.

I don't do that.

"Then all of a sudden, wham! He brought his hand up and smacked me in the face, really hard." I hear a catch in his voice. "I thought he'd broken my nose. I started yelling, covering my nose, but he told me I better shut up if I knew what was good for me. So I just sat there and kept as quiet as I could. I guess I was in shock. Like this can't be happening. 'If you stay quiet I'll take you home,' he said. 'But I gotta run an errand first, okay?'

"I couldn't speak. He drove on while I sort of sat in a daze, like I was just a regular passenger getting a ride. My nose was killing me but I tried not to cry. Soon he was on McFarland, and then he pulled onto the interstate. I still thought, okay, maybe there's a chance he'll do his errand and then drop me at home. But he drove and drove. I was trying to keep calm and not show him that I was scared. I saw cars driving past us, and I made eye contact with a few people. I thought maybe I should open my window and scream or try to signal for help. Because I knew I was in trouble. We'd gone five miles, maybe more. I even thought of opening the door and jumping out. I may have put my hand on the door, near the lock. But he was watching me like a hawk, with that lazy eye of his—that made him scarier. And that's when he reached under the seat and pulled out a gun. A pistol. It looked real. 'Not such a Superman now, are you? You try to yell for help or do anything funny, I'll blow your brains out.' He said it so calmly. Like . . . like killing some kid was the same to him as swatting a fly. 'Go ahead and cry, baby. But I'll kill you if you try anything.'"

Sam stops speaking then. He still stares straight ahead, like he's in a trance. I want to say something—but what? What do I say to this?

"He kept on driving. At one point he finally pulled off the interstate. 'What do you want with me?' I asked. I wanted to know. I wanted it to be over with, whatever it was. He pulled behind a closed-down gas station. I thought, he's going to kill me here."

Attempted murder. Kidnapping. Here it all is. I feel like I might puke.

"'Please don't hurt me,' I said. I don't even know if he could understand a word I said. I was blubbering and trying to choke words out. . . . It was terror. Total terror."

Right then we finally look at each other. Sam's eyes are dry, but he looks deflated. It takes all my willpower not to slide my hand over to his. To touch him. To say, "I'm sorry." Nothing I could do feels good enough. But maybe he can see how I feel, and maybe that's enough. I hope it's enough.

"It was almost a relief when he told me to shut up and get

in the back. There was like a little cramped backseat behind the main two seats. No one could sit there comfortably, but he cleared away some stuff. He made me lie down the whole way, with my head near the passenger side so he could keep an eye on me from the driver's seat. And then he drove off again. He drove and drove. I thought we must be driving hundreds of miles away. It got dark out."

By then, back in Pine Forest, we were probably being grilled by the police. By then everyone was in a panic. It was hard to believe that all these things were going on at the same time.

"At one point I fell asleep. But then I woke when I felt the truck slow down. I kept my eyes shut. I knew he was watching me. The truck finally stopped. I opened my eyes then. He smiled at me. Not that evil, creepy smile. I can't describe it. But it was like he was trying to turn into someone different from what he'd been the past few hours. His voice was different, too. I'll always remember it. He said, 'Wake up. We're home.'" Sam pauses, shakes his head. "'Home.' Can you believe it?"

Right then I see my mother's car rounding the bend in the road. Her car lights are on, though it isn't really that dark yet. "My mom's here," I say, but I don't move. I feel like I'm chained to the ground.

"Yeah," Sam says, watching as the car approaches.

Even when she parks, we both keep sitting there. I take

another sip of water, and then offer one to Sam. He takes it and sips and hands it back to me, and I take another gulp, knowing that I'm drinking in tiny particles of Sam now, the way he was drinking in particles of me. *Connected.*

"Josh?"

"Yeah?"

"If you don't want to hang out with me again, I'll . . . I'll understand."

Mom honks her horn. I guess because she's in a rush, or maybe she thinks we don't see her. As if on cue, Mrs. Manderson's car swings into view.

"Why would you think that?" I say.

Sam doesn't look at me, just shrugs.

I stand up and gather my stuff, and he does, too. We both walk toward the gate. All I can think to say is, "We should play again sometime."

Sam doesn't say anything at first. But at the gate he stops and says, "You sure?"

"Yeah," I say. "I'm sure."

At home, I get started on my schoolwork. I begin with the algebra problems, but nothing makes sense. It's like I'm reading a foreign language: *Julie rode her bike for 6 1/4 miles on Tuesday. On Thursday, she biked 3 1/10 times as far as on Tuesday. How many miles did Julie bike on Thursday?* Who cares. I skip ahead but it doesn't matter—the questions are all like this.

Sam's at home by now. He doesn't have homework. He's not in school yet. Sam's not in school because he didn't ride his bike fast enough. If Sam had ridden his bike faster—no that's not it. If he hadn't stopped . . . if he hadn't gotten a flat. If I'd stayed with him . . . If I'd mentioned the white truck. If we had just stayed home. We should have stayed home.

I try and get back to my work but the problems keep tripping me up. And I can't stop thinking about Sam's story. It's like a person's life could be turned into a problem set, like the dumb ones in my algebra text. *Sam rode his bicycle 2.5 miles that day. He rode in a car for over 120 miles. He was gone from home for 1189 days. X is the life he would have had, if he'd only stayed at home. Solve for X.*"

I stand and rip the paper into pieces. I don't even bother to clean it up. I walk to my bed and I lie down and I close my eyes and I put my pillow over my face because I'm crying now and I have to let it out and I don't want Mom or Dad to hear me.

When I finally stop, I go the bathroom and wash my face, careful not to look at myself in the mirror.

I sit back down at my desk and close the algebra book. There is other homework to do, luckily.

CHAPTER 7
Adults

Beth

After the party disaster, I wear my Central Soccer sweat-shirt to school every day. I walk the halls with the hood up, staring down at the ground, not looking at anyone. In class, I talk as little as the teachers will allow me to. It's not easy. It seems like everyone in the world is always trying to get at me—with their hellos and the questions, their casual asides, their jokes. All the stupid chitchat of daily life. I just want to be left alone.

During lunch, I hang out in the library and steal bites of a sandwich. I spend sixth period in there, too. I've told Coach Bailey my ankle still hurts, and I know she doesn't believe me. But she can't force me to practice. All she says is "Are you okay, Beth?" and I say I am and I walk away.

When the bell rings on the Wednesday before Thanksgiving, I sit and wait till the halls clear. When I think it might be safe, I walk to my car, unbothered by anyone, wondering if I can get through the rest of high school this way. But then I see Ainsley and Darla waiting for me. They're dressed in their warmer soccer clothes. Chita is nowhere in sight.

"Shouldn't you be practicing still?" I say.

"Coach B. let us out early, since tomorrow's Thanksgiving," Darla says.

"So what is this then, an intervention?" I say.

"Kinda," Darla says.

"We're worried," Ainsley says, tugging at the green strand of her otherwise blondish hair.

"I know you are. But don't be." I sit up on my trunk. Darla plops next to me, and Ainsley paces around in front of us.

"You got big Thanksgiving plans?" Darla asks.

"I'm going to work on my college application," I say. They already know I'm only applying to the University of Alabama. "And, um, my dad's visiting." For weeks it felt like it was so far off. For weeks I could pretend it wasn't going to happen. But now, saying it, I know it's a reality, and my heart starts racing a little, the way it does when the teacher slaps down a quiz on your desk. "I have to sleep on an air mattress because my aunt Shelley is visiting, too, and she's staying in my room. It's a big family get-together."

"That will be nice," Ainsley says. "Besides the air mattress, I mean."

I shrug. "It's Sam's first Thanksgiving with us since . . . since he got back. My mom's . . . Well, it's a big deal for her. For all of us, I guess."

"How *is* Sam?" Ainsley asks.

"Yeah," Darla says.

"Fine," I say. I ask about their plans to change the subject. Darla's headed to a big family gathering outside of Atlanta, and Ainsley's staying in town, with just her mom and little brother. A small gathering. I envy that.

"Well, I better get going," I say.

"Beth," Darla says. "You're not mad at us are you? Did we do something wrong?"

I shake my head. "No. I just . . . I just kind of want to be alone."

"Well, when you feel like . . . you know we're here for you," Darla says.

"We miss you."

I miss me, too, I want to say. I miss the days when we could just kick the soccer ball around or just goof off or talk about nonsense. I miss the times when my friends didn't ask me how I was doing ten million times a day. But I don't say anything. I just accept their hugs good-bye and then drive off.

I'm supposed to head home and help Mom get ready for tomorrow. But I drive downtown, along a street lined with old trees and old houses that have been converted to offices for lawyers, court reporters, doctors, and therapists.

I park in front of one and sit. There is where I came a few afternoons a week in the first year after Sam vanished. Dr. Rao's office.

Oddly enough, we didn't talk about Sam much at these

sessions, although that's what I was supposedly there for. Dr. Rao would just sit quietly, eyeing me with a professional smile, expecting me to do all the talking, and then I'd feel like I needed to talk, so I'd blather on about school or something, and she'd scribble notes down on a pad of paper. Sometimes I wanted to snatch that pad and see what she was writing. *What? You have me all figured out?*

One day I refused to talk. It was like a game of chicken. The silence lasted for many minutes. So she spoke. "I have a brother," she said.

Great, I thought. *Here we go.*

"Nathen," she says. "He lives in New York. I miss him." There was a picture of them together on her desk, posing on top of a tall building in New York, the city view spread out behind them.

"But you visit him," I said.

"Yes, I do, and he visits me. But when he's not around, I think about him." She paused, maybe waiting for me to say something. When I didn't, she said, "Do you think about Sam?"

Of course I knew that was coming. "Yeah," I said. "But I don't want to."

"Why not?" she'd asked.

I stopped again, wondering if I could speak the truth. But I knew that's what she was there for, so I gave it to her: "Because he's dead."

I expected her to wince or something, but she just nodded. "And why do you think that?"

Because it's easier to think that. It's easier to let go. But I didn't say any of that. I just shrugged, and she didn't press.

That was the last day I went. Mom protested at first, but in a way I think she didn't mind not having to spend the money.

I get out of my car and sit on the trunk. At four o'clock, a mother and a child walk out the office door and off down the street. Soon the door opens again and out walks Dr. Rao, stylish in a dark suit with a scarf tied at her neck, her silky dark hair pulled off to the side.

I watch her walk toward me. At first she doesn't notice me, but just as she's about to walk by she stops short.

"Beth?"

"Hi," is all I can say.

"How are you? What are you doing here?"

"I was just driving by, I guess."

She knows I'm full of it. "It's good to see you. I talk with your mother now and then."

"Yeah, she says you suggested the shrink Sam's seeing."

"Yes, Dr. Saylor." I wait for it—for her to ask about Sam. That's what everyone else does. The world revolves around Sam. But she doesn't. She says, "Do you want to chat inside?"

"No. I need to get home and help Mom with Thanksgiving stuff."

"I'm about to head to the grocery myself. It's going to be a madhouse."

"Yeah. Well, it's good seeing you," I say.

"You too, Beth." She smiles at me. She pauses, but I know if I don't say something she'll walk away.

"It's funny," I say. "When Sam was gone, I hated going home. My stepdad and me always tiptoeing around Mom, never knowing how sad she'd be that day. So I joined soccer, and a few clubs. Hung out at my friends' houses. It was like I had two lives. One good one. One not so good one. But now . . . I don't know. Now everyone knows what happened, and they won't let me forget it."

She moves closer to me, sets down her satchel, and leans against the trunk. "Things have changed," Dr. Rao says. "Do you like being at home now?"

"No," I say, finding it a relief to speak honestly, even if what I'm saying makes me feel ashamed inside. "I mean, sometimes. But the thing is . . . It's just that everything is about Sam. His tutor is always there. Our lawyer sometimes. Mom is home all the time, hovering. Neighbors are always stopping by. Complete strangers send him gifts—like piles of stuff. It's all Sam, all the time. And no one gives a . . . no one cares about me. I know that makes me sound awful."

"It doesn't."

"Don't get me wrong. It's nice to see Mom so happy. My stepdad, too. But . . . I don't know. Something's off. Mom wants us to move on with our lives, but how can we? How can we pretend nothing ever happened?"

Dr. Rao doesn't say anything. She was never someone who needed to fill the air with words.

"What . . . what happened to my brother?" I ask. "What happened to him there?" I see that man's awful face, the scraggly beard, the dead eyes, and I feel a chill tingle up my back. I know Dr. Rao doesn't know much more than I do about the case; maybe she knows even less. But who else can I ask?

Dr. Rao just looks concerned, calm.

"And why did he stay there? I read one article online that says he went out by himself all the time. He even had friends. So why wouldn't he try and escape? That's what everyone wants to know, but no one can ask him. We can't talk about any of that at home. But . . . I just can't get past it."

"Give it time, Beth. Give *him* time."

"That's what everyone says," I say, disappointed that this is her only response. We both just sit there for a bit—kind of like when I'd sit in her office years ago, defiantly silent. But I don't want her to leave yet. "My dad's coming tomorrow," I say.

She lets that settle in the air. "Are you excited to see him?"

"He's only coming because of Sam," I say. "It's been three years since Sam disappeared and Dad never even called me. And before that, we hadn't seen him in two years. So, it's been five years. I shouldn't even call him Dad. He doesn't deserve that name." The anger in my voice surprises me.

"Beth, I don't have magical words," Dr. Rao says. "But I can say, as a parent myself, that your father loves you. He may not have always shown this, for whatever reason. And he may not have seen you for a while, for whatever reason. But trust me, he loves you."

I shake my head, let out a little laugh. It's true, she doesn't have magical words. She never has. But I never expected to hear the usual crap from her. I flip my hood back over my head and jump off the trunk. "Well, I better get going."

"Beth."

I open the car door. "Yeah?" I say, not looking back at her.

"Will you talk to your mother about scheduling a visit? You're dealing with a lot. Your brother, your father. Of course things are confusing now. I'd like to help."

No one can help, I think. I don't nod, I don't say anything, I just get in my car and drive away. At a stop sign, before I turn the corner, I look in the rearview mirror, quickly, and see her still standing there, watching me slip away.

If you take away Sam vanishing and everything, then my family's story isn't that unusual. Big deal, two parents divorcing. Tons of kids at school had divorced parents. Plenty of kids had stepparents.

Dad was always the fun-loving one. He'd crack open a beer

when he got home from work each day, and by the end of the night five or six cans would be stacked on the counter. But I don't remember him being a drunk or anything like that. He was always quick to laugh, making jokes, teasing. Mom was the one frowning, angry and annoyed. Always cooking or cleaning or washing, barely resting to watch the news on TV.

They argued a lot, but Dad always seemed to treat these fights as jokes—he never took anything seriously. He'd spend a lot of time out with his friends, calling at the last minute telling Mom he'd be home late. Once, when he did this, she took his plate of dinner from the table and threw it down the driveway.

It was rainy the night they told us they were divorcing. They told me separate from Sam, because he was so young and probably wouldn't get it.

Mom's eyes were red, worn out from crying. But they were dry at that moment while we sat on the couch. Dad was the one crying. I'd never seen him cry, so I was frozen in fear. Mom gave the usual speech that all divorcing parents tell their kids: "Sweetie, sometimes even when two people love each other—well, that's not always enough."

"Your mother wants a divorce," Dad said. I noticed that it was not *we* want a divorce.

I asked why, fighting tears. But what do you say to a nine-year-old whose life you're ruining? None of their explanations mattered. I ran out of the room, out the kitchen door, into the hard rain. I ran to the big oak tree in the front yard and took shelter there, even though it didn't really protect me. It was Mom who came out. "I'm so sorry." She hugged me and cried and we both got soaked. I looked over her shoulder and saw Dad, watching from the garage. Safe and dry. I wanted him to be the one hugging me, but he was already miles away.

Dad moved out. For a while we'd see him on weekends. Or else he'd call and we'd talk on the phone and then Mom would get on and they'd fight.

After the divorce was official he moved away, back to Ohio, where he was from. He got a job there selling real estate. He took us for ice cream the day before he left. When he dropped us off and told us he loved us, Sam started screaming, "Don't leave!" I had to pull him off Dad. When he drove away, I thought my heart couldn't bear it. I missed him immediately. And Sam, Sam was hysterical, and I tried to hug him and calm him down but he just kicked at me and yelled "Go away!" And it killed me because even though I knew he was in pain, nothing I said or did could make him feel better or undo what had happened.

Kind of like now.

I wake on the air mattress and hear the noises from the kitchen—coffee cups clinking, Mom and Aunt Shelley talking, the oven opening and shutting with a metallic squeak. I hear the TV, too. I'm in the living room-slash-dining room, tucked in my little corner of home till Aunt Shelley leaves. She made the usual protestations last night about taking my room. "No, let me sleep on the air mattress. Beth needs her privacy."

Don't get me wrong, I love Aunt Shelley, a lot. She's the only family Mom has, really, besides some stray cousins I've never met.

Aunt Shelley's what you would call a character. She's tall, big-boned, and has this flop of poofy blondish-graying hair. She has big lips that she covers with this purple-red lipstick, and slightly crooked teeth. I know this makes it sound like she's hideous, but it works somehow—she looks charming and unique. She sells real estate in Nashville. Aunt Shelley is a lot older than Mom. She'll turn fifty in January. Both Mom's parents died years ago, so Shelley's kind of motherly toward her, but not in a strict way—more like a mom who wants to be her daughter's best friend.

With Dad coming, it's a relief she's here, putting us at ease with her jokes and laughter.

When I walk out of the living room, Aunt Shelley greets me, holding her coffee mug with two hands. "How'd you sleep, hon? You sure that air mattress is okay?"

"Morning," Mom says, putting a casserole dish in the oven. Thanksgiving dinner is at two. Or at least that's when Dad is expected. He's flying in today, to Birmingham from

Ohio, then renting a car and driving down. He's staying at the Hampton Inn near the interstate. It's a quick trip, barely twenty-four hours. Today he'll just join us for dinner, and tomorrow he'll come for breakfast.

He'd wanted to stay the entire weekend, but Mom said that would be too much disruption right now.

Aunt Shelley always liked Dad. They stayed in touch after the divorce, which Mom wasn't thrilled about. It was Aunt Shelley who gave him advice about real estate, helped him get started. I think she kind of had a crush on him, just in a way that she enjoyed his attention. Dad was a flirt. He was good looking. Not tall but wiry with dark wavy hair and bright brown eyes, always a little facial hair that Mom said he grew to cover up his weak jawline. He had olive skin, too, almost like he was Italian, but he wasn't. Sam took after him, looks-wise, though he inherited the same pasty skin that Mom gave me.

"Sam and Earl went to the grocery store for me," Mom said. "Maybe you and Shelley can tidy the den, and set the table?"

"Sure," I say. In the den, the Macy's Thanksgiving Day Parade is on TV. I feel a glob of dread in my stomach that I know is only going to spread the closer it gets to two.

Shelley and I tidy up and then I deflate the air mattress and put my stuff back in my room. I set everything in my closet and that's when I see those stacks of presents and cards I got when I came back to school. I never even opened any of them, just tossed them in there like dirty clothes.

My phone pings and I see a message from Donal: "Happy Turkey Day!"

I've pretty much avoided Donal, like everyone else, these past few weeks. Soon, pretty much everyone at school will hate me. And I don't care.

I walk to the kitchen and get a Hefty bag from under the sink. I go back to my room and open my closet and start scooping all the gifts and cards and crap into the bag. I cinch the bag closed and walk back down the hall, then outside, to the trash container, and dump it in.

By around one thirty, we're all dressed and waiting. Mom and Aunt Shelley are in the kitchen. Sam and Earl and I are in front of the TV. Stupid football is on. Sam watches it like he's interested, but he looks at the screen blankly. Maybe he's nervous about Dad, too.

I see Earl look over at me a few times, like he's worried about me or something. I wonder how he's feeling about this visit. He seems calm, but then again, he always does.

I keep looking at my phone. 1:35. 1:38. 1:41. *Stop*, I think. 2:00. My stomach starts churning. 2:02. 2:05. 2:12. My heart rate kicks into overdrive. He's late. As always.

Then, at 2:17, I hear a car door slam. Sam sneaks a quick look at me, then turns away. On the TV, a quarterback runs in for a touchdown; the crowd goes wild.

A knock at the kitchen door. Aunt Shelley answers. "Well, Hank, look at you. Handsome as ever." Earl stands, and Sam follows him toward the kitchen, but I stay seated.

"And you're as gorgeous as ever," Dad says to Aunt Shelley. That voice. I still know it, with that Midwestern nasal sound mixed with just a touch of Southern twang.

I push down a flash of tenderness. I keep my face stony and join everyone else near the kitchen door.

Sam has to go first. I know the moment calls for that. But before Dad says hello, before he even looks at us, he gives Mom an awkward hug. Then he turns to face us. He's in jeans, a button-down, and a tan blazer. He looks the same as I remember, but with more gray in his hair. His beard has flecks of gray in it, too. The same, but older, more tired. He looks at me first, a quick flash, but then he sees Sam.

"My boy," he says, almost whispering. Sam goes to him and they hug tightly. Dad pats Sam on the back and then just takes him in. "You're so big. So handsome. . . . Like your old man." He flashes that grin at all of us, his audience. Then he turns to me. "Beth," he says, inching closer. "Beautiful like your mother." He looks back at Mom and lets out a little chuckle. Then he looks at me, but he seems nervous. "Can I get a hug?"

I nod and he hugs me tightly and I remain mostly limp, my hands barely on his shoulders. When he pulls back, he says to all of us, "It's so great to be here. Diane, Earl, thanks for letting me come—thanks to all of you. Thanks for letting me be a part of this."

"We wouldn't have it any other way," Shelley says.

"We're glad to have you," Earl says, sounding subdued.

Dad rubs his hands together. "It smells damn good in here."

"I hope you're hungry," Mom says.

He nods, and I see him staring at Sam, like he's trying to figure something out.

We move into the dining room and Mom, Shelley, and I help bring the food to the crowded table. Turkey, ham, stuffing, cranberries, green bean casserole, a tossed salad, sweet potatoes, and regular mashed potatoes, plus homemade rolls. A feast. But I don't feel hungry. My stomach is in knots.

"Hank, do you want to lead us in prayer?" Mom asks, after we're all seated.

I see Dad pause. He hardly ever went to church. It was always just Mom and me and Sam. And then we stopped going altogether once Sam disappeared.

"Me?" Dad says. "Uh, sure. Okay." We join hands and close our eyes.

Dad clears his throat. "Dear God, thanks for bringing us all together on this fine day. Thanks for this delicious food. Thanks for these wonderful people. . . . Thanks for my . . .

for our beautiful daughter, Beth, who's grown into a lovely young woman." I open my eyes, but everyone else has theirs closed. I'm a little surprised he mentioned me first, before Sam—his only reason for being here in the first place.

"And thank you, God, for returning our boy to us. Thanks for answering our prayers. Amen."

"Amen," we all say.

"Okay, let's dig in," Dad says, letting out a relieved laugh. He winks at me, then at Sam, holding his gaze.

"Amen to that," Aunt Shelley says, taking a swig from her white wine.

Even though I'm not hungry, I sample a little of everything. For a good while, we just sit around and eat and talk about how good the food is—a safe topic.

Earl asks Dad about his business, and soon they're having a boring discussion about real estate, which Aunt Shelley loves. I can feel Sam fidgeting next to me. Sitting there, I wonder what Thanksgiving was like for him all those years. Did he and that man celebrate it, somehow? Or was it just another day? And I wonder if Sam's thinking about that, too—how a year ago he was somewhere else, maybe eating turkey, maybe not, and all of those unknowable things make me feel queasy all of sudden, and I start coughing, gagging on the cranberries I was eating.

"You okay?" Mom asks, and I grab my water and nod.

After we clear the table and pack up the leftovers, it's

time for dessert. I help Mom and Shelley bring in the apple pie, the ice cream, and the chocolate cake. It's all too much. I don't think I can eat anything else.

Once we're settled back with our dessert, we eat quietly until Dad says, "So, Sam. Your mother says you're working with a tutor."

I see Shelley kind of shoot him a look—like she's warning him to be careful. Mom is looking at Sam, smiling—but it seems fake, like she's holding something back.

"Yeah, Lane," Sam says. "She's nice. I like her."

"That's great." Dad takes a bite of his pie, then looks back at Sam. "And you're seeing a therapist."

Sam nods. Mom's smile is gone. Now she's staring at Dad, but he's still watching Sam. The air in the room feels weird now—like there's a bad smell we're too embarrassed to acknowledge.

"Sam's adjusting really well," Earl says, piping in.

"We're taking things one day at a time," Mom says.

"That's great," Dad says. "That's all you can do. One day at a time."

Mom has always stressed that talking about any of this is off-limits. But maybe Dad didn't get the memo.

Or maybe he did and he's defying her.

"Why don't we move into the den," Mom says, pushing back from the table so hard that the table rattles. She starts grabbing plates.

"Sure," Dad says.

I help Mom, rinsing the dishes, then putting them in the dishwasher. When we lock eyes, she gives me a tense smile. Shelley helps, too, while the others settle back in front of the TV, watching football. I can hear Dad and Earl talking. Outside it's getting dark. Finally, we get the kitchen into reasonable shape and join everyone else in the den.

"So, Sam. You playing any soccer?" Dad asks.

"No. Not really."

"Sam's a great artist now," Mom says, the edge from her voice gone. "He draws these wonderful pictures."

"You should see some of his sketches," Shelley says. "Sam, show your daddy some of your work."

"I'd love that," Dad says.

"Okay," Sam says, sounding kind of embarrassed.

"Wow, an artist in the family. Maybe you can draw my portrait?"

"Sure," Sam says.

"And Beth is applying to Alabama for next fall," Mom says, sounding a little too cheerful. I can tell she wants the focus off Sam. That's the only reason she brought me up. I mean, we've barely talked about college. "And she's still super involved with soccer. Her team has a real good shot at making the state championship this year, right, hon?"

"I guess," I say.

"You're a midfielder?" Dad says.

How does he know? "Yeah. More of a defensive midfielder."

"That's great. Midfielders—those are the real workhorses on the team. You must be strong."

"She is," Mom says, "and fast."

I fight the urge to roll my eyes. She's acting like an expert, but she's barely been to any of the games. Earl sometimes came, and he explained Mom's absence as being related to Sam. ("It all reminds her too much of him.")

"Any young men in the picture? A pretty girl like you, I bet boys—"

"Stop it," I say.

"What?" Dad looks at me and cracks a smile, then glances at Mom and Earl in a confused way, like he's seeking their guidance.

"Stop pretending you care about me."

"Beth," Aunt Shelley says.

"What?" I say, my eyes laser focused on Dad. "I know you only came down here to see Sam. I was here for three years and I never saw you, but the minute Sam comes back, you're dying to be here."

"Beth, calm down," Mom says.

"No," I say. I feel my skin burning, and my adrenaline kicks in, like during a game when the ball is coming toward me. "It's true. Sam's the only one who ever mattered to him. To anyone in this house. Including you, Mom."

"Beth, honey," Aunt Shelley says.

"Don't expect me to jump up and down and act all happy that you've actually acknowledged me. You're all here because of Sam. You only care about Sam." I stand up from the couch. A kind of fury is building inside me, but my throat tightens and I feel my eyes welling up. But Dad's still smiling at me, trying to be an adult.

"You shouldn't have come," I say to him.

"Stop it, Beth," Sam says.

My father looks down then, unable to meet my eyes. I feel a vein throbbing at my temple and I wonder if I look crazy to him, to all of them. "You're not my father. You're a stranger to me," I say, still feeling fury, but also a hard burst of sadness. Because what I've said is true. He is a stranger. I don't know him at all.

"Stop it!" Sam says again.

I turn to him, and his wet and angry eyes only push me to keep going. "And what about you? You just mope around like a ghost and we have to pretend that everything is fine and normal, and it's not. None of this is normal."

"Stop, please," he says, softer this time.

"Beth," Dad says.

But I can't face him anymore. I can't face him or Sam or anyone else. I walk away toward the kitchen, then out the kitchen door, through the garage and down the driveway and into the street. I start walking up the hill, away from our house.

The cool night air feels good. I breathe deeply, feeling charged up but also exhausted, like I just ran down the field. And as I walk, that sadness blooms in me and it takes all my energy to keep moving. After a few minutes I hear Aunt Shelley calling after me. I keep walking, but she catches up.

"Lord, slow down, girl. I might have a heart attack."

I ease my pace, but I keep walking, my arms crossed against the cold. For a while Aunt Shelley just walks along with me. Then she puts her arm around me. "You're having a hard time of it, aren't you?" I don't say anything, because my throat is lumpy and dry. "I can't imagine what it's like, having to deal with all this adjustment. The years of ups and downs. You're a stronger girl than I was at your age."

"I'm not strong," I say, enjoying the feel of her arm, the smell of her flowery perfume.

"Oh you are, and you know it. You'll get through this. All of you will."

This. Whatever *this* is. Like it's something physical. Like it's a place that we can just drive past.

"I wish Dad hadn't come," I say.

"You don't mean that."

"He's always loved Sam more. Mom too."

"Honey," she says. "Listen to me."

I stop at the crest of the little hill but keep facing forward.

"Love's not a pie. There aren't limited pieces to go around. Your parents love you both equally, just in different ways. When you're young, I know that love can feel like a burden, or it can show itself in funny ways. But trust me, that love is overflowing."

I think about Dr. Rao, about what she said earlier, and start to feel a little bad that I stormed off.

"You know, I speak to your daddy. A few times a month."

"You do?" I say.

"I probably shouldn't tell you all this, but I've had some wine. Plus, you're almost an adult now. Heck, you're *already* an adult, the stuff you've gone through." Shelley starts walking, so now I'm the one following her.

"Yeah, he calls me a few times a month, sometimes more. He has ever since he left Tuscaloosa. And after Sam vanished he called a lot. He was a wreck. I hate to say it, but he sort of became a bad drunk again. He's better now, I think. But during that stretch, he'd call me, a mess. He always said it was his fault that Sam went missing. If he'd only been there, this would never have happened."

Would that have made a difference? If he had stayed? Probably. It would have altered the entire future.

"But he didn't worry about me. He hardly called," I say.

"He wanted to. But he was . . . I don't know, afraid. Ashamed. Like I said, he felt like it was his fault. And your mother had Earl. She didn't need him."

"*I* needed him."

"I know you did. I'm not excusing him. But he . . . I guess he couldn't face you. He couldn't face your disappointment in him. He should have gone to see you. But he kept staying away, kept putting it off."

Hearing all this, I don't know what to think. All these years I pictured my dad barely thinking of me. A stranger.

"Sometimes I couldn't knock sense into him. He's not a perfect man, Lord knows. He's got his problems. We all do. But I just thought you should know that he's never stopped being your father."

We walk on. It's completely dark out now, the streetlamps casting crescents of light on the street. I can see inside the houses we pass—dining rooms full of people, or people camped out in front of the TV, scenes of togetherness. We used to run around this neighborhood on summer nights, playing kick the can and elaborate hide-and-seek-type games. Hiding in backyards, in pool sheds, under cars in garages. Running around alone in the dark. Back when we thought bad things happened to other people. Back when the worst thing was having to come in at night, having to brush our teeth and take a bath and go to bed.

"We really do have so much to be thankful for, you know?" Shelley says. Our neighborhood is a big circle, and we come to the base of the second, steeper hill that will lead us back to our house. When we reach the top I see that Dad's car is gone. I've spent weeks dreading this visit, and now I want to run down the street, call out to him, beg him to come back.

I wake at the crack of dawn, the light from the sun barely poking through the curtains of the living room. All the theatrics from last night come flooding back to me and for a minute I feel frozen under the covers. But then I think of Dad. He's not coming for breakfast anymore—all because of me. I realize with a stabbing sensation that I can't leave things broken between us. I have to see him before he leaves town.

I crack the living room door open and smell coffee. I walk to the den and see Shelley on the couch, with an afghan over her legs. The TV is on, the volume so low it might as well be on mute. A mug rests on the coffee table.

"They're already showing Christmas movies, can you believe it? Even at this hour," she says.

I sit down next to her and she puts her arm around me and starts rubbing my shoulder. It will be Christmas in a month. Another occasion to mark—Sam's first Christmas back at home. Presents and tidings of good cheer.

Unless I've ruined everything.

"I want to see Dad," I say. "Will you take me to his hotel? Will you go with me?"

Shelley grabs her coffee, takes a sip. "Your mom would kill me."

"If we go soon, we could get back before anyone wakes up. We can say we went for doughnuts. I need to see him. If you don't take me, I'll just go by myself."

She sighs and looks at the ceiling as if asking for divine assistance. "Okay," she says. "Just let me get some decent clothes on."

We drive down Skyland, toward the Hampton Inn near the interstate. The sun casts a pink glow in the sky, peeking through the morning clouds. Hardly any other cars are on the roads at this hour. It's a quick drive. When we pull up I say, "Can you stay in the car? I think I want to see him alone."

"Sure, honey," she says.

I walk into the small lobby. There's a skinny guy in glasses behind the counter. "Can I help you?"

"Can you tell me what room Hank Walsh is in?"

He hesitates, like maybe he's not supposed to tell me that information. I push my hair behind my ear and smile. "I'm his daughter."

"Oh, okay." He types information into the computer. "Room Three fifteen."

"Thanks." I head down a dimly lit hallway to the elevator and take it up to the third floor. I knock. No response. He must be asleep. Or maybe he's gone. Maybe I've missed him. I knock again, louder. *Please be there.* And soon I hear feet shuffling toward the door, and finally he opens it. He's in a T-shirt and jeans, his eyes tired from sleep, his hair flattened. But when he registers me he looks shocked, and then his shock turns into a genuine, gentle look of happiness, like he can't believe his eyes and doesn't want to make a move or I might vanish like a dream.

"Beth. What—what are you doing here? What time is it?"

"It's early, I know. But I wanted to say good-bye."

"Here, come in." He stands aside and I walk in the room, which has two queen-size beds. It's sort of a mess. Clothes strewn on the floor. A few empty beer bottles resting on the bedside table. And on one of the beds are all these papers. Newspaper clippings, magazine pages, some spilling out of envelopes, some resting on top of folders. I walk over and get a closer look.

Right away, I see pictures of Sam. And of him. Russell Hunnicutt. That mug shot. I look over at Dad, and he eyes me sheepishly, like I've caught him at something.

"What's all this?" I say, even though it's obvious. I remember Bud Walker telling Mom that he would save all the press, but Mom said she never wanted to see any of it. I'm shocked about how public our lives have become these past few weeks.

"Just stuff about the case. About Sam. I know it looks obsessive, but I had to keep track of everything. I wanted to know. . . . I thought knowing everything might help me understand. But it hasn't really."

I walk to the other bed and sit on its hard mattress.

He takes a chair from the little round table by the window, pulls it closer to the bed. He smiles at me, and his dimples are like Sam's, and I almost want to reach out and hold his hands, but I don't.

"I'm sorry for what I said yesterday," I say.

Dad shakes his head. "You don't owe me an apology. I owe *you* one. For . . . for being a terrible father."

It feels good to hear him admit this, but also sad. "Aunt Shelley told me you always asked about us. About me."

"It's true."

"But why," I say, my voice catching. I swallow. *Be strong.* "But why didn't you come see me?"

He looks away, tearing up.

"These past three years, it's just been . . . It's been hard. Mom was . . . sometimes she just wasn't there." I'd never admitted this to anyone, but on some days, I wanted to shake her, wanted to shake her so she'd look at me and see that she still had a daughter right there in front of her.

Dad's full-on crying now, the tears shining in his beard. "Your mother is a good woman, Beth. A good mother."

Not while Sam was gone, I want to say. But my flash of anger softens, and I know he's right.

"Some people aren't really cut out to be parents," Dad continues. "But she is. And she did all the hard work. The saying no. The discipline. I just wanted to be the good guy. The fun dad."

We don't talk for a few minutes, but I can tell he has more to say. When he gets the tears under control, he sniffles, then says, "I'm a little afraid of you. Of her. Because when I look at you both, I see what a failure I am. I see you, and you're a smart, strong young woman, and none of that comes from me." He takes a deep breath. "And it hurts me. I may be an adult, but I have my pride. Sometimes I . . . can't face the truth about myself." He looks up again, wiping his eyes.

Something spills open inside me. Like that day, years ago, when I thought Sam was never coming back. But this feeling is different. It's like a warmth spreading around.

"Dad . . . Is Sam going to be okay?" I ask.

He stares at me for a few seconds, like he's searching his brain for the right answer. "I hope so, honey. But I know one thing. He needs you. He needs his big sister. Maybe more than anyone."

This is what Shelley said, what Mom says. But I still don't know how I can help him. I'm just trying to get through each day. Whatever happened to Sam—there's no how-to guide for us to consult.

My cell phone pings a message, and I know it's probably Mom, awake now, wondering where we are. "I better get going," I say.

"Oh, okay," he says, and I can hear the disappointment in his voice. "But can I . . . Can I hug you first?"

Yes, I think. Of course. To touch him, to smell him even, would feel so good, I know. But I make him wait a few seconds before I actually say "Yes."

We both stand and he embraces me, gently, and yes, it feels so good. Something I wish I had from him every day for the rest of my life. After a few seconds I pull away. "I'm still mad," I say, though inside all I feel is warmth.

"Okay," he says, nodding, wiping his eyes with his hand.

"But I didn't . . . I wanted to see you. I'm not sure when I'll see you again."

"Can I . . . can I call you?"

"Yes," I say, breathing deeply. I want another hug, but I have to leave. "Have a safe trip back." I walk past the bed covered with all those horrible clippings. I open the door.

He says, "I love you."

I pause. I look back at him, standing in that room, waiting. "I love you, too," I say, and then I'm gone.

While waiting for the elevator, a door opens down the hall and two old people come out. They smile at me as they approach.

"You have a nice Thanksgiving?" the man asks.

"It was okay," I say, hoping my voice doesn't crack.

"Where you visiting from?" the lady asks.

"Oh," I say. "I'm here seeing my mom. My dad and I—we live in Ohio."

"How nice," she says.

"Family should be together over the holidays," the man says.

The elevator arrives and we ride down in silence. Once we get to the ground floor, I get out and the man says to me, "Have fun with your momma."

"Thanks, I will," I say, and it's nice, I think, these brief few moments when I was a different person, a different Beth, who had a whole different life.

But when I get outside, when I get in the car, when Aunt Shelley starts driving, I know I belong in this life. With Mom and Earl and Shelley. With my father. With my friends. With Sam.

"Well, we can't come home empty handed because your mom just texted me asking where in the hell we were." So Shelley drives us to Krispy Kreme doughnuts and we load up. "Just what we need after yesterday's meal," she says, shaking her head.

Before we go in the house, I hand her the doughnuts. "Can you carry these?" She nods and I go to the trash bin. I know this is gross and crazy but I dig around and find the bag I dumped in there yesterday.

"What on earth?" Shelley says, eyebrows raised at me like I'm disturbed.

"Don't ask."

Everyone's still in their rooms when we go inside. Shelley sets the doughnuts on the counter. "I'll make some more coffee," she says.

Back in my room, I dump it all out on the floor—the cards and stuffed animals, a candle, slips of paper. Even just glancing at the messages, I know they're from the heart. I sit down by my bed and just look at it all. That warmth from earlier—I feel it spread through me again. I close my eyes but the tears still pour out and I cover my mouth with my hands because I don't want Mom or Shelley or anyone to hear me. Because they won't understand that this feeling overwhelming me right now isn't sadness, but something else. Something I can't even define, but which feels a little like relief. Relief that I'm returning to myself. Like I know who I am again.

CHAPTER 8

The Most Awful Story in the World

Josh

Saturday of Thanksgiving weekend, Sam calls and asks if I want to see a matinee, and then maybe hang out at his house after. All I've been doing is homework, so I say yes. Mom drives me to the mall, which is mobbed with shoppers.

"Is Nick coming?" she asks.

"No, he was busy."

I can see her take this in, scrunching her forehead, like she's confused, or worried. Before she can say anything, I get out of the car. "See you later!"

The movie theater's pretty crowded. When we find our seats, I just focus on the dumb ads on the screen. A few times, I sneak looks around, but from what I can tell no one from school is here. Good. Since playing tennis that time, Sam and I have hung out a bit. We played tennis once more, watched a movie at his house one Friday night. Nothing Nick or Raj or any of those guys need to know about. Finally, the lights go down and the previews begin.

The movie ends earlier than we thought, so we have half an hour to kill before Sam's mom picks us up. We get coffees and walk around the mall. We round a corner where the pet store is, and I see this guy and girl, around our age, holding hands, walking toward us. My heart jumps a little, thinking it's Nick and Sarah, or someone else from Central. But when they get closer and walk past us I realize I don't know them at all.

"I had a girlfriend," Sam says, like seeing the couple jogged his memory.

"What?" I ask, not sure if he said *had* or *has* and feeling confused either way.

"Her name was Kaylee."

After that day at the courts, Sam hadn't told me any more things about Anniston. I kind of thought that might be the last of it, like maybe it was a one-time thing. Now I feel a mix of nervousness and pride. Nervousness because does he have other awful things to tell me? But pride because, well, he's choosing me. For some reason, he trusts me.

"I met her at the mall with my friend Tony."

Tony? Who's Tony?

"Tony and his mom would go to the mall each Saturday and sometimes Rusty would let me go."

A girlfriend. A friend. Trips to the mall. In some of the articles I read, it sounded like he had some freedom. But all I can think about is that man hitting him in the nose. The man who pulled a gun on him. How did he get from that place to this other place?

Sam continues, like this is just a normal thing to talk about. "Rusty gave me money for food and art supplies or whatever. And that's where I met Kaylee, at this supply shop. She was buying paints. She had this dyed red hair and all these piercings. I thought she was really pretty. Tony thought she was too goth, but I thought she was perfect."

I look over at him and he has this peaceful grin on his face. "She gave me this funny look when she saw me in the shop. I looked lame to her, she told me later. I had on these khakis, I guess they were baggy and dorky. And this cap I always wore. That Rusty made me wear when I went out. Anyway, she came right up to me. She was bold—I liked that. She asked me what I drew, and I told her I wasn't very good yet, and she said she was taking an art class at the community college and I should take it. Rusty wouldn't let me, I knew. But I got her number."

"Back up a second. Who's Tony?" I ask, even though I'm still trying to process Kaylee.

"Tony was my friend. He lived upstairs in the same complex, with his mom. They moved there a year after . . . after I got there."

"Are you . . . I mean, do you talk to them? To Tony? Kaylee?"

"Mom doesn't want me to have any contact." Sam gets all

solemn-looking then. He sits down on a bench and kind of stares off. I sit down next to him. "I asked Mom if I could have a cell phone, but she says not yet—that's why I always have to call you from the landline. She thinks I'll try and get in touch with them. But I never got to explain anything. I never got to say good-bye."

"Wow," I say, wondering what they felt when they learned the truth about Sam. Shock, I'm sure. Maybe some guilt. All this time they'd known a kidnapped kid. I want to ask him why he didn't tell them anything. Why he didn't ask for their help. Sam's dumping out pieces from a puzzle box and I'm scrambling to pick them up and put them together.

"I bet my mom's here," Sam says. "We should get going."

When we round a corner, I see the GameTime store. The place we were riding our bikes to that day. I hadn't made that connection till now. But Sam keeps walking.

Once we get to Sam's house, I think we're going to play video games or something, but Sam says, "I thought I'd try and draw you today. Is that okay?"

"Okay," I say, thinking that sounds kind of boring. And also kind of weird. Why does he want to draw *me*?

Sam grabs his sketch pad from his room and, since it's not that cold today, we go outside to the backyard.

"So I just sit here?" I ask.

"Basically," he says. "Look off to the side a little. But we can talk. I can talk and draw at the same time. I'm talented like that," he says, winking, then looking back down at the sketch pad.

I sit there as he starts using his charcoal pencil to go to work. It makes me feel kind of awkward the way he stares at me so much. I know he has to, to look at my features and all, but still, it feels invasive. To break the silence, I say, "You never told me how your dad's visit went."

He doesn't respond at first, but he furrows his brow. "It was fine. No big deal."

He continues sketching, and I sit there, watching him watch me. If he gets to look at me so closely, then I figure I can do the same. Even though we're the same age, I notice that Sam looks older. He doesn't show it off, but I can tell he has strong arms. And he has bits of stubble sprouting on his chin. If I shaved now it would only cut away peach fuzz. I notice, too, little nicks in his face—one on his lip, one on his eyebrow. Where those piercings were. Gone now.

He stops drawing, stares over at me, then looks away, toward the shrubs that line the back of the yard. I worry that I did something to upset him—did he notice me studying him? When he starts drawing again, I'm relieved. "I learned to draw from the TV," he says. "When Rusty left for work each day, he'd turn the channel to PBS. 'This is educational. Watch it. Don't change the channel, or I'll know,'" Sam says, deepening his voice to imitate Rusty. "I was so dumb. There was no way he'd know if I flipped the channel. But by then I believed everything he told me."

By then. How much time had passed *by then?* What had happened to Sam *by then?*

"There was always some drawing show on later in the day, after *Sesame Street.* This guy with curly hair and a mustache would stand in front of an easel and draw and show you how to do it, step-by-step. He was no Picasso. But I got hooked. The idea that you could create something out of nothing. Just take a blank piece of paper and do anything. When Rusty got home that night, I was nervous but I asked him anyway, I asked for paper. To draw, I told him. I told him about the show. I think he was a little suspicious at first. But he gave me a pencil and a few sheets of notebook paper, and that's what started it all. I mean, it was a way to fill time. A way to stop thinking about..." But he stops. "My hand's getting a little tired. You mind if we go inside?" he asks.

Inside, Mrs. Manderson has made cookies, and we start wolfing these down. Sam's aunt is there, too, and she makes a big production out of meeting me. "I'm so glad Sam has such a nice friend," she says, embarrassing both of us, I guess, because we don't look at each other.

"Can we watch TV, Mom?"

"Okay, but not too loud. Earl is napping."

We sit on the couch and flip channels—past football, past infomercials, shows about fixing up houses, cooking shows, till we get to a movie.

"Oh, I love this," Sam says.

On screen I see that tall actress with the funny name. She's with some guys dressed like soldiers and carrying big machine guns, walking down through a dark and abandoned-looking base.

"What is it?"

"*Aliens*. It's awesome. And the first one, *Alien*, is great, too. We'll have to watch that sometime."

The movie is intense but I like it. At one point, the little girl that they rescue says something about how her mother always told her there were no monsters, no real ones. "But there are." I look over at Sam, and he's just staring at the screen.

After the movie ends, I call Mom to come get me because Sam and his family are going out to dinner with their aunt for her last night in town. As we sit and wait, Sam asks, "Can I keep drawing you? It may take me a few rounds. Is that okay?" He says this so eagerly, like he's afraid I'll say no.

"Sure," I say. I'm still not sure why he wants to waste his time on drawing me, but I'm glad he does.

On the way home, Mom says, "It feels so funny to me, driving back over here." She means this side of town, our old neighborhood. We left almost a year after Sam had been gone. Mom had gotten her job at the firm, and she worked downtown, so she said the move was to be closer to work. But I knew she wanted to live in a nicer neighborhood. And maybe get away from the sadness and drama that seemed to hover over Pine Forest. When we drive across the river, she seems relieved and gives me a pat on the knee, like we just escaped from something.

Central's football team is in the play-offs. That's all anyone talks about at school on Monday, the Big Game. It will be on Saturday, in Montgomery. Some people are organizing overnight trips. At lunch on Monday, Nick and the guys talk about going. "My dad said he'd get us a hotel room and drive us down," Nick says.

"I'll have to ask my parents," I say.

But that night, at home, while we're eating dinner in front of the TV, I don't ask them. I don't even mention the trip. Because I don't want to go. I know I'm being kind of stupid about it, because to most people it would seem like a blast. But Nick would just talk about Sarah all the time. Or worse, maybe Sarah would go, too, with a group of her friends. And Madison J would be there, too, then. I just don't want to deal with it. Plus, I have so much homework.

On Tuesday, I say, "Yeah, my mom says I can't go."

"That sucks," Nick says. "You want my mom to call her?"

"Nah, it's no use," I say, and he looks at me for a moment,

like he's suspicious of something. But he doesn't press me about it anymore.

Friday afternoon there's a pep rally. Sixth period is canceled. We all pile in the big smelly gym, climb up the bleachers. I sit with Nick and the guys, and then Sarah and Madison and a few other girls worm their way to our section.

The rally starts. I used to love these, but today the noise and the cheerleaders jumping around and all the shouting grate on me. All of the stuff from my school life seems off to me, for some reason—less enjoyable, somehow inconsequential. It might have something to do with Sam, but I'm not sure why.

Principal Rhone gives a speech, the players are introduced, each one running out like a hero. Everyone stomps their feet on the bleachers. Even I do, because I want to at least pretend to have school spirit today.

After it's over, we all empty out of the gym into the big hallway outside. Sarah has her arm around Nick. They're shameless now. I see Madison staring over at me, and I look away. But she approaches.

"Hey, you're going to Montgomery, yeah?" she says.

"No, I can't," I say.

"Oh," she says, looking disappointed. "I thought Nick and you guys were all going?"

"They are. I'm not."

"That's too bad," she says.

I look and see Sarah playfully swat at Nick, and he laughs and backs away and she starts chasing him around. I roll my eyes and look back at Madison, but she's looking at them, too, but smiling, thinking they must be cute. When she turns back to me, she says, "You want to hang out sometime?"

"Uh." I look away, at Nick, then back to her. "I mean, I probably could," I say.

Instead of looking pleased, Madison's smile wipes away. "Don't sound so enthusiastic," she says.

"It's just things are so busy now," I say, which I know is lame because we're *all* busy.

I worry she's about to persist, about to bring up something we could do together specifically, but she just turns and walks away. For a second I feel bad, and then I feel relief.

Dad will be picking me up soon so I head to my locker. At the bottom of the stairwell, I glance down the hall and see Madison fiddling in her locker. Instead of going upstairs, I walk over to her. Almost no one else is around.

"Hey," I say. I expect her to be mad or something. But she just looks normal, like nothing happened just a few minutes ago.

"Sorry about earlier."

She continues fiddling with things in her locker, like its contents are fascinating.

"It's not that I don't want to hang out," I say. "You're really nice."

She lets out a little laugh. "What every girl wants to hear."

"I'm sorry. It's just that . . . like I said, I'm so busy—"

"It's okay, Josh. I get it."

"Get what?"

She glances around, then lowers her voice. "I know you don't like me. I mean, I know you don't like me *that way*. I suspected for a while. Like, at homecoming, at the game, you kept staring over at that guy—the kid who went missing? You barely would look at *me*. And then, at the dance, you didn't kiss me, didn't even try. You spent the whole night looking at Nick, or glued to his side when he wasn't with Sarah. I was like, what's wrong with me? But I'm not stupid. I get it now. And I'm not going to tell anyone."

"Tell anyone what?" I say, my voice sounding all scratchy.

She looks kind of embarrassed. "I still want to be your friend," she says. "I just wish you had told me."

"There's nothing to tell," I say. But my heart starts pounding, pounding.

"I'm here if you want to talk about it," Madison says.

I feel my face catch fire. And then two loud seniors run by, banging the lockers with their hands, acting like jerks. So I walk away, fast, up the stairs, taking them two at a time, adrenaline carrying me. I get to my locker and fumble and finally get it open and then I just stand there, catching my breath, hoping my heart slows down. My phone rings. "I'm here," my dad says.

I walk outside, still sort of in a daze. I fight the urge to go back inside, find Madison. *How did you know? How did I give it away?* But I just stand there until Dad beeps the horn and waves.

On the drive home, Dad asks the usual questions. And I answer the usual way. "Okay. School was okay. I'm okay." But I'm not really listening to him. I've been so dumb. Afraid of myself. My own feelings. Of course I don't like Madison that way. I'm different.

"What are you thinking about?" Dad says.

I look over. I could tell him. Mom too. But no one really needs to know. It's like one more item in the Box. Things that give me happiness and comfort and peace, but which no one needs to see.

"Nothing," I say.

The next day, Saturday, I'm back at Sam's house, sitting on the patio while he draws me. Mrs. Manderson made us hot chocolate. I'm wearing my jacket, and Sam has gloves on, the kind that have holes cut out for the fingers. I don't know why we don't go inside, but he prefers it out here.

Sam looks at me before he starts, like *really* looks at me, and I have to look away, because I wonder if he can see the truth about me in my eyes. Like Madison could. Does he know? Would he care? Soon he starts drawing, his pencil making soothing sounds across the paper. I just listen to the noises of the neighborhood. Cars going up the streets, a screen door slamming a few houses away. A mother yells for her kid. But overall it's quiet. Too quiet. I don't hear the pencil anymore. I look back at Sam. He's stopped drawing and is sort of staring off like he's prone to do.

"Everything okay?" I ask.

He nods. But he doesn't start drawing. "I'm just a little tired. I don't always sleep too good."

"That sucks," I say, and I want to ask why, but I know. "We can stop if you want."

He doesn't respond. He chews on his pencil, then just holds it there, on the paper. He's staring ahead again. "It was about a month in. Or five weeks," he says. "I tried to keep track of the days, but it was hard."

For a second I have no idea what he's talking about, but then I realize where his mind has gone. Back to Anniston.

"Russell woke me up when I was sleeping. He woke me up every few hours at night. I guess to mess with my head. Sometimes for other reasons."

He looks at me then, to see if I understand. *Other reasons.* And by this I know he means the abuse. I nod at him, while a knot seems to tighten in my chest.

"That night, he told me to get dressed, to come with him outside. I hadn't been outside yet. I'd been inside all that time. Tied up. Duct tape on my mouth for a while. But by then he'd stopped doing that."

By then.

He pauses, maybe to see if he can continue. I nod again, slowly, giving the go-ahead.

"He walked me out the door, through this courtyard. He told me to be quiet. 'You tell people you're Sam Hunnicutt if they ask. My nephew. My brother's kid I'm taking care of.' I could tell it was late. Most people were asleep. Most of the lights were out. I thought about screaming, but I didn't. I was so scared." Here his voice cracks a little, but he recovers himself and goes on. "He pushed me along up some steps, then into a parking lot. I saw his truck. It was red, not white. I guess he'd painted it. He told me to get in. I got in the backseat and laid down. 'Put this on,' he said, giving me a bandanna to wear as a blindfold.

"He drove for a long while. It was late but I was too scared to be tired. The truck went up some hills, steep ones, then down some curves. I had no idea where we were going. Finally, he slowed down, pulled off onto a gravel road. I heard him curse and stop the car. 'Stay here. Don't try anything.' He took the keys. But I wouldn't have done anything. I was paralyzed. He got back in the car and drove on for a little bit more. Finally, he stopped.

"'Get out,' he said. He yanked the blindfold off. I climbed out of the backseat. It was dark out, but from the moonlight I could tell we were in the woods, by some pond or something. You could hear bugs, a loud whirring sound. It felt good to be outside. To have the air on my skin. I'd been trapped in that apartment for weeks.

"'Sit down,'" he said, motioning to a spot of grass not far from the water. So I sat.

"'Lay back.' I did as I was told. By then, I knew resisting would only make things worse. He sat down next to me. I closed my eyes and pretended I was somewhere else, like I always did. On a camping trip with my dad or at the beach with my family, at Gulf Shores. I could feel Rusty watching me, but not doing anything. I mean, I knew—I knew he'd dragged me out here for a reason. But then . . . Then I heard. . . . I heard crying. I opened my eyes. He was staring out at the water, just crying like a kid would, all messy and ugly. I shut my eyes again, because I didn't want him to see me looking at him. I braced myself. I thought about Six Flags, eating cotton candy till my teeth hurt. Then I felt him move on top of me, still crying, and all of a sudden . . . I felt a pressure on my throat." Sam stops, like he has a choke in his voice.

"I remember opening my eyes, looking up at him. He was still crying, but I realized right away that he was choking me. My first instinct was to resist, but he squashed his legs on mine, and he was so huge, so strong. I felt like I was being pressed down by a boulder."

My hands are cold. I'm cold. I'm shaking.

"I know this sounds weird, but right then I felt like . . . a

244

kind of relief. He was going to kill me, but it was okay, because it meant that it was all over. All of it—it was going to stop. I'd go to heaven." Right then a tear falls from Sam's eye and he wipes it away quickly.

"I felt myself losing consciousness. But then, I don't know . . . I saw something." He sits up in his seat. "Like they say, your life flashes before your eyes. And in that flash I saw Mom. And Beth. I saw them, sad and alone without me. In our house—in *this* house," he says, looking behind him, then back ahead. "And I knew then that I had to fight. I don't know where I found the strength. I was almost out of breath, and blacking out, but I fought. I started slapping him with my free hands. I kicked. I punched. And finally his hands were off my throat. He was off me. I started coughing. Throwing up. I rolled to my side and just gasped for air. I couldn't believe it. I wasn't dead. I rolled away from him. I tried to stand, but I felt too wobbly. I heard him stand up. I started screaming. He kicked me, yelled at me to be quiet. I balled myself up, but he came and yanked me to my feet. I thought—here's where he's going to finish the job. He held me by the collar of my shirt and stood in front of me, breathing heavy. His face was still wet with tears. He looked like a maniac.

"And that's when I started begging. Please please please. I was bawling. But I tried to calm myself down because he had to listen to me. He had to. I told him I'd stay with him.

I wouldn't run away. I swore I wouldn't tell anyone. I'd do what he said—if . . . If he let me live."

The lump in my throat makes it hard to breathe, but I don't let myself cry. Sam needs me to just listen. He has to let this out.

"He put me back in the truck. He started driving away, back down the gravel road. He didn't say anything for a while. I was surprised he hadn't blindfolded me. He pulled over again, the car still running. I could tell his brain was still firing, he was still thinking about what I'd said, like could he believe me. He said, 'If you try and leave, I'll kill you. You got that?' I guess I wasn't quick enough because he yelled 'Answer me!' I said yes, I understood. I told him I wouldn't, but I knew he still didn't totally believe me. 'I'll kill you. But I won't stop there.' He took out his phone. 'I'll kill your mother, too.' Then he flashed his phone at me, and there was . . . there was Mom. A picture of her leaving our house." Sam stops and sort of lets out a high-pitched sob, before he gathers himself and wipes his eyes again. He sniffles, takes a breath. "I mean, part of me was so happy to see her. I didn't have any pictures, and there she was. But then I realized that Rusty knew who they were, where we lived."

A cold chill creeps through me, thinking of it—Rusty, here again, in this neighborhood. Watching Sam's family. Maybe watching me.

"But that wasn't the end," Sam says. "Rusty said 'And I'll

kill your sister.' He flipped to another photo. It was Beth. She was standing somewhere, maybe at school. And Russell was smiling at me. He was enjoying it. 'Yeah, that's right. I know where they live. I know everything.'"

Sam looks at me then. He wants to tell me something more but I can sense him hesitate. He takes another breath. "He put the phone away. 'You got that?' he yelled. I nodded, I was crying again, crying like crazy. 'Answer me!' he yelled. And so I finally said, 'Yes!'"

We both go quiet. The urge to reach out, hug Sam is so strong that I'm holding my breath. But what if his mom is watching, or Beth, or Earl? I move fast. I scoot my chair closer to Sam so that we're only inches apart. I reach out and touch his shoulder and squeeze. "Sam, I'm so sorry. I'm so sorry this happened to you." I don't know what else to say—those are the only words that come close to how I feel, and they're a mile off.

"I can't tell Beth any of that," Sam says. "I can't tell Mom. I can't tell Earl. I can't tell my dad. I could never tell them any of that."

No, think. *No, you can't*. And part of me wishes I didn't know any of this either. But it's too late. I know it, and I have to know it.

Mrs. Manderson comes out just then. "Aren't you boys cold? You want some more hot chocolate?" She looks at us, smiling and cheerful, totally oblivious to what we've been

247

talking about. Sam is facing away, probably hoping she doesn't notice his eyes or read something else on his face. "Sam?" she asks again when we don't answer right away.

He closes the sketch pad and pulls it to his chest. He turns and smiles at her convincingly. Like he's flipped a switch. It amazes me how quickly he can do this, and it makes me sad, too. "Sure," he says, like nothing has happened, like he hasn't just told me the most awful story in the world.

CHAPTER *9*
Superman

Beth

It's the Monday after Thanksgiving weekend. The bell for sixth-period *finally* rings. I get my duffel bag from my locker. For a while I just stand there, acting like I'm fiddling with something as the halls empty out. The bell rings again and I walk around, up and down the halls. No one stops me for a hall pass.

About ten minutes later, I finally head to the locker room. It's empty, as I'd hoped. I change into my soccer clothes— track pants, because it's chilly out, a long-sleeve dry-fit shirt, my cleats. I tie my hair back. I also put on the ankle brace my physical therapist gave me, just to be extra safe. Then I leave and walk to the soccer field. Coach Bailey is already having everyone stretch. She turns and sees me and smiles.

"Beth!" Darla shouts.

I look over and flash her a thumbs-up, and she smiles and flashes one back. Ainsley waves. I look around and spot Chita, but she's just staring ahead, focused on her stretching.

"Your ankle good to go?" Coach asks.

"Yep," I say, and I lift my track pants and show her the ankle brace. "I have this just to be careful."

"Okay then. Good to have you back," she says.

Stretching hurts. I'm stiff—stiffer than the others. At one point, Coach Bailey comes and pushes down on my back and I groan, completing the stretch as far as I can take it. But it feels good to be out here, around my teammates, the cool air like a balm on my skin.

After practice, Chita rushes off, clearly avoiding me. Not that I can blame her. Coach Bailey comes up to me as everyone clears out. "You're doing well."

"A little slow," I say, and I feel so done.

"That's okay. Don't overdo it." She pats me on the back.

Ainsley and Darla are holding their bags, waiting for me, and we walk together toward the back parking lot. They know they don't have to say anything. That we can just walk peacefully along. Like going back to the way things were.

"Hey, Beth!"

I stop and see Donal, chasing us down.

Ainsley smirks at Darla. They walk on ahead, and I want to yell at them not to leave me. I still hadn't told any of them about the kiss, but it's like they *know*.

"Hey," Donal says, running up, his red hair shining in the fading afternoon sun. He has a few tiny flecks of grass on his forehead, like green confetti. Even though it's cold out, he's in his maroon soccer shorts, with a tight black shirt on top that hugs his chest. He squints those blue eyes at me.

"Glad to see you back out there," he says.

"Yeah, it's good to be back." I start walking again.

"Did you have a good Thanksgiving?"

"It was fine," I say. "I saw my dad—he came down from Ohio."

"That sounds nice."

I don't say anything, just continue to walk along.

"Hey, can you stop for a sec?"

I stop. He's grinning, but I can tell he's nervous because he's cracking his knuckles. He was doing that when we were studying. Right before we kissed. I feel a pang of sadness. Something had been stirring inside me that day—maybe inside both of us—and then it all got shoved aside.

"Do you want to, maybe, grab a—I mean, go to a movie sometime?"

"A movie?"

"Yeah, you know, a moving picture, with actors and explosions and car chases and all kind of fantastic stuff."

I want to smile and laugh. I want to say yes. But I know it's not just a movie. It's a date. The truth is that I'm behind in schoolwork. I'm out of shape on the field. And my family—Sam. These are the things I need to focus on. I can't deal with anything else. Those feelings that stirred that day—well, it's better to set them aside. I can't even deal with them for now. "Um, a movie," I say, stalling. "I mean, I have a lot going on right now."

"It's okay if you don't want to," he says.

"It's not that I don't want to," I say.

"But you don't want to," he says, looking away. "Clearly."

I just stand there like an idiot.

"I'm sorry that I kissed you that day," he says. "It was a mistake."

"Donal," I say.

"I'll catch you later," he says, and I can hear the hurt in his voice. He turns and starts running back toward the field.

"It wasn't a mistake," I say, but he's too far away to hear.

When I get home Mom is in the kitchen, prepping for dinner. She asks how school was, as usual, and as usual I tell her it was fine. Better than it's been in a while, except for the incident with Donal. The sourness of that like a smudge on an otherwise spotless day.

"Where's Sam?" I ask. We hadn't said much to each other since Thanksgiving weekend.

"Out back, drawing," she says.

Of course. Every day, he's out there—even in the cold—with that sketchbook. It's like he hates being indoors.

"You should go say hello," Mom says.

"I don't think he'd want me to," I say.

"Don't be silly," she says.

Today, I don't feel like arguing. Plus, I think Mom's right. It's what I should do.

Like Shelley and Dad said—Sam needs me.

I set my bag down and walk out to the patio. "Hey," I say. He glances up at me and I can tell he's unsure why I'm there.

"Hey," he says, then goes back to his drawing.

"Can I see?"

He shrugs. I move behind him. It's the start of a drawing of Josh. "That's really good," I say.

"It could be better. I need him to sit one more time."

"Cool," I say. I don't know how to talk about drawing. "So, would you want to kick the ball around?"

"The soccer ball?"

"No, the golf ball," I say, trying to be jokey. But he doesn't smile. "Yeah, the soccer ball. I need more practice."

"I'd like to finish this," he says.

"Oh, okay. Some other time, then."

"Sure," he says, but he's just humoring me.

He keeps sketching, acting like I'm not even there, and I walk back inside. I guess I can't blame him. Mom's on her cell, and so I take my bag and walk back to my room. At the end of the hallway, Sam's door is open—it's usually closed. I set my bag inside my door and look toward the kitchen. I can hear Mom still on the phone. I walk into my room and look out my window and see Sam still at the patio table.

Quickly, I walk into Sam's room. It doesn't seem very lived in—no dirty clothes on the floor, and the bed is tightly made. On his little desk a few textbooks and notebooks are stacked in an orderly way. I walk over and flip open one of the notebooks, but it's just study notes from his tutoring, some stray doodles.

I guess I'm looking for something—something that can help me figure out the new Sam.

I go to his closet and ease the door open. It's pretty bare in there, with just his new shirts hanging, a few sweatshirts. All the old stuff is gone—maybe thrown out, or donated somewhere, put in the attic. The hamper is filled halfway with dirty clothes. And next to that, kind of squashed in a corner, is a knapsack. The one he brought back with him from Anniston. I creep back to the doorway and look down the hall and still hear Mom on the phone. I go back to the closet. I think about grabbing the knapsack, opening it, but right then I hear the door to the patio squeak open. I shut the closet and dash quickly back to my room and shut my door, my heart pounding.

On Saturday, I'm taking a break from homework and watching some girl-in-peril movie on Lifetime. Sam's outside as usual, with Josh. Finishing that portrait, I guess.

The phone rings. I hear Mom answer in the kitchen, where she's at the table going through receipts or something. She sounds upset, so I turn the volume on the TV down slightly so I can hear.

"No, I don't think that's possible," she says. "I'm sorry, no—" and then she's quiet again. On TV, a blond girl is running up some stairs. "Look, I told you, that's not a good idea. How did you even get this number? . . . Uh-huh. Well, I'm sorry. . . ."

I put the TV on mute.

"No," Mom says in a louder voice. "Please don't call here again, I mean it." Then she hangs up.

I turn the volume back up a bit on the TV. The girl is bawling, slamming a door. "Who was that?" I shout.

Mom doesn't say anything at first. Then she shouts, "A telemarketer."

I get up off the couch and walk in there. She's just staring off. "You okay?" She seems not to hear me. "Mom?"

"Yeah," she says, finally looking at me, then back down at the receipts and checkbook spread before her. "Yeah," she says again. I don't push her, even though I know she's lying to me. I go back to my movie. I sit on the couch just as the blond girl swings a baseball bat and knocks a guy on the head.

Monday, at soccer practice, Coach announces that Ainsley is out with the flu. She's our usual goalie. And Ronda, the backup, has a doctor's appointment. "Beth, I need you to fill in today," Coach Bailey says.

"Me?" I protest.

"Yep," Coach says.

I put on the pads and accept my fate. It's not bad at first, even if my hands start to hurt, not used to the ball slapping them so hard. I make a lot of blocks though. And each time I prevent a goal, I start laughing. I guess I'm surprised I'm so good at it.

Then it's Chita's turn. She's our best kicker; she scores the most. I bounce on my heels as she lines up her shot and connects with the ball. I guess right, catching the ball with a thud against my chest. I can tell by her expression that she's pissed.

"Nice job!" Coach Bailey yells.

A few minutes later, Chita's back. I ready myself, as she lines up again. She runs toward the ball, then stops short, dribbles, then takes her foot back and kicks, sending the ball right at me. I can't get out of the way, and then—BAM! The ball smacks me right on the side of the head. Dazed, I cup my hands to where the ball hit, just above my ear, and I stagger to the side. Soon everyone surrounds me. Coach Bailey gently peels my hands from my head, looks at my face. "You okay?"

I nod. My head throbs, but I'm fine. Just a little shell-shocked. "Here, let's get you seated," Coach says, taking me by the shoulder and guiding me to a bench on the sidelines.

"I'm sorry," Chita says. But I know she'd been aiming right at me. I give her a quick scowl. Someone gives me a cup of water and I take it and chug.

"Okay, everybody, back out there. Beth, you're done for the day," Coach says, heading back to the field. But Chita stays and sits next to me.

"I said I'm sorry," she says again. "I didn't mean to—"

"Yeah you did," I say, cutting her off.

For a few seconds, no one says anything. But then Chita says, "Well, you gotta admit, I have pretty good aim."

There's a silent moment of shock. And then I start laughing, and I see her face relax, and she laughs, too, relieved. What she said was not that funny, but our laughter is like a ball rolling down a hill, gathering speed, and soon we're both in hysterics, so much so that my belly starts to hurt and I have to lift my head up to catch my breath and calm down.

After a few minutes, Chita says, "That felt good."

"Yeah," I say, smiling over at her, my knee knocking hers playfully.

Again, we sit in silence for a few minutes before Chita starts talking again. "You were always the one we went to," she says. "When we had problems and stuff. Like when I came out to my mom. You always knew what to say. So when Sam came back, we just wanted to be there for you."

"I know," I say, the shame making my face burn. A breeze blows through as a cloud covers the sun, casting us in a brief cold shade. "I just . . . I wanted to deal with all that in private. At school, with you guys, I didn't have to think about him and stuff at home. And then suddenly, I did. And you guys kept treating me like I was this fragile thing. It was so weird. And I just wanted you guys to be normal so that I could be normal. I don't—I didn't want you all to pity me."

"It's not pity, dumbass," she says. "It's like love, I guess."

"You're such a cheeseball," I say.

"And you're such a jerk," she says.

"I know," I say. "That's why you love me." I reach out and grab her hand and hold it and squeeze it, and she squeezes back. We both sit there like that, not looking at each other, because I guess this is all a little embarrassing, for both of us. "I'm a mess, but I'm getting better, I think." I pull her in for a hug.

"Careful," she says, "people might think you're gay, too."

I laugh. "Who cares," I say.

But after a few more minutes, we unclasp our hands, because both of us can only handle so much corniness.

"I'm glad you're back," she says.

"Me too," I say.

"Because for a while there I thought you might join the cheerleading squad or something crazy like that."

"Oh yeah, totally, I had my pom-poms and everything," I say, laughing again.

Right then Coach yells for Chita, because there's still some practice time left. Chita smiles at me and runs back out to the field.

===

Back at home, I set my bag down in the kitchen and pour my-self a glass of water. As I drink, the phone rings. I look at the caller ID on the landline, an Alabama area code. I'm about to pick up but then it stops ringing. That's when I hear Mom's voice down the hall, in her room. I creep down there.

"Yes, your mother called the other day. Uh-huh," I hear her say. I stand by the door, straining to hear. "No, I'm sorry. It's out of the question. . . . I'm sorry. He needs stability right now, and this would only upset him. You seem like a nice young man, but I wish you'd listen to me. He won't be able to see you. Please, stop calling." Mom sounds exhausted, but also angry. "Good-bye, I'm hanging up now. Don't call back." I creep back down to the kitchen. Mom walks in a few minutes later, carrying her purse and jiggling her keys. "Oh, you're home."

"Yeah."

"I'm going to go pick Sam up at Dr. Saylor's. You have a good day?"

"Uh-huh."

"Okay, we'll be back in a bit."

I listen as the car starts and pulls out of the driveway. Who would be calling for Sam? I grab the cordless and look at the number again, typing it into my cell phone. My heart starts racing as the line rings once, then twice, three times, and then a boy's voice answers: "Hello?"

"Hi," I say. "Who's this?"

"Who's this?" he says back.

"You just called here?" I say. "You spoke to my mom."

Silence. "Oh, hi. Are you . . . who are you?"

"I'm Beth."

"Sam's sister!"

"Yeah," I say. How does this kid know who I am? "Who's this?"

"I'm Tony. Tony Johnson."

I pause for a minute, searching my brain, but his name doesn't ring a bell. "Who are you?"

"I was . . . I'm Sam's friend. I live with my mom, in the same complex where Sam lived. In Anniston."

Lived. You can't call it lived. He sounds so nonchalant that I feel a flash of irritation. "Why are you calling?"

"Does your mom know you're talking to me?" Tony asks.

"No."

"Well, my mom called last week. We're coming to Tuscaloosa this weekend. My aunt is getting married there. I thought . . . I thought it would be nice if . . . If I got to see Sam while we're in town." He's quiet, waiting for me to respond. In a softer voice he says, "He was my best friend," almost like he's embarrassed to use those words.

"Best friend?" I say back to him. How could a boy who was held captive by a maniac have a best friend? It's insane.

"We lived across the courtyard, upstairs," he says. "I . . . I really want to see him. I never got to say good-bye. I mean . . .

260

we were all . . . I had no idea what was really going on."

I feel like shouting at this kid. Like, what do you mean you had no idea what was going on? How stupid are you? "I agree with my mom," I say. "It's not a good idea for you to see Sam."

Silence on the other end. Then, "Can I see you? Can *we* meet?"

I'm about to say no. Mom would never allow this. But, I realize, I don't have to tell her. And maybe, I don't know, this might help me understand something about what happened to Sam. "Yes," I finally say.

"Thank you," he says, "thank you," sounding relieved and grateful. "Can you meet Saturday morning? We've got the wedding that night. It's a quick trip."

"Saturday. Sure." Already I have second thoughts. What am I doing, meeting with this kid, this stranger?

"Where?"

The mall, I think, and then realize I might see someone I know there. I tell Tony to meet at Monnish Park, Saturday at one. I tell him where it is.

"Okay," he says. "Thanks, Beth."

But I don't say anything. I just hang up and sit there for a moment. The house is quiet, I'm still alone. I walk to Sam's room. I open the closet and I see the knapsack, same place it was the other day. It's light brown, with a few dark scuff marks on the sides. I sit down on the floor and hold it in my lap. This backpack is all Sam brought back with him from that place, besides the clothes on his back, and it feels light. I know the sketchbook was in here. But there must have been something else.

I take a deep breath. I know what I'm doing is wrong. But after talking with Tony, I want more answers. I unzip the main compartment.

It's empty except for a flash of baby blue. I feel inside and it's cloth, soft and worn. I pull it out and unfurl it and see it's a T-shirt. A Superman T-shirt. It's small, like a kid would wear.

It's the shirt Sam wore the day he vanished.

And in that moment I can see him all those years ago, smirking at me before he closed my door, before he left us, before our lives changed. I press it against my face and sniff. It smells kind of sour, like it hasn't been washed in a while.

I wonder if this was Sam's only connection to home.

I stuff it back in the knapsack, which I then return to the closet, as close to possible as where I found it. Right then I hear Mom's car door slam, and I rush to my room and close my door.

I hear them come inside. I hear Sam go into his room and shut the door.

Sam, I think. I'm trying. I'm trying to understand. Really, I am.

===

At school, I still spend my lunch hour in the library. I just can't deal with all those people in the cafeteria, most of whom I still want to avoid. Today, as I settle in at a study table and start doing some homework, I see Grace enter the library, her eyes searching around, and I think about ducking my head. But she spots me and walks to the table and sits down.

"So this is where you go," she says, gazing around the big room, like she's never been in there. There are a few other kids here, and Mrs. Jansen, the librarian, is typing things on a computer at the information desk. "Can we talk?" she says.

One of the kids shushes her, and Mrs. Jansen stares over.

We haven't spoken since that horrible party, so why now?

"I've got some studying to do."

She sighs. "Fine." She gets up and walks to another table. She takes out a notebook and starts writing. I try and focus on my work, but I keep stealing glimpses at Grace, scribbling ferociously. Finally, she rips the sheet, folds it, and walks back over. "Here," she says, flashing a pleading look. I take the note and she walks out.

I set the paper down. I'll read it later, I think. But as I study my chemistry text, I keep seeing the folded square in the corner of my eye. I can't focus with that note sitting there. So I shut my book and unfold the note and read:

Beth–

Until we can have a real conversation, I just wanted to say I'm sorry about that dumb party and the way Tark and the others treated you. I really enjoyed spending time with you and I thought we were going to be friends again, but if you don't want to, I understand. But I don't want you to think that I was being fake or anything. I really have missed you and I wish I could go back in time because I wasn't a good friend to you after Sam disappeared and I'm sorry about that. I really am. And I want to make it up to you. Maybe we can talk or hang out again soon. (I hate writing!) Talk to me soon. Please?

Your friend,
Grace

I fold the note and put it in a pouch in my backpack. I try working, but mostly I sit there, staring off at nothing, and it's like a knot in my stomach loosens—a knot I never knew was there.

===

The next day at school, instead of going to the library, I go to the cafeteria. My belly churns when I step inside, the noise and smells a bit much for me to take. I see Chita in our old spot, with Darla. I see Donal and Brendan and the other guys.

I walk over close to Grace's table and motion for her. She gets up and heads toward me, a cautious look on her face. "Hey," she says. She looks back at her table. "We can clear a spot for you?"

"No, it's okay. I'm going to sit with Chita and those guys," I say, gesturing over to the table. "But I wanted to thank you, for your note."

She smiles. "I really do hope we can hang out sometime," she says. "Or something."

"Sure," I say. "I'd like that."

"Good," she says. I can tell she wants to hug me, but I can't deal with that, not in front of all these people

"Can it be just us?" I ask.

"Of course," she says.

"Thanks." We just stand there, not sure what to say. "Well, I better join my friends over there."

"Yeah," she says. "I'll see you."

We both walk to our respective tables, the places where we belong.

"Any space for me?" I ask when I get to mine.

Chita nods, and scoots down and clears a spot on the end of the table. I'm relieved she doesn't make a comment about me talking with Grace.

"Is your head okay?" Darla asks.

"I'll live, no thanks to her," I say. Chita elbows me.

Donal hasn't yet looked up from his food. He probably hates me. I unwrap the sandwich I brought and start eating, and eventually everyone starts talking about whatever it was they were talking about before I intruded. It's fine just to be there, sitting at the table, a part of them.

The bell rings and Chita says, "See you at practice."

She walks off, the table clears, and it's just me and Donal, who's still finishing his lunch. I get up to leave, but I stop.

"It wasn't a mistake," I say.

He looks up, and he knows what I mean. He's chewing something still, and kind of has a dumb look on his face, but it's cute, too—like he's trying not to break into a big grin and chew and talk, all at once. I grab my stuff and bolt before he can say anything and I make it to my next class just as the second bell rings.

Saturday turns out to be a windy, cold gray day. I regret suggesting the park as a meeting place, but I'll make do. I wear a sweater, my heavy coat. I tell Mom I'm going shopping, which is believable only because Christmas isn't too far away.

On the drive over I try to imagine what Tony looks like. But he's a blank. Like most everything about Sam's time in Anniston.

I park in the little lot and sit in the car. No one else is here, due to the cold. Perfect. The trees are mostly bare, except for the tall skinny pines, which line the edges and provide a kind of barricade against Fifteenth Street. The shrubs that shield the park from the back of Central's football field are bare, too, so I can see the school in the distance. It's a little depressing.

Soon a white Honda drives up, a woman at the wheel, a shadow of another person in the passenger seat.

I get out of my car.

"Hello," the woman says as she steps out of her car. She's African American, wearing a tan overcoat and high-heeled boots. "Lorraine Johnson," she announces, walking over and extending her hand.

"Beth Walsh," I say, shaking her hand.

"This is Tony," Lorraine says, and the boy shuffles forward awkwardly. He's lighter-skinned than his mother, with close-cropped dark hair, and sort of bulgy and intense-looking brown eyes.

"Hi," I finally say.

"Hi," he says.

His mom looks around at the park, puts her hands in her coat pockets. "You kids going to get cold out here?"

"We should be okay. And we can always sit in my car," I say.

She eyes me suspiciously. "Thanks for meeting with him," she says finally, forcing a smile and pulling him next to her. He's staring at me with those eyes and it makes me a little uncomfortable, so I focus on Lorraine. "We felt horrible about everything, you know," she says. "We had no idea. It's just . . .," she continues, trailing off. "How is he? How is Sam?"

Now that I'm face-to-face with these people, that anger I felt a few days ago feels misplaced. "He's okay," I say, which seems true enough.

"That's good," she says, forcing that smile again. "That's really good. Right, honey?" she says.

"Yeah," he says, staring at me like he's in awe or something.

She looks down at him like she's sad for him, like she doesn't want to let go. "Well, anyway," she says. "I'll pick you up at two? That way we can get back to Aunt Gisele's place to dress." She turns her attention back to me. "My sister's getting married tonight. Her second marriage, but still." She hugs Tony, and I can tell they're close, that she's a good mom. All that goodness, I think, near so much evil. It doesn't make sense. She says, "You two have a good visit."

We watch as she drives off, till her car vanishes around a corner gas station. Then Tony looks back at me with those sharp, big eyes. He has on a green jacket that doesn't seem warm enough for this chill. I take in the park. "Let's find a bench?" I say. We walk to the nearest one, right in front of a rickety swing set and slide, and sit. Tony keeps fidgeting. I smile over at him. I want to tell him to relax.

"So," I prompt. "Sam was your friend."

"Yeah," he says. "Sam Hunnicutt. That's what he said his name was."

"Oh," I say. My belly clenches, but I know this is just the beginning. I want the blanks filled in, but I'm afraid to read the sentences once they're complete.

"We became friends pretty quick. He was the only other kid my age in the complex when we moved in. I guess by the time we met he'd been there for a year."

"You didn't . . . You didn't suspect anything was wrong?" I ask.

He looks down at his hands. His nails are bitten. "No," he says. "Sam was quiet, but just, like, a normal kid. And Mr. Hunnicutt—Rusty. I mean, he was kind of grumpy and overprotective. But he seemed okay. He seemed normal."

"But he wasn't," I say, more sharply than I mean to. I'm here to listen, I remind myself. Listen, and try to—try to what? *What am I here to find out?*

"Yeah. We'd play video games and he always said Rusty didn't allow it and he always felt bad when we did, and finally we stopped doing that because I think he got in trouble once when Rusty found out. Rusty thought video games rotted your brain or something."

"So, everyone thought Sam was . . . his son?" Saying this makes me want to vomit.

"No, his nephew," he says, sounding sad. "Sam called him Rusty. Or sometimes he called him Uncle. When he called him that, you could tell it felt weird to him." His big eyes look desperate. "You gotta believe me. It seemed normal. I mean, Rusty was really strict. I'd hear him yelling at Sam sometimes. But otherwise, they got along really good. I'd see them laugh together. Make fun of each other, but in a . . . you know, like friends do. It just seemed like nothing was wrong."

Surely Tony's memories are messed up. There's no way this can be right. Sam was a captive. A prisoner. I inhale a deep breath of cold air. Tony must realize I'm upset because he doesn't say anything else. He starts nibbling his nails.

Off in the distance, I take in Central High. Seeing it grounds me for a moment. I spent so many days there, while Sam spent his in that apartment, with that man. But now that man is in prison, locked away, and Sam's with us. We have him back. I feel some of the knots loosening inside me.

"Sam didn't go to school," I say at last. "What did he do all day?"

Tony quickly pulls his hands away from his mouth. "He

told me he was homeschooled. I guess that was weird because Rusty worked all the time, so when was he ever there to homeschool him? But I didn't think much of it. Sam had these textbooks, he'd show me, but we didn't talk about school and stuff. I just thought he was lucky."

"*Lucky?*"

Tony shrugs, starts biting his nails again before he catches himself. "Yeah. I hated school. I mean, it's better now. But people would call me Obama. No one was really that mean, but I was sort of . . . Well, you get it. But Sam never made me feel weird. Plus, we both had one parent, sort of, so we bonded that way."

My belly kind of lurches when I realize he views that "one parent" as Russell Hunnicutt—not Mom.

"What did he say about his mother? His parents?" I ask.

"Uh," he says, sounding hesitant.

"It's okay," I say. *Breathe*, I think, so that the queasy feeling I have won't make me want to roll into a ball on the ground. "Go on."

He won't look at me, and I can tell he doesn't want to say anything, and I almost wish he wouldn't. "He said they died in a car wreck when he was a baby. When they lived in Ohio," he says, his voice quiet.

"Died," I say, like this is a new word I'm just learning.

"He talked about his aunt a lot, though, and his cousin. His cousin Beth. You."

Cousin. Cousin Beth.

"A lot makes sense now. He talked about you all the time. I mean, I like my cousins okay, but we've never been *that* close, you know? Once I found Sam sitting at the picnic table in the courtyard, crying. I asked him why and he told me it was because he missed his aunt and cousin."

It's so much to take in. Cousin Beth. These fake worlds he had to create.

"These reporters all came to our complex, after the truth came out. After they took Rusty away," he says. "They wondered how we couldn't know that we had a kidnapped kid there. They made us feel like . . . like we were criminals."

I picture the cameras, the reporters, invading their territory like they did with us.

"Those days, after it all happened, Mom and I just sat on the couch with the TV on, pretending like none of it was true. And one day she just finally started crying like crazy, and I did, too. Because we just felt . . . We should have known. We should have . . . saved him." His voice trails off and he stands up, suddenly. He walks around for a little bit, and I think he might be crying, but I stay frozen to my seat. Finally, he walks back and settles back onto the bench, beside me.

"I really miss Sam," he says.

I do too, I realize. I miss my brother—who he was. Because the Sam at home, I don't really know him.

But I want to.

"What was he like?" I ask. "I mean, as a friend?"

Tony's quiet for a bit, like he's surprised at the question. "He was nice," Tony says, his voice brightening. "He was funny. I mean, I guess he could be quiet. And a little nervous sometimes when it came to Rusty." He shakes his head. "He was so different from the guys at my school. They're so loud and annoying, and Sam wasn't that way."

He could have been, I think. But that part of his personality had been snuffed out. He wasn't allowed to become a normal teenage boy.

"I miss him," Tony says again.

"I know," I say, hoping I sound comforting. It's dawning on me that Sam's return has affected so many people besides just me and my family. "Maybe one day you can come visit."

He lights up when I say this, and for the first time that day he smiles. And I picture him and Sam, together, and I feel grateful toward this kid. For maybe being the one bit of brightness in this horrible life Sam had with that horrible man.

Mrs. Johnson drives up right then. Has it really been an hour? Tony sees her, too, and his smile vanishes. She steps out of the car and waves at us. Together, we walk to the parking lot. Before she says anything, Tony says, "Beth says maybe I can visit one day, and see Sam."

She gives me a kind, sad smile, like she knows this probably won't happen but appreciates me saying it anyway. "Thanks again for speaking with Tony. With us."

Tony steps toward me and I'm surprised when he hugs me. At first I don't know how to respond, but I hug him back. I feel a lump in my throat as I pat him on the shoulder. I pull back from him, not wanting him to see me upset, so I wave and start walking across the parking lot. When I'm almost to my car, I hear Tony shout, "Wait!" I look over as he opens the door to the backseat of his mom's car and digs around until he pulls out a manila folder. He jogs over to me. "Here."

"What is this?" I say. When I open it I see it's full of drawings. Drawings of me, of Mom. Of Dad. Even Earl. Drawings of our house. Drawings of Sam, all of us together. Some are just pencil, but some are in color. They're really good. And there are so many of them. Sam must have spent hours on these. I feel an ache in my chest, thinking of him in that awful place, finding these moments to draw—to draw us. His family.

"Sam gave me these to hold on to. He told me that Rusty didn't like him drawing pictures of his aunt and cousin and stuff. I guess it makes sense now."

"Thanks," I say.

Ho nods, gives me another smile. "Bye for now," he says.

After they drive off, I get into the warmth of the car. I look through the drawings again, more closely. Happy scenes of family life—all of us posed in front of the house. Mom and Sam under the oak tree in the backyard. Then there are these solo portraits. I come to a picture of me, from the waist up, and I can tell this is Sam's attempt to imagine me older. Didn't he tell me he tried to do this, but he threw them away, that they were no good? In the picture, my hair is shorter, like I wore it back then, but the color is so precise—I'm amazed he could do this with color pencils. My eyes look a little off—maybe too round, and my lips seem too full and perfect. But I can recognize myself in it. *Cousin Beth.*

When I get home, I tuck the drawings under my jacket and walk to my bedroom, where I stuff them in the bottom drawer of my desk. I'll think of a better spot later. After that, I realize the house is dead quiet. I walk around and through the kitchen window I spot Mom out on the patio, in her coat. I go outside and join her.

"Oh, you're back early," she says, sounding a little flustered, quickly stamping out a cigarette. There are already three butts in the ashtray.

"I know," she says. "It's horrible. Please, promise me you won't ever smoke."

"Don't worry," I say, sitting down on one of the cold chairs.

I finally get a good look at her eyes, and from the redness it's clear she's been crying.

"What's wrong?" I ask. For weeks Mom has been so calm, so cheery, so focused on moving forward with life.

She smiles over at me. "Nothing," she says.

Obviously I don't believe her. I want to show her Sam's beautiful drawings. The way he kept us alive. But that would mean telling her about Tony. And I know that's a bad idea.

"All I ever wanted was for Sam to come back," Mom says. She leans back in her chair. "I never thought about what would happen if he did. Some days, I look at him and I know it's Sam. But it's not *Sam*. Our little rascal. And I just need to get over that. *That* Sam is never coming back." Her voice catches, like she's about to cry, but she fights through it. "But the alternative—of him never coming back? Well, I'll take this any day. Right?"

"Yes," I say, feeling my throat tighten. Superman, I think. He's Superman. For surviving. For making it back home.

She starts crying for real then, little sobs that cause her chest to lurch. I reach for her hand, and she grabs mine, then takes a deep breath and straightens her back, refusing to break down further. Sitting here, I think about all the times Earl and I held on to her as she sobbed and moaned, her sadness so intense it was like she was in physical pain.

It's weird, that I've been so annoyed with Mom lately. For being home so much. For cooking dinners and baking cookies. My clean clothes stacked on my bed when I come home from school. Because Sam is back, and so is my mom. I can see that now.

"It's cold," she says, like she's snapping awake. She wipes her eyes. "Let's go inside and order a pizza. I'm too tired to cook tonight." She smiles, her puffy red eyes the only trace of the past few minutes.

"Okay," I say.

Mom orders the pizza, and right when she hangs up the phone Earl comes home from some renovation north of the river. Mom stands and they hug, because I think Earl can tell she's been crying. He pulls back and brushes her hair from her face, kisses her. That stuff used to gross me out, but today I'm grateful for it. We're not falling apart, are we? We're going to be okay, like Mom says.

When the pizza comes, Earl cracks open a beer, Mom too, and they go to the den with plates and napkins.

Sam walks in and grabs some slices and plops them on a plate. "You want a Coke?" I ask. I'm at the fridge, letting cold air escape, and he comes and takes it from me, then walks away.

I shut the fridge and stand there. I want to call him back and say, *I met your friend. He misses you. And I saw your drawings. I have them in my room. I love them.*

And I think again about how amazing Sam is, that he carved out some happiness somehow, even in that place.

CHAPTER 10

Alien

Josh

"Can't I see it?" I ask.

"Nope," Sam says. "Not till it's finished."

It's Friday afternoon. I had Dad drop me here after school because Sam needed to make touchups to the portrait. It's been a busy time at school, so I haven't been able to come over. We're in the living room, and it's quiet. It's too cold today to even *think* about doing this outside. Sam's sitting across from me on a plush upholstered chair. I'm on the couch, which is kind of hard and uncomfortable.

The same couch where I sat while that policewoman interviewed me years ago on that day in July. Where I didn't say a word about the truck. I chew on my lips and look away, feeling my face getting warm.

Sam says, "You okay?"

"Huh?" I say, turning to him.

"Your face is a little red."

"It is?"

He smiles. From then on he goes back and forth from me

to the sketch pad. I still feel a little ridiculous posing this way. But Sam said he wants to give it to me as a Christmas gift, which is just weeks away.

I try to think of things other than the last time I sat on this couch. Like next week at school, when we have midterms—three half days, two exams each day—and then we go on break until the new year. I'll need to study all weekend. Or maybe not *all* weekend. I mean, I'm doing great in all my classes. Plus, I've always aced my exams. Surely I can have *some* fun. Nick is probably hanging with Sarah. And Raj with Madison. I could ask Max and Ty to go to a movie. I look over at Sam, still deep in concentration. An improbable idea comes to me, but I give it a shot. "Hey, you want to come over tomorrow night?"

"Tomorrow night?" he asks, looking up again from the drawing. He's never come inside my house. I've never invited him until now.

"Maybe you could sleep over. We could watch *Alien*, like we talked about."

He stares at me for a second, maybe surprised, maybe trying to figure out a way to say no. "Yeah, that would be fun. I just . . . are you sure it's okay with your folks?"

"Yeah," I say, even though I haven't asked them.

"I have to run it by my parents."

"Okay."

I haven't had a sleepover since this past summer, with

Nick. It's like once we started high school, those things were childish. But with Sam, we have our own realm, in a way. Normal rules don't apply.

"My mom may freak out if I am not here at night. She's still a little overprotective," he says.

"Well, if you don't want to come," I say.

"No, no, I do. It will be fun."

"Yeah," I say. I click my phone for the time. It's just after five. Dad will be here soon. "You almost done?"

"Yep," he says.

I try and lean over to sneak a peek, and he snatches it away, smiling. "Jerk," he says.

His hands move swiftly now, like he's just scribbling. He looks happy, concentrating on his task. And all that stuff he told me seems so far away from us now. You'd think that someone who'd been through all that would be so obviously messed up. But I look at Sam—focusing his eyes on the sketch, a slight smile forming as he looks at his own handiwork—and it's like I can forget anything ever happened to him.

"Done." He looks up and flashes another smile and closes the sketchbook.

The next day, around noon, while I'm studying, Nick texts me.

Want to go to a party tonight?

What party? I text back.

Rob Moore's parents are away and he's having some people over.

I'm a little surprised he's not going with Sarah. And then I'm surprised there's a party the weekend before exams. And then I'm confused. I text back: **Who's Rob?**

He goes to TA. Remember??

Oh yeah. TA is Tuscaloosa Academy, the private school. Then I remember that Rob took some summer tennis clinics with us. I didn't know Nick was that friendly with him.

Come over at seven.

I don't text back right away. **I can't,** I eventually type.

Why not?

I think about an easy lie. That we're having company over. That I really need to study, which wouldn't be that far from the truth. But I'm sick of lying. **Sam's coming over. To hang out.**

No response for about five minutes. **U there?** I text.

Ur really hanging out w that freak?

I hold the phone for a bit, just looking at the words. Why would Nick say something like that?

Not a freak, I type back.

But before I can type anything else, I get another text from Nick: **Whatever. Later.**

I just sit there, holding the phone. I don't know why Nick's being this way. Angry and jealous and kind of mean.

I set the phone down. I don't respond.

===

Sam comes over at seven. His mom walks him to the door. I can see her eyeing the foyer and den, checking out our house. It's nicer than the one in Pine Forest.

"What a lovely home," she says, sounding genuine but also kind of annoyed.

"Thanks," Mom says. "You want some coffee, or a glass of wine?"

"No thanks, I better get going. We're going out to dinner." Sam's mom hugs him so tight and for so long that it's like she thinks this is the last time she's ever going to see him. After the hug, Mom walks her to the car. No telling what they're talking about.

Sam and I go upstairs and dump his duffel at the base of my bed. I'd already blown up the air mattress for him.

"Want to start the movie now?"

"Yeah, sure," I say.

In the den, I sit at one end of the couch and Sam sits at the other. I find the movie on Netflix and we start it.

Alien is creepy, kind of like watching a haunted house movie, except everyone's on this weird spaceship. Later, when Sigourney Weaver is in the shuttle escaping after everything has gone to hell, I say, "Don't tell me the alien is in there with her." But it is. I dig my hands into the cushion, but then it's all over, she's safe in hypersleep, until she's rescued and has to battle a whole bunch of aliens in the next movie.

I flick on the light and it's like we're coming out of a bad dream. "Intense," I say.

"It gets me every time," Sam says, watching the credits.

We order our pizza and once it comes we just flip channels and watch stupid stuff, not really talking. Mom comes in and checks on us after a while. "You guys sleepy yet?" It's midnight. I hadn't realized we'd wasted so much time just vegging in front of the TV.

"Not really," I say.

"Well, just shut out the lights when you're done. Your father and I are hitting the hay," she says.

A little bit later, after I let out an audible yawn, Sam says, "Let's go to your room."

Upstairs I sit down on my bed, and Sam starts digging around in his bag. He pulls out a paper sack and holds it up, grinning like he just opened a present.

"What is it?" I say.

He opens it and yanks out these little mini bottles of liquor. Jack Daniel's, Bacardi, Wild Turkey, Absolut, Dewar's.

"Wow," I say, surprised that Sam has this stuff. "Where'd you get all that?" I feel excited and nervous all at once.

"Found them at home, a whole bunch. Might have been my dad's. There was a whole bag in the back of the pantry. You wanna have some?"

Mom and Dad are asleep, at the other end of the hall. I've really only had sips of drinks and beers at parties with

Nick and the guys. I can't say I've ever been drunk. "Sure. Why not?"

We each crack open a Jack Daniel's. I can only take small sips. It's bitter and burns my throat. Sam chugs his, then opens another. I start to wonder if he drank and smoked and did stuff like that in Anniston. Nothing would surprise me anymore about his time there.

I dim the lamp and put on my pajamas in the bathroom— boxers and a T-shirt. When I come out Sam's just in his boxers, sitting Indian style on the air mattress. I want to stare but I know I shouldn't. I go to my bed and crawl in. I take another sip, then another, finishing the bottle. I see two empties by the air mattress. Sam grabs his sack, digs around, and tosses me a Wild Turkey, which tastes only slightly different from the Jack. I feel a buzz now, a dizziness. Like I'm cut loose from my actual life, calmer, almost giddy. I stare over at him, at his shirtlessness. He's a little glassy-eyed, looks kind of goofy. But also cute. I take my T-shirt off then, feeling less self-conscious.

"Man, every time I watch *Alien.* . . . Every time I think somehow they'll all survive. I know how it ends, but I still root for them to get away. Like, that scene with Parker and Lambert, I'm always like, 'Run! Run!' But they never do. They always die. That's stupid, isn't it?"

"No," I say. "Not at all." I know what he's talking about. Like, what if I had run out of that backyard and seen the white truck's license plate as it drove by, and what if I had reported that?

But I didn't.

Sam crawls under his covers, so I flip off the lamp. The glow from the streetlight sneaks through the blinds, so I can see the outline of Sam down beside my bed. I feel myself start to doze, lulled by the alcohol, but Sam starts talking.

"I called Kaylee the other day," he says, sounding suddenly serious. He's quiet for a few seconds, then says, "Her dad wouldn't let me speak to her. He told me to never call again."

I don't say anything, but I hear Sam take another chug from one of the bottles. I wonder why he thought of her now. "I really cared about her. She's the only girl I ever did it with."

Did it with. It takes me a few seconds to realize he means sex. And I feel queasy all of a sudden. Sam, who had his life taken away from him, has had sex with a girl. I start to wonder about Nick and Sarah and my other friends, and then about all my classmates. All of them doing it. Everyone having sex, drinking. Is everyone normal and I'm like the one who's the total loser, who's never done anything exciting in his life? Even Sam, after what he went through—he's done stuff that seems so far off to me.

I haven't even kissed anyone.

I feel small in my bed, and I'm glad I'm in the dark under the covers.

"Josh? You awake?"

"Yeah."

"Have you ever, like, done it?"

"No," I say, and it feels surprisingly okay to admit that to Sam. The old Sam might have laughed at me or made a joke. But not this Sam.

"You're the only one who knows about Kaylee," Sam finally says. "I haven't even talked about her to my therapist."

I don't respond.

"I really miss her sometimes."

"I'm sorry," I say.

I see him unwrap the covers and stand up. He walks toward my bed, around to the other side. "You mind if I just lay here for a little bit. It's easier to talk this way."

"Okay," I say, my heart starting to rev.

He lies on the side next to me, but not under the covers, and I feel my body shift a little to his side of the bed, his weight pulling me toward him. I close my eyes and listen as he talks.

"Kaylee was . . . well, when I was with her. It just felt like I was in another place," he says.

Another place. Does everyone feel that way, when they're with someone they like, someone they love? Sam's so close I can smell the alcohol on his breath, can smell the musky scent of his body next to mine. I scoot away a little and reach over to the bedside table and grab the Wild Turkey, still mostly full, and take a few sips.

"Can I have some?" he asks.

"Finish it," I say, and he does.

After a long silence, I think maybe Sam is asleep. But then I feel the bed shake as he props himself against the pillows a bit more. I see his hand going under the covers, just a bit. Outside, I hear a car drive by. So late for this neighborhood. I close my eyes again when I feel Sam's hand on my hip, at the waistband of my boxers.

I don't know what's happening, but I do.

Maybe if I wasn't drunk I'd leap up and lock myself in the bathroom, but I don't. I just lie there, eyes closed, and let it happen. His hand, it's warm, it creeps into my boxers and finds it, and he starts tugging. It hurts at first but then it doesn't.

It doesn't hurt. It feels good. So good.

I know this isn't what he wants. It's what I want. It's what he somehow knows I want. I listened to him talk about Kaylee, and now I get this.

"Don't," I say softly. But he keeps going, keeps at it till I gasp and shake a little and then it happens and I feel like I might yell out or something because it's so different than when I do it. It's like he knows exactly when I can't bear his hand anymore, and he lets go and rolls off the bed, goes back to his air mattress, climbs under the covers.

We both just lie there in silence for what seems like a long time. It's like how I felt after the movie earlier. My heart racing and racing and then it's over, and my heart slows and slows.

Maybe Sam's fallen asleep. I pull my boxers off and sort of wipe myself, and then drop them on the floor, on the other side of the bed. I'm tired. So tired, and a little drunk probably, because my head spins when I collapse on my pillow. And I'm glad I feel so funny because then I don't have to think about what just happened. It's so quiet, the only noise the sound of Sam breathing.

When I wake up Sam's not there. But his stuff is. The bed's unmade. Why didn't he wake me? I don't hear any noises in the house so I rush to the bathroom, totally naked. I don't look at myself in the mirror, but I wash myself with a hot rag. Out in my room I change into a clean pair of boxers, my jeans, a T-shirt.

I hear a faint noise from the front yard. I crack my blinds and I see Mom and Dad, and Sam, all of them dressed. They're wandering around cleaning things up because someone has toilet-papered our house.

No, not someone. Probably a whole group. They've thrown toilet paper over the trees, over the shrubs, around the mailbox, everywhere, making it look like a snowstorm came through overnight.

I put on my shoes and go downstairs and out the front door.

It's a mess.

Mom spots me first. "Morning," she says, sounding surprisingly amused.

Sam and Dad are slowly unwrapping the toilet paper from around the biggest tree in the yard. I try to catch Sam's eye, but he keeps to his task.

"Here, have at it," Mom says, throwing me a Hefty bag.

I start on the mailbox, unwrapping the soggy paper, which comes off in gloppy, messy clumps. While I do this, I keep glancing at Sam, but he never looks my way, and I realize he's doing that on purpose. He can't look at me. I feel my face flush, thinking of his hands on me. I turn away and grab strips of paper off the ground. Some of the streams of toilet paper, the ones high up in the trees, won't be easy to get down. The rain or the wind will have to do that. For weeks, we'll be reminded of this, and the neighbors, too.

I keep grabbing the toilet paper. It seems endless, but that's okay. If I focus on getting every speck of the stuff then my mind won't flash back to last night. How good it felt. How weird it was. How guilty I feel.

"Who could have done this?" Mom asks out loud, but I don't think she expects or even wants an answer.

It's not like this happens in our neighborhood. Looking up and down the street, all the other yards are untouched.

Only high school kids do this dumb shit, to other high school kids. And only to people they know.

And then it clicks.

Nick.

Nick did this. And whoever he was with at that party. Because they knew I was with Sam, not with them. Because they knew Sam was here. *Sam the freak.* I feel a crackling in my chest as I grab yet another glob of paper and force it into the bag.

I look at Sam, he's saying something to my dad, who pats him on the shoulder as they both keep collecting the paper.

When we get the yard as clean as possible, we go back inside and Mom toasts us some bagels and brings out the cream cheese. Sam and I sit on the stools by the counter and watch her, not talking, still not even looking at each other. When we're done with our bagels, he packs his bag in my room while I watch TV downstairs. I see Mrs. Manderson drive up.

We all walk Sam out to the car and Mom and Dad and Mrs. Manderson kind of chat and laugh about obviously be-ing toilet-papered, despite our cleanup efforts. "There's been a rash of these lately," Dad lies. "I guess it was our turn."

I see Dad look over at Sam, like he's worried about him for some reason, but Sam's a blank. Mrs. Manderson's gaze swivels, and a flash of recognition registers across her face, her eyes squinting ever so slightly. She clears her throat, says, "You'd think people would have better things to do with their time."

"You'd think," Dad says, clapping his hand on Sam's back.

"Anyway, did you boys have a nice time?" Mrs. Manderson asks.

"Yes, ma'am," we both say at the same time.

Sam looks over at me, for the first time that morning. He's giving me a slight smile, but then it's like he suddenly remembers last night and he frowns and looks away. Still, he sticks his fist out and we fist-bump, like we always do, like nothing happened between us. And when they drive off, Mom cups her arm around my shoulder and we walk up the front walk. She stops to stare up to the top branches of the trees where the toilet paper that was too high to remove is, little white strands waving around in the morning breeze.

"He's a nice young man," she says.

All day Sunday I cram for exams and try not to think about the sleepover, but I feel a guilt pressing down on me. Can you hate something and like it at the same time? Because I do. And it's like these feelings are battling in my stomach—making me smile one minute, and then making me tingle with shame the next, again and again. And then I think of how Sam wouldn't look at me this morning. Because he was embarrassed. Or maybe he was disgusted by me. Disgusted because I let him do it, even though I said *don't*. Disgusted because I liked it.

The only way I can stop these thoughts is by studying harder, so I do. My eyes start to feel exhausted from reading my notes again and again. The book stacks on my desk, towers of information. I feel like my brain might explode.

When I wake on Monday morning, I sit in bed, immediately thinking about my exams for today—Spanish and algebra—all the formulas and rules and phrases and grammatical rules held in place, ready to spill out.

I jump in the shower and scrub and wash my hair and hope the water washes away any bad thoughts or feelings I have. I want to ace my exams.

I see Nick during the algebra exam, and I don't even talk to him, and he doesn't talk to me. And that's all the convincing I need to know it was him and the rest of my friends. I see them all—Max and Raj and Ty and Nick—after the test is over and classes are dismissed. They're at Raj's locker, talking. Normally they'd wave me over, but they don't and I keep walking. I don't want to confront them about what I know they did.

While I wait for Dad to pick me up out front, I think about them out in the dark that night, rolls of toilet paper cupped in their arms. While they trashed our yard, was I asleep? Or was Sam next to me on the bed doing what we did?

Once back at home, I continue to study, cramming my brain with facts, nothing but facts.

I finish my last exam on Wednesday. School is over for the year. Christmas break. I should feel happy and free, but what I feel mostly is tired, and slightly uneasy. I'm chatting with Dad in the kitchen, eating mini pretzels before dinner. We're waiting for Mom to get home, to see if she wants to eat out. And that's when the house phone rings, and I know it's Sam. "For you," Dad says.

I take the phone and go into the family room. My heart thuds. Normally, Sam calling wouldn't be so weird. But I haven't heard a peep from him since Sunday.

"I have the portrait done," he says. "Can I drop it off tomorrow? Mom has some errands after lunch and she can drive me over." Hearing his voice, a tightness in my body eases. "Sure," I say. I'd almost forgotten about the portrait.

"Okay then," he says. "See you tomorrow." Then he hangs up.

I stand at the window, with the phone still pressed to my ear, because when I hang up I know Dad will want to keep chitchatting in the kitchen. I'm glad Sam called. I just wish he'd said more. He sounded kind of cold, but maybe I imagined that.

Later that night, at home, in my room, I think back to the call. I'm not crazy—Sam sounded angry. And as I lay on my bed—in almost the same spot as the other night—I start thinking that it's likely he hates me now. He hates me because of what happened. He will give me the drawing and that's it, I'll never see or hear from him again.

And I can't call Nick or the other guys, because they hate me, too.

And it's like something physical starts raining down on me. Shock and fear and sadness, pricking me like cold drops of water. Still dressed, I get under the covers and I start shivering, like when you have a fever, and I close my eyes and just try and breathe in and out, in and out. My body eventually slows down. But I feel heavy. I feel like I can't move. I can't even summon the energy to undress.

I start to doze, but my brain won't let me fall asleep. I think about how happy I was just a few days ago, watching *Alien* with Sam, and then those moments when Sam passed me the little bottle of liquor, smiling. Before things got weird. I wish I could go back, and do things differently. Not just the other night, but years ago, that day, when I saw the man in the white truck and did nothing. But I know I can't. And I feel that heaviness again, and the heaviness finally drags me under to sleep.

The next day, when I wake up, I see a note from Mom on the kitchen counter: She's at work and Dad's on campus, grading exams. I make some coffee and let it flow through me, waking me up. Somehow, I feel better. I feel okay. And then I realize it's probably because I'll see Sam soon, and maybe he won't be so mad about everything. Maybe things will be okay after all. So I sit around and watch TV, waiting, feeling both hopeful and anxious.

Around noon, Mrs. Manderson's car pulls up. I see Sam get out, carrying what must be the drawing, wrapped in brown paper. The car drives off, which surprises me. I thought this was just going to be a quick handoff. I open the door and greet him, the muscles in my body suddenly feeling rubbery.

"Hey," he says. "Mom's running a quick errand, but she'll be back soon."

"Okay," I say, trying to sound casual.

He comes in and we settle on the couch in the family room. He's holding the wrapped portrait against his chest and looking down. He's barely made eye contact since I opened the door. I feel all of those heavy feelings from yesterday rushing back in. "I hope you like it," he says. He unwraps it, but keeps it faced away from me. It's in a frame. He stares at it, like he's having second thoughts about parting with it. Then he slowly turns it around.

It's under glass, in dark gray pencil, and yes, it looks like me. Seeing it, the tension in me loosens. In the portrait, I stare off to the side, the way I did in his backyard, and there's a slight smile on my lips. The strands in my hair are ruffled as they would be after a long day, and my eyes—it's almost like I'm looking at myself in a mirror. Sam has gotten me exactly right. "It's so good," I say.

"It's okay if you don't like it."

"No, it's ... it's great, it really is. It's ... like, I can't believe you can do something like this. It looks just like me."

"You sure it's okay?" he says, looking at me now, but in a shy way, a slight hopeful smile on his face.

"Yeah," I say, looking back at him, and I can see how stupid I've been. He doesn't hate me. He's my friend.

He needs me.

I look back at the drawing and stare at it for a bit, because as much as I wanted Sam to look at me, I feel shy, too, and I don't know what to say to him now. The stuff from the other night—it's still hanging in the air. I can't talk about it, and I know he can't either. So I focus on each detail of the drawing, each swerve of the pencil.

"Mom says I can take art classes, eventually," Sam says, breaking the silence. "I mean, I basically taught myself."

"Yeah, you told me that," I say. "From the TV. While you were ... in Anniston." I look over at him, and he's nodding gently.

"You can tell me stuff, too, you know," he says. "Things about yourself."

He looks serious. I know he means it. I can tell him things, if I want to. I can tell him I'm gay. He already knows it. And he's giving me an opening, isn't he? But there are still things he doesn't know. About the white truck. And I realize that I want to get it out of me. It's like the alien from the movie, waiting to burst through my chest.

"That day," I say, then pause. I feel a little sick to my stomach, but I know I have to go on. "When I rode my bike back home, after I fell off. Well, a little bit later, he drove up next to me. That man. Russell Hunnicutt."

Sam's eyes flicker at the name, then narrow a little.

"He offered me a ride. But I didn't get in. I guess he gave me the creeps. I rode off." I'm speaking quickly, feeling the urgency to get it all out as fast as I can. "But then I looked back and saw that he was following me. I jumped off my bike and hid in someone's backyard, in one of those houses along the road that goes to Pine Forest. I sat there and waited and he drove by slowly, like maybe he was searching for me. I stayed for a few minutes, then when I came back out his truck was gone. I rode home, fast, in case he came back." When I stop, I take a deep breath because I feel like I just ran a sprint. But I'm not done. I'm about to tell the worst part. That I didn't tell anyone about this. Not my parents. Not Beth. Not the police.

"I know about all that," Sam says. "That first night, when he took me. Rusty told me."

"What?" I say softly, because it still feels hard to breathe.

He swallows. "He told me that he'd wanted to get you.

That you were his first choice. But that you got away. And then he drove back to Skyland. He knew I was still out there, alone. And he saw me. He saw me walking on the side of the road." Sam looks toward the window.

My heart is pounding. It could have been me. It *should* have been me. The terror of Sam's words slam into me like a blast of cold air.

But I have to go on.

"Sam," I say, and I start shaking. "I never told anyone. I never told the police or my parents or Beth. I didn't tell anyone about the white truck. About seeing him."

His eyes dart back to me, face scrunching. "You didn't? Why not?"

"I don't know," I say, wishing I felt even the slightest bit of relief. Instead, I feel sick. "I thought . . . I thought I was overreacting. Like maybe this man was just trying to help me, and he was an innocent guy and I'd just get him in trouble. Plus, I never got a look at the license plate or anything."

A car horn blares. Mrs. Manderson.

"I have to go," Sam says, spotting her car through the window.

"Please," I say, though I don't know what I mean. Please stay? Please forgive me?

He gets up and walks toward the door. I follow, and he turns back to me before going out.

"I'm sorry," I say. I want to hug him or something, so that my body will warm up, so I'll feel better, but I know he wouldn't let me. He stands by the door, poised to leave, looking at me blankly.

"It's okay, Josh," he says. But the expression on his face says that it's not okay, at all.

The car horn beeps again. He opens the door and leaves.

I go back to the couch and lie down. I stop shaking after a while. When I finally get up off the couch, I pick up the portrait resting on the coffee table and take it upstairs to my room. I hide it in my closet because I can't bear to look at it anymore.

CHAPTER 11
Gone but Not Gone

Beth

Driving home from the movies, the streets are mostly empty since it's late. It was my first night out with the girls in forever. We saw a dumb romantic comedy—Ainsley chose it—and I ate too much popcorn, and then after we just talked in the parking lot, even though it was cold out. It felt like old times—just the four of us, no cares in the world now that school was out. Excited about Christmas, which is only a few days away.

I turn into Pine Forest. Lights are on in the first few houses I pass, which is weird at this hour. Then I notice our neighbors peering out their windows, looking in the direction of our house. And when I drive a little closer I see the news trucks and vans. Five or so. Reporters and cameramen hovering about, staking spots.

Just like in October.

I slam on the brakes and just idle in the street.

Oh God. Oh God.

After a moment, I press the gas again, turn slowly at the

corner, easing past some reporters into our driveway. Even before I can get out of the car I see Earl racing out from the kitchen door. He gets to me fast, before all the reporters by the driveway can hurl their questions at me. "Come inside," he says, huddling me against him.

"What's going on?" I ask once we're in the kitchen. "What's happened? Is it Sam?"

That's when I see Bud Walker, in the living room on his cell. "What's he doing here?" I ask, feeling that horrible tightness in my chest.

"Shhh, it's okay. Come into the den." He guides me in there, and Mom is sitting with Sam on the couch. *Thank God.* Sam looks shell-shocked, his hair messy, his eyes kind of glazed over, but he's there.

"What's going on?" I ask.

"That man," Earl says softly, like he's trying not to wake someone. "Russell Hunnicutt. He was killed today. Another inmate stabbed him in the prison."

I hug Earl, to steady myself as the blood rushes around my head, a whooshing sound drowning everything out around me. When I'd seen all those news trucks, I thought something awful had happened to Sam. And now I'm trying to process what Earl has just said. *Killed.* The man who took Sam is gone from this world. It's like stumbling off a cliff and then a hand reaches out and jerks you to safety at the last possible second. The rush in my head slows and I feel steadier. When I pull back, I say, "He's really dead?"

Earl nods. "I guess it happened earlier tonight, but the sheriff's office only called about thirty minutes ago. And now the media knows," he says, motioning outside.

Mom comes over and hugs me. Over her shoulder, Sam looks shrunken in. Maybe that's how I look, too.

"We tried your cell," Mom says.

It takes me a few seconds for her words to register. "My phone was on silent, because of the movie."

"I figured," she says. "Come, sit."

I look over at Sam, hoping I can see something in his eyes that will give me some clue as to how he's feeling. And maybe then *I'll* know how to feel. "Reporters are calling," Earl says, "wanting our reaction. That's why Mr. Walker came over."

"What are we going to say?"

"Nothing," Mom says, like that is the final word on the matter.

I look back at Sam. "Are you okay?" I ask.

It takes him a second, like no one has asked him this yet and he's surprised, but he nods. "I can't believe it," he says softly. Mom sits back down and pulls Sam close against her, but his body seems limp.

I can hear Bud Walker on the phone in the living room. Earl takes a seat in his recliner. We sit there in tense silence, like we're waiting out a tornado. I keep looking at Sam, but his eyes are closed now.

One by one we hear the news trucks leave. Eventually Earl goes and talks to Mr. Walker, quietly, so we can't hear what they're saying. He finally leaves and Earl comes back and sits down. And then we're all sitting there again, no one saying anything.

It's weird because we should be happy, shouldn't we? And yet it feels like we're at a wake. A wake for the man who destroyed our lives.

I glance over at Sam but his eyes are still closed, like he's asleep.

Earl stands and starts turning out the lights and that snaps us out of our spell of silence. Mom stands and goes to lock the kitchen door. It's just Sam and me on the couch, the room lit only by the small lamp on the desk. But even in the dimness, I think I see a tear leaking down his cheek, and then, quickly, his hand flicks it away.

"Let's get some sleep," Mom says, walking back into the den.

We both stand from the couch, Sam's eyes open now, and that's when Earl flicks the desk lamp off, and we're all in darkness.

I wake up all of a sudden in the middle of the night. I sit there and wonder why my body shook me from sleep. Then I hear a crashing sound. *Jesus*, I think, a cold fear rippling through me. I hear a door opening, voices. Then I hear a kind of wailing. A boy's wail.

Sam.

I jump off the bed, open my door, my heart pounding. I look down the hall, Sam's door open, light spilling into the dark hallway. I take a few quick steps and I'm at the doorway. I see that Earl has Sam in an embrace on the floor at the foot of the bed, while Sam moans and thrashes around, trying to get free. It's scary, like watching some animal in a trap. I just stand there, frozen and uncertain, my body itching to do something useful.

"Calm down, buddy," Earl says. "I got you. I got you. You're okay."

Mom is hovering over them, her face stricken as she watches Earl try to calm Sam. She keeps trying to touch Sam, but he keeps thrashing.

I see that the mirror over his dresser is cracked, dangling askew. The whole room is a mess. Picture frames and books and clothes on the floor. Marks on the wall. I'm still afraid, but it's a different kind of fear from a few seconds ago. That was the fear of not knowing. Now I feel afraid, seeing my own brother act like someone having a violent seizure. Sam's face is wet with tears and pinched with rage. He's still fighting Earl, trying to get free. But then he almost goes limp, so sudden it's like someone has pushed an off button. He stops moaning. Mom squats to the ground in front of him and takes him from Earl, cradling him in her arms, his eyes open, looking at the ceiling.

"I miss him," Sam says, his voice faint and cracked.

"Shhh," Mom says.

Did I hear him right?

"I'll never," Sam says, his voice faint and cracked.

"Shhh," Mom responds.

"I'll never," Sam says. His voice sputters, the way it does when you're in a crying fit and try to speak. "I'll never . . . see him . . . see him again."

My legs feel suddenly weak. I look over at Mom, holding Sam, and she's stroking his head, but her eyes are on Earl, and they look at each other like two people who've just witnessed a horrific accident—with fear and shock and uncertainty.

"Oh God," Sam moans again. "I want it to stop," he says. "I want it to stop." Sam opens his eyes and fixes his gaze on me. His face is wet and red, his jaw shaking a little, but he just looks at me in a way that's hard to describe. Like he's pleading with me to help him.

But I'm frozen. I don't know how to help him at all.

"Here, come on," Earl says, gently lifting Sam from the floor. He and Mom settle him onto his bed. Earl stands while Mom sits next to Sam.

I shake myself into action and start cleaning things up off the floor—clothes, a few frames, books.

"Leave that, Beth," Earl says, so I just drop everything in a corner.

"Beth, will you go to my bathroom and get an Ambien," Mom whispers.

I do just that, glad to have a task, first grabbing a glass of water, then cupping the pill carefully in my hand when I walk back to Sam's room. Mom nudges Sam gently and says, "Here, baby, take this." He whimpers a slight protest, but Mom asks him again and he takes it and gulps down the water. He lies back down and closes his eyes.

I just stand there till Earl says, "Go back to bed, sweetie."

Back in my room I don't sleep. I just sit on my bed. I keep seeing that man's horrible face. The mug shot. He's dead, he's gone, but I know he's not, really. He might never be.

The next morning, Sam is calm, like nothing ever happened. But I feel wrung out. Mom cooks us breakfast—pancakes and bacon—and we all eat in silence at the dining room table.

The news vans are gone. They've moved on to the next thing. But Mom says we shouldn't turn on the TV. My phone's still somewhere in my purse, on silent. I don't care. I don't have the energy to talk to anyone.

Later, Sam settles in the living room with that sketch pad. Mom and I work on the Christmas decorations—pulling out boxes of ornaments, hanging the stockings on the fire-place, putting out the ceramic Nativity set. Meanwhile, Earl works in Sam's room, painting over the marks on the wall, cleaning up the traces of last night, eventually taking the cracked mirror to the trash can outside.

Aunt Shelley gets here at lunchtime. We help her lug in her suitcase to my room, and then two big bags of presents, which Sam and I start placing under the Christmas tree. "Oh, Shelley," Mom says, shaking her head, looking at all the gifts. Mom begged everyone not to go overboard. She said that the only present any of us needed this year was Sam being home. But she's smiling, surrendering to the occasion.

After lunch, Mom and Shelley spruce up and grab their purses. "I have to get some last-minute things," Mom says before they leave.

I stay in my room, wrapping my gifts. A candle and some slippers for Mom. A scarf for Aunt Shelley. A nice brown belt for Earl, because his usual one is falling to pieces. And for Sam I found this sketch booklet, with a hard backing, nicer than the one I've seen him using. It's more like a notebook, he could even write in it if he wanted. I also got him a soccer ball, since I took his old one. I hope he'll have use for it one day, if he goes back to school. When he goes back.

When I finish my wrapping, I go out to the den. Earl's watching TV in his recliner, and Mom and Shelley are still out shopping.

"Where's Sam?"

"Out there."

"Isn't it cold out?"

"Yeah, but he bundled up. He says he's okay."

I look out at him, sitting there, staring off calmly. "Do you think . . . last night—you think that will happen again?"

Earl looks at the TV, like he's barely paying attention to me, but I can tell by the way he scrunches his eyes that he's thinking. He rubs his beard a little and says, "I don't know. I hope not."

"Are you happy that man was killed?"

Earl's quiet at first. "I guess in some ways, yeah. But part of me wishes he had to rot in prison. That would have been the true punishment. A life in prison, knowing that Sam is out in the real world. That he's getting better."

I'm about to ask about what Sam said, about missing him. Missing Rusty. But Mom and Shelley walk in right then. Shelley is carrying a few bags. "Nothing to see here," Shelley says, walking past us to my room.

"Want to help make cookies?" Mom asks me, smiling to maybe distract me from the redness of her eyes.

"Sure," I say.

Shelley hovers about the kitchen while we bake, talking away like she does, but it's soothing, like listening to music. Earl comes in and grabs a beer. Sam finally comes inside, too. He grabs a Coke from the fridge, cracks it open, and stands there, smiling and watching us. I watch him back, wondering if he's really feeling okay, or if he's holding something in. How can he seem so happy now, after the past few days?

When the cookies come out, Sam helps me ice them with sugary frosting—one bowl white, one bowl reddened with food coloring.

"Remember when we used to wake up at like four in the morning, so excited about Santa?" he asks.

"Yeah," I say, relieved that he remembers those happy years. They haven't been snuffed out of his memory. "How did we ever believe that?"

"Once you said you saw the glow of Rudolph's nose coming from the roof, that you heard the hooves and stuff."

"I did?" I ask, laughing.

"Yep," he says. "I was so bummed you saw it and I slept through it. The next year I slept in a sleeping bag in your room so you could wake me up if it happened again."

"I remember that now," I say. And I do: the two of us little kids, trying to stay awake by talking to each other, but eventually falling asleep. I remember waking up to Sam shaking me, "Get up, get up, time to open presents," his eyes wide with wonder, his hair messed from sleep. I remember him taking my hand and dragging me to the living room, where our treasures awaited. How old were we then? Was Dad still around? It feels like my life but also someone else's—like something I read in a book.

Once the cookies are done, we watch movies in the den. *A Christmas Story*. Mom makes lasagna for dinner, which we eat on plates on our laps while watching *It's a Wonderful Life*.

After the movie, feeling full of Christmas spirit, Earl flips off the TV and we all just sit there and look at the tree, its colored lights flashing.

"Remember that time when Sam got so excited about the presents he puked all over the floor?" Shelley says.

"I did not," Sam says.

"You did!"

"I remember," I say. "Dad had to clean it up, and then *he* puked."

Sam puts his face in his hands and shakes his head.

"I remember, too," Mom says, smiling to herself.

And on we go like that, trading stories of past Christmases. Even Earl chimes in, sharing memories from before he knew any of us. But of course we don't mention the past few Christmases. And I try to squash down any thoughts about what Christmas was like for Sam, with that man.

We call it a night, and once I'm ready for bed I remember my phone. I have some texts, and a missed call from Dad. I call him back, hoping it's not too late.

"Hey, honey," Dad says when he answers.

"Dad," I say. It feels good to hear his voice. We've texted a few times since Thanksgiving, and each week he e-mails me. Just stupid stuff—like about the house he showed that day, and how cold it was and then asking me about school, and soccer.

"You doing okay?"

"Yeah," I say. "I wish you were here."

"Me too."

"Earlier, we were talking about that time, when Sam puked."

"Oh, lord have mercy," he says, laughing.

We talk for a bit before he gets silent. "How's . . . How did Sam take the news?"

I know right away he means the news about that man being killed. I lower my voice a little. "He freaked out," I say. "But he's okay now." I wonder if it's true even as I say it.

Dad sighs. "Well, I'm glad that . . . I'm glad that man's dead."

"Me too," I say, even though I don't know how I really feel.

"Will you do something for me tomorrow?" Dad says.

"Sure."

"Will you hug Sam for me?"

"Of course," I say.

There's no snow on Christmas morning—there never is—but a winter chill came through overnight, dropping the temps below freezing, and we're all bundled up sitting by the tree. Earl has even started a fire in the fireplace, our first of the season. The logs crackle as we open gifts.

I receive gift cards, a necklace from Aunt Shelley, a few

sweaters, some novels. Sam seems to like his soccer ball, even bouncing it on his head a few times. He also says he loves his sketchbook, flipping through the pages and touching the paper, maybe imagining how he will fill them.

"This is too much," Mom says, looking at all the wrapping paper littering the floor after we're done.

"Wait, there's one more," Shelley says, handing Mom a card, looking proud and mischievous.

Mom rips it open. "What on earth?" She flashes around what looks like a ticket. "What is this?"

"You're going on a cruise with me next week. That's what it is," she says.

"Shelley, I can't," Mom says.

"Yes, you can," Earl says. "You deserve a vacation."

"It's my fiftieth birthday present to myself and I'm not going alone."

"But Shell—"

"Mom, you're going," I say, excited for her.

"Oh my God," she says. She stands and hugs Shelley, but then looks over at Sam, like she's worried about his reaction. "I can't leave the kids, though."

"Oh for Pete's sake," Shelley says.

"We'll be fine, Mom," I say. But I know she's not worried about leaving me.

"Yeah, Mom," Sam says, sounding like he's annoyed she's even worrying. "You have to go. We'll be okay."

She nods, still unsure.

"Well, it's settled," Shelley says.

Earl grabs a trash bag and we start piling in the wrapping paper, ribbons, boxes.

"Ready for some breakfast?" Mom asks.

"Wait," Sam says. He walks down the hall and into his room. He comes back with four little packages all wrapped in red tissue paper. Each one is marked with a sticker that bears our names. He passes them out. "Go ahead, open them," he says.

I tear away the paper and, wrapped inside, is a little framed colored-pencil drawing of the whole family—Shelley included—posing against a bright yellow backdrop, or maybe an otherworldly sky. It's even better than the sketches I saw, the ones that Tony gave me. Somehow Sam has captured how we all really look—our cheekbones and hair and smiles, though the bright colors of our clothes, and the yellow hovering behind us, somehow make us look like we are posing in some fantasy world. "I love it," I say. "It's beautiful."

"Oh my God," Shelley says slowly, then turning her portrait so that we all can see it. It's much the same as mine—the whole family—but hers is also slightly different. We're wearing different clothes in hers, and everyone is set against a lavender background. Everyone's is different, I realize.

"These are gorgeous, honey. Gorgeous," Mom says.

"A true artist indeed," Shelley says, getting up and hugging Sam.

We set them all in a row along the mantel. I watch Sam as he watches us admire his art, and it's like I can see relief spreading through him, and also a kind of happiness that I realize I haven't seen in him before. I give him that hug then, the one from Dad. But it's from both of us, really.

When we pull apart, I stay in the den while Sam joins everyone in the kitchen. I want to look at the pictures on the mantel a little more. And only then do I notice something. We're all smiling, in every picture—me, Mom, Shelley, Earl. Everyone except Sam. In each picture, Sam stands there, gazing out, not frowning, really, but looking blank, like his mind is miles away.

CHAPTER 12

A Better Place

Josh

It's a few days before Christmas and we're in the family room finishing a late dinner when the news comes on and the anchor from Channel 4 announces that Russell Hunnicutt has been murdered by another inmate while in prison. His mug shot flashes on the screen. Then a shot of the prison where it happened.

The anchor throws it to a reporter speaking from outside Sam's house. The reporter talks, filling the air with what little information she has. Behind the reporter, I see the house, lit up.

"Good," Mom says.

Dad gives her a funny look.

"What?" she says. "He was a horrible man. Good riddance."

Dad still looks at her funny, but he seems too flustered to say anything. I look back at Mom, and she has this fierce, determined look on her face, and for some reason this gives me comfort.

"Don't you think at least Diane and Earl can have some peace," Mom continues, "knowing that the man who did this to Sam can no longer harm them anymore?"

"He was locked behind bars. He was probably going to be sentenced to life in prison," Dad says, sounding exasperated.

"So? He would still be able—"

"Can I call Sam?" I ask, breaking into their argument.

Mom looks over like she's just remembered I'm there, and her face softens.

"Not now," Dad says. "Give them some time, okay? Give them some space."

"Okay," I say. It was a stupid idea anyway. Sam doesn't want to hear from me. Not after what I told him.

I take my plate into the kitchen and leave Mom and Dad to their argument. Up in my room I wonder about Sam. How he feels about what happened to Rusty. Is he happy? Upset? Shocked? I wish I could call him and ask. I wish I could be there for him. I think about that awful story Sam told, when Rusty tried to kill him. And all those other days and nights when he put Sam through so much pain.

Rusty's dead now. That man who was just a few feet away from me all those years ago. I wonder if he died instantly, or if he bled to death, slowly and painfully, so that he had time to think about the horrible things he did. And if it was slow, did he think about Sam at least a little bit, and did he feel sorry? Did he wish he could go back to that day, too? Go back and just leave Sam alone.

The next night Mom and Dad are hosting a small little holiday gathering, like they do every year. The house is all decorated, candles are lit, appetizers are out on the side tables, and Dad has set up a makeshift bar in the kitchen.

I was planning on staying up in my room, but Mom knocks on my door. "You dressed?" she asks, barging in. When she notices I'm still in sweats and a T-shirt, she says, "Josh, people will be here any minute!"

"Why do I have to come down? They're *your* friends."

"You know Nick and his parents are coming over."

I knew that, they've been invited for years. But I was hoping Nick wouldn't come this time. That he'd make some excuse to stay away.

Mom leaves and I jump in the shower. I start to feel nervous, which is stupid, because why should Nick make me feel nervous?

Once I'm dressed and presentable, I go downstairs, where I can already hear voices. It's a kind of torture, walking in the living room and having to say hi to everyone, answer their small-talk questions. A few of dad's colleagues and their spouses. Mr. Spencer, the head of Mom's firm, and his wife. And the Lanzanos. Nick's parents make a big production about seeing me, asking me about exams, that sort of thing, and I see Nick standing back. He got a haircut, finally, but it's almost weird seeing him without his dark brown bangs falling in his face. He has on these dark gray dress pants and a button-down, and he looks kind of dorky, but then I realize I probably do, too.

I'm careful that he doesn't catch me watching him. At one point, amid all the chatter, I spot Nick by himself, eating almonds from a bowl. I know he can sense me staring, and he's careful not to acknowledge me. He even seems kind of nervous. I feel a kind of power then. I avoided him at school, but I feel bolder here, safer in my own house. I want to point out the front window, up in the trees, where stray strands of toilet paper still hang and blow in the breeze. "You did that," I want to yell.

But I go over and just say, "Hey."

He lifts his head, "Hey." He shoves a few more almonds in his mouth.

"Nice haircut," I say.

His resolve slips, and maybe my words cut through his nerves, because he smirks at me and says, "Ugh. Mom made me. She says I looked like a hippie."

"You kind of did," I say, enjoying the jab.

A few of the adults start laughing, really loud, and then I see our moms looking over at us fondly, like they plotted getting us together and they're celebrating the achievement. Mom waves at us.

"Can we go to your room? I'm over this," Nick says.

"Sure," I say. I mean, I'm not thrilled to be alone with Nick, but at the same time I feel annoyed at our moms, watching us like we're two cute puppies.

When we get to the stairs Nick says, "Hold up." He goes to the kitchen, and he comes back walking fast, carrying two bottles of beer. "Go, go," he says, and we both rush up the stairs.

When we get to my room I shut the door. He hands one of the bottles to me and I hesitate before taking it. It just reminds me of what happened with Sam. But I don't want to be lame, so we clink the bottles together, and I pretend to take a sip from mine.

"Not fair they're the only ones who get to have a good time, right?" Nick says, pulling out the chair at my desk and sitting.

"Right," I say, sitting on the edge of my bed.

After a moment, it's like we both realize we're stuck in my room together because we just sit there in awkward silence. It's funny how quickly we went from being best friends to being—well, what?

"Do you wanna watch something on Netflix?" I finally ask. I'd rather do that than talk, even if a ball of anger is starting to bounce around inside me.

Nick doesn't respond. He chugs a few sips of his beer. "Not really," he finally says.

I start tearing at the paper of the beer label, which is mushy and comes off easily. "Why did you guys do it?" I ask. I feel kind of bad, throwing that accusation out there, because what if I'm wrong? But I'm not wrong. I can see it in his face, the brief flash of panic, realizing he's caught.

"I don't know, we were drunk," he admits. But he won't face me.

"It's still up in our trees," I say. "Like, who does that to his best friend?"

He rolls his eyes. "You don't even want to hang out with me. You're always with him. With Sam. Ever since he got back."

I flash to a vision of Sam, in this very room, without a shirt on. I stare down at the floor, hoping my face doesn't redden.

"Like, what's your fascination with him?" Nick says.

"What do you care?"

"It's like . . . I mean, you always told me you hated him, and now he's back and you just drop everything to hang out with him."

"He needed . . . a friend," I say. "He needs someone to talk to. After what happened."

"Gross," Nick says. "I don't even want to *think* about all that."

"You don't understand," I say, which is the truth, but I'm not sure I can explain it to Nick. "That day he disappeared, I was with him."

"I *know*, you told me that a million times."

"It's my fault," I say.

"What?"

"It's my fault he got . . . It's my fault. I left him."

"That's stupid. It's not your fault." He looks over at me, and I can see that he thinks I'm being ridiculous. "It's his own fault," he says. "He's a guy. Guys don't—that stuff doesn't happen to guys."

"*You're* stupid," I say. "It does happen. It did." My mind flashes to that moment Sam told me about, by that pond when it might have all ended for him. But it didn't. He fought. He lived. "He's not some freak, or someone you can just make fun of. He's strong. Stronger than us. He's a *survivor*." I stop, anger burning out of me.

"Okay, okay."

We're both quiet for a few minutes, the noise of the party downstairs creeping through my bedroom door.

"And so what if I spend time with Sam," I say finally, feeling calmer now. "You're always with Sarah."

Nick sips the last of his beer, then leans forward. "You're mad at me for having a *girlfriend*? You can have one."

I can hear some laughter downstairs, the clinking of plates.

"I can't have a girlfriend," I say quietly. "I don't want one. I'm . . . I'm gay." The words slip out so easily, and somehow I don't feel my face redden.

I'm not ashamed to tell him—I'm relieved.

His face softens with surprise. "You are?"

I nod.

"Why didn't you tell me?"

"I'm telling you now," I say. I take a breath. "You're the first person I've told," I say, which is true, even if Sam knows, and Madison, too. Still, I'm amazed at how good it feels.

"When did you figure this out?" he asks.

"I guess I've known for a while. But I was . . . I don't know. Confused."

He nods. "My uncle's gay," he says.

I let out a little laugh, and he does, too.

My beer is still full, so I say, "Here, finish this," and hand him my drink. Nick hops from his seat and grabs it from me and settles back and chugs.

"You know," I say. "Sam has changed."

Nick looks annoyed that I'm bringing up Sam again.

"He's actually pretty cool. He's not the way . . . the way he used to be." I want to tell him so much more about Sam, but there's so much I can't say—about what happened to him. About what happened between us. "He didn't deserve any of it. He didn't ask for it."

"If you say so," Nick says.

We don't talk anymore about Sam, or me being gay, or whatever's going on with us. I grab my iPad and we both sit on the floor and lean against the bed and watch a zombie movie until Nick's mother yells up the stairs that it's time to go.

"You better hide these," he says when he stands, grabbing both beer bottles from my desk. I take them and shove them under the bed.

"Have a good Christmas," he says.

"You too," I say.

But he doesn't move. "Listen, I . . . I still don't know. . . . It's okay if you want to spend time with Sam, but I'm not so sure I'm ready for that. But, I mean, *we're* good, aren't we?"

"Yeah," I say, and it's true, though I'm not really sure how things will be once we go back to school. "Promise not to tell anyone what I told you? I just . . . I don't want the whole world to know yet."

"I won't tell anyone," he says. "And . . . I mean, thanks for telling me. I want you to know I really am cool with it."

"I know," I say, feeling something altering in the air between us, but in a good way. Nick's looking at me like he's just now really seeing me.

His mom yells up again, and Nick yells an irritated "Coming!" He turns back to me. "I better go."

We bump fists and then he walks down the hall, down the stairs.

Alone in my room, I try and picture me and Sam with Nick and my other classmates. The picture is still fuzzy. But it's not so unlikely, maybe.

That is, if Sam ever speaks to me again.

===

Christmas morning is sunny and cold. We get up early, and Mom cooks a big breakfast—bacon, biscuits, scrambled eggs. When I was a kid I'd be jumpy to open presents, but today I feel older, like I've moved on from caring about that. The presents can wait. We eat, drink coffee, listen to Christmas songs on this CD Mom's had for what feels like a century. Then we open gifts. I get clothes, and some thick tennis socks. From the garage, Dad hauls in this chair that Mom wanted for the living room, and he also gives her some new jewelry. Dad always says he doesn't need or want anything, but this year Mom and I gave him some new hiking shoes, plus a gift card to Home Depot, where he loves to go on Saturdays.

That morning, I'd opened my closet for a sweater and I saw Sam's portrait, but I left it there. I wasn't sure what to do with it, but now I know. Whatever Sam thinks of me now I know he spent a lot of time on that picture. It doesn't deserve to just sit in a closet. So when Dad starts picking up the wrapping paper, I say, "I've got one more, for both of you." I race upstairs and grab the portrait from my closet and bring it downstairs.

"What *is* this?" Mom says. She takes the picture and holds it up. She and Dad stare at it, smiling, looking from the picture to me and back again. "It's wonderful."

"Wow," Dad says softly. "Looks just like you."

"*You* did this?"

"No," I say. "Sam did it."

"Sam Walsh?" Mom says. "*Sam* did this?"

"Yeah," I say, feeling proud.

"I had no idea," Mom says so faintly I almost can't hear it.

Their expressions darken a little—or maybe I imagine that? "Lovely," Mom says. And then I see her eyes are tearing up, and she hands the drawing to Dad and stands and hugs me. She keeps crying, sobbing actually, so I hold on to her, not sure what's wrong. I manage to steal a look at Dad over her shoulder, and it looks like his eyes are wet, too.

Mom finally calms down and releases me and picks up the picture again. "It's stunning. It really is. Thank you."

"You should thank Sam," I say.

She smiles over at me. "We will."

Dad stands up and pats me on the shoulder. "We need to find the perfect spot to put this," he says.

Mom and Dad walk around downstairs, trying to figure out where to hang it. I gaze out the window, and think about Sam opening presents, his first time back with his family. I want to tell him that my parents loved the portrait. I know it will mean a lot to him. But I don't pick up the phone. I just wait, hoping I'll hear from him, uncertain if I will.

But Sam does call. The day after Christmas. The landline rings and I know it has to be him, and I feel a lot like I did the other day when he came over—relieved but nervous. "Hey,"

I say. I want to bring up Russell Hunnicutt, but what do you say about something like that? "You have a good Christmas?"

"Yeah," he says.

"I gave the drawing to my parents, and they loved it. Like, really loved it."

"That's great," he says, but he sounds sort of disinterested.

I don't know what to say, and Sam is quiet, too, and as the silence builds I wonder why he even called. "Listen," he finally says. "I . . . I need your help."

"Okay. With what?"

"Um. Well, can you come for a sleepover on New Year's Eve?"

"Sure," I say, though I'm kind of surprised Sam would even want to after last time. "But what do you need my help with?" I ask.

He doesn't say anything for a bit. I almost think the line is dead, and then he says, "The thing is, I need you to go somewhere with me."

"Where?"

"Anniston."

"Anniston," I murmur.

He tells me his mom is going on a cruise with his aunt in a few days. He says Earl has to work on New Year's Day—that he has a big project that has to be done, even if it means working on a holiday. "It's my only chance."

"Your chance for what?" I ask.

"They'd never let me, but I have to go, Josh. I have to go there. You understand, don't you?"

"I think I do," I say, because that's what he needs to hear. But I don't understand at all.

"So you'll come with me?"

It's like that day, when he persuaded me to go to the mall. When I knew it was a bad decision, and I said yes anyway. I get that queasy nervous rumbling in my belly.

"Please?" he says.

"Sam, I don't know . . . I mean, I'm not sure it's a good idea."

The silence builds like a wall.

"Forget it," he says. "It's okay. Forget I asked." He hangs up.

"Sam?" I say, but I know he's gone.

After the phone call, I don't feel like doing much, so I camp out in the family room in front of the TV. For now, Mom and Dad have propped Sam's portrait on top of the fireplace mantel. But I don't want to keep looking at it. I get up from the couch and turn it around so all I can see is the back of the frame.

Hours go by, the light of day fades to evening, and that's when Mom comes in and asks if I'm okay.

"Fine," I say. The dumb movie I was watching ends.

"Dad and I are going to Home Depot, you wanna come?"

"Nah," I ask.

"Okay, suit yourself." She smiles, then notices the portrait. She walks to the mantel and flips it back around, then looks at me, confused.

I finally hear them drive off. I flip the channels and stop at Channel 4, the station out of Birmingham. The news has just started. A house fire on the west side. Scenes from the Galleria Mall, where people are returning or exchanging all their gifts. Then there's an old lady on-screen, next to an old man. "An exclusive interview you'll only see here on Channel 4," the anchor says. "The parents of the murdered child abductor Russell Lee Hunnicutt." The old woman on-screen has curly gray hair, thick glasses, a jowly face. The old man has on a cap over bushy white hair. They sit on a couch in a room with crummy-looking wood paneling.

A male reporter is interviewing them. "How are you coping?"

The man shakes his head, chews his lip.

The woman speaks first, with a country-sounding voice. "Our son's in a better place now."

"I know what he did was wrong," the father says, his voice gruff. "But that kid . . . he could have left. All them years, he could have left."

That's not true! I want to shout at the screen.

The wife looks over at him, nods her head, then looks at the reporter. "They have their son. But *our* son's dead."

I force myself to sit there and keep watching, even though anger swells in me.

"Do you have anything to say to the Walsh family?" the reporter asks.

The old lady is crying, wiping her eyes with a tissue. The old man shakes his head. "I dunno. . . . I just hope that boy and his family . . . That they get some peace now."

I flip the TV off. I can't watch anymore. I just sit there in the dark, waiting for Mom and Dad to get back.

Peace. That's what they hope this death has given Sam and his family. And maybe it has, for Sam's mom, his step-dad, even Beth. But I know it hasn't for Sam. Not really.

Still in the dark, I grab my phone and call Sam's house. His mom answers and a few seconds later she puts Sam on.

"Yeah?" he says.

I don't say hello. I just say, "I'll go. I'll go with you to Anniston."

CHAPTER 13

January

Beth

In a group text the day before New Year's Eve, it's decided that the girls and I will attend the New Year's Eve party at Brendan Olson's house. **He says it's going to be small,** Ainsley writes.

Mom left that morning for Florida, where she'll meet up with Aunt Shelley for the cruise. It's just me, Sam, and Earl for a whole week. Earl says yes, I can go, but that I have to be home at twelve thirty. "Don't make me stay up late, worrying. I have to work tomorrow," he says, looking at me all serious-faced before he lets loose a grin.

Sam has invited Josh to stay over. I guess they're just going to watch movies.

"Can Chita sleep over after? I'm giving her a ride to the party."

"Of course, if her parents are fine with it."

I go back to my room and text: **Okay, I'm in.**

===

Brendan lives in Woodridge, across the river, not too far from where Darla lives. She walks up just as Chita and I park along the street.

"So where are his parents?" Chita asks as we walk up to the door.

"They went to their lake house or something," Darla says.

So it's just me and the girls, and Brendan and the twins, Jake and Jackson, and a handful of other seniors on the soccer team. And Donal, who answers the door. "Welcome, lasses," he says, exaggerating his Irish accent, waving a cup of beer at us. He kind of looks drunk already and it's just eight.

"Can I get you something?" he asks, looking only at me.

"A water," I say, the thought of alcohol making my stomach churn.

Through the kitchen window I can see into a large backyard lit with strong floodlights, where some people on the team are playing a pick-up game. This was the idea—soccer, beer, hanging out, pizza, and watching the ball drop in Times Square on TV. Low-key and chill.

Donal hands me a bottle of water from the fridge and cracks open a can of Bud that he pours in cups for himself, Chita, and Darla. Then we head out onto the back deck. It's only in the fifties or forties, a lot warmer than it had been at Christmas. Chita sets her beer down on the deck floor and joins the soccer players in the yard, and Darla ambles up to some of the other kids milling about on the sidelines. Donal settles next to me, leans against the wooden rail. "It's nice to see you," he says.

"It's nice to see you, too," I say, feeling embarrassed all of the sudden.

"Christmas was good, with your family?"

"Yeah," I say, thinking about the presents, the food, the memories. It *was* good. But hovering off to the side was the news about Russell Hunnicutt. Mostly I could forget it, but at times it was like a physical thing we could spot, briefly, off to the side.

"And your Christmas?" I ask.

"Yeah, just me and the folks. It was good, though my mum misses home this time of year."

"I bet," I say. "I mean, it's such a funny time of year."

"How do you mean?"

"Well, everyone is so happy. But also sad. Like your mom missing home. And I kind of missed my dad. I mean, he called. But we talked a lot about the years past, when we were all together. Before . . . well, before any bad stuff happened."

For a while, we don't say much, just watch everyone kicking the ball around.

"I can't believe this year is almost over," Donal says. "It'll be January in a few hours."

In January, I always thought of Sam. His birthday month.

Everyone else always marked it as a new beginning. But for the past few years it was another painful reminder—so soon after Christmas—that Sam wasn't there to eat birthday cake and open presents. "My brother Sam will be fifteen in a few weeks," I say.

"How's he doing?" Donal asks, sounding careful and concerned, knowing that in the past I hardly ever talked about him.

"Fine, I think," I say. Because what do I know, really? I can't help thinking back to that night. *Make it stop.* The way he looked at me, like he was begging for help. But then the way he acted like nothing had happened.

"He's lucky to have you," Donal says.

And I smile at him for saying that. But I'm not sure if I believe it.

I set my bottle of water down on the railing. I need to take my mind off of Sam. "I'm gonna go play," I say, walking down the steps and out into the yard, joining the others so that I can run and sweat and not think about anything.

Later, after we gorge on pizza, everyone's settled in the TV room, watching all the insane people in Times Square. The stereo is blasting, and some people are dancing around a little, acting drunk and silly.

It's getting close to midnight, so I go out on the back deck again to get some air, to get away from the noise. It's chillier now, the deck lit only by a dim bulb by the door. A few minutes later Donal comes out. He has two cups of champagne. "Always prepared," he says, looking at his watch.

"Good thinking," I say. I guess a little champagne won't hurt. We clink the plastic cups and eye each other as we both take long sips.

"You having fun tonight?" he asks when we set the cups down and both gaze out at the darkened backyard, up at the blue-black sky, where just a few stars glitter.

"A lot of fun," I say.

"I'm glad," he says. *Glod.* He sort of gently shoves his shoulder into mine, and I gently shove back, and I finally look at him, his blue eyes gazing at me in a way that makes me kind of tingle.

"I'm *glod*, too," I say.

Donal laughs. "Still mocking me accent, I see."

"Nah," I say. "I like it."

He lets that sit, then says, "I like you."

Even though it's not surprising, I can't stop smiling.

"I'm sorry if I—"

"Don't be sorry," I respond.

"Yeah?"

"Yeah," I say. I nudge a little closer to him.

Inside I hear Brendan yell that the countdown is starting.

Donal says, "Do you want to go inside?"

We both turn so we're facing each other now. "No," I say.

We can hear everyone shouting out the numbers, counting down.

Donal cracks his beautiful smile at me. "You know what has to happen at midnight, don't you?"

Inside, the chants: "Three, two, one!"

And that's when I lean toward him and he leans toward me and I hold on to him and then we kiss, the noise from the party inside like a sound track to this moment. Everyone always says you feel fireworks when you kiss someone. And maybe that's true. But it's not *all* you feel. I feel like I'm alive in a world that's only about happiness and laughing and exhilaration, everything else blocked out. And I want this feeling.

I want Donal.

"Wow," Donal says, his eyes closed, smiling in a dorky way that I find sexy. I lean my head against his chest, and he pulls his arms around me. We don't say anything. I just enjoy the moment, feeling warm and safe and happy.

I feel his hand stroking the back of my head, twirling my hair in his fingers.

I pull back, so I can see him. He still has that smile on his face. Maybe I have one, too.

Finally, I turn toward the house and that's when I see everyone peering at us through the kitchen window, clapping and cheering and cracking up, and Donal and I break apart, laughing.

"Those jerks," he says, still beaming, like he's embarrassed but also glad they caught us.

"Happy New Year," I say to him.

"Happy New Year, Beth."

"I guess we should join the others," I say.

"I guess," he says, pretending annoyance.

He grabs my hand and pulls me gently back inside the house.

When we walk in, Chita smirks at us until I stick my tongue out at her. Brendan has put on that dumb Prince song even though 1999 was a million years ago, and everyone's going crazy, and Donal and I join in, dancing and jumping up and down, feeling like the year ahead will bring us nothing but good times. It's what everyone believes on New Year's, isn't it? A fresh start. Hope for better things to come. And I actually do feel it, caught in the moment. But even then I think of Sam. I hope he feels this way, too. A new year in his new life. Moving forward.

CHAPTER 14

The Other Kid

Josh

"Wake up."

I open my eyes, and I see Sam crouching above me. "Wake up," he whispers again, though I was already sort of awake.

It's New Year's Day. Last night we rang it in by watching the ball dropping on TV with Sam's stepdad. After that, I brushed my teeth and then when I got back to Sam's room, he was in bed, shirtless. Without the coating of Jack Daniel's, I felt nervous. There was room in his bed for both of us, but I saw he had set out a sleeping bag on the floor, and my flash of disappointment was overtaken by relief. We lay in silence for a while, then Sam said, "Thanks for doing this, Josh. Thanks for coming with me."

I didn't say anything back.

"You awake?" he says again now. But he knows I am. I look at my phone. It's a little after seven. I can see a grayish morning light poking through the window shade.

"Earl just left. Coast is clear."

"What about Beth? And her friend?" I ask.

"They're still asleep. By the time they wake up, we'll be gone."

I get out of the sleeping bag. I'm a little stiff from being on the floor all night. Sam's packed his backpack and he's dressed. Even his bed is made. I see a piece of paper, folded, on his pillow. A note saying not to worry, he'll be back later, sorry. Sorry because we're basically stealing Beth's car for the day. She leaves the keys on a hook by the kitchen door. Sam knows how to drive—Rusty taught him, believe it or not—but he doesn't have a license. "I'll drive the speed limit. I'll be careful."

I pull on my jeans, and ruffle a hand through my messed-up, flattened hair. I hate not showering, but we can't risk that. I pack all my things into my duffel and lace up my sneakers. My stomach growls but I'm not hungry. I'm too anxious to think about food.

"Ready?" he whispers.

"Uh-huh," I say, but I'm not.

He opens the door gently, and then pulls it closed when we're in the hall. He puts a finger over his lips. I don't need reminding to be quiet, but part of me hopes that Beth wakes up and foils everything.

We step quietly down the hall, and when we pass Beth's closed bedroom door I think about bumping against it, but I don't. All I can do is follow Sam. We walk on through the den to the kitchen. Sam grabs the keys hanging on the rack, opens the kitchen door. Out we go. Beth's car sitting in the driveway, waiting for us.

There's still a chance for Beth and her friend to wake up. Or maybe Sam's stepdad will come back, having forgotten something. Sam unlocks the car and climbs in. He sticks the key into the ignition, the engine giving a rev. Maybe Beth will wake up now. Maybe she'll hear. Sam motions for me to get in, so I open the door. I pause, glance at the kitchen door, and then I climb in and slam the door too hard. Sam backs out, puts the car into drive, and somehow he looks natural doing this, like it's old hat for him. I look in the rear-view mirror, hoping to see Beth running from the house after us. But she doesn't.

I could beg Sam to stop. But I know nothing can stop him. And I can't back out. I have to go with him. It's the least I owe him. The very least.

I think of the last time we set off together, over three years ago, on our bikes. And then I think about the last time Sam headed toward Anniston in a car. I still don't know why he wants to go there. But there's so much I'll never understand.

As Sam pulls onto the interstate, I try and calm myself. Everything's going to be okay. And we're together at least— he's not alone. We'll do this—whatever *this* is—get it over with, then go back home.

And we'll be safe. We'll be fine.

===

Sam drives the speed limit all along the interstate. It's early and it's New Year's Day, so there aren't many other cars out. We don't speak. Maybe he's thinking about what awaits him in Anniston.

After we pass Bessemer, its ugly shutdown steel mills off in the distance, Sam starts talking, like he'd been in the middle of a story and was picking up where he left off.

"I never went inside Kaylee's house," he says. "But I know where it is."

"Is that where we're going?" I ask.

He nods, staring ahead at the road. "Rusty stopped messing with me once I started seeing Kaylee," he says. "He even acted happy for me, or pretended to. At first. But one night, after I came back from a date, he got up from the couch and was real quiet and weird, just staring at me. He had this lazy eye and it would twitch when he was mad or upset, and it was twitching right then. So I knew to be careful. And I was right to be. He said something about my piercings, how they made me look like a fag. 'Does your girlfriend know she's dating a fag?' he said. Normally, I didn't say anything back. But that night, I dunno. Something snapped. I said, 'Fuck you.' His eye twitched and he threw a punch at me. He missed, though. I was ready for him." I see Sam, his jaw clenched, hands tight on the steering wheel, like he's reliving that moment and ready to fight again. "Then I grabbed his arm. I'd gotten stronger. Doing push-ups and shit while he was at work. I grabbed his arm and twisted it and he let out this babyish sound, like he was in pain, and then I punched him a few times in the face. He broke loose and backed up. He was holding his face where I hit him, and he looked at me like he was afraid of me. I'd never seen him look that way. It felt so good."

He stops, and I think that's the end of the story, and part of me is relieved. But part of me knows I have to listen. And after a wave of silence, he starts in again.

"I was about to walk to my room . . . and he said to me . . . He said, 'She doesn't love you. She'll never love you. No one will ever love you. Not after what I've done to you. I'm the only one who will ever love you now.'" Tears trail down Sam's cheeks.

"It's not true," I say. My throat kind of closes up. I want to say more—to explain to him why Rusty was so wrong—but if I speak, I don't know if I can come up with an explanation that makes any sense to him, or to me.

Sam wipes his eyes and then focuses on the road. We drive along in silence for a good while, before he starts up again. "It was a few days after that he got his idea."

"What idea?"

"Of replacing me. Finding another kid."

"Oh," I say, my belly doing a violent flip. I think about the other kid he tried to take, the one who fought back, who managed to look at the license plate. I wonder if he has nightmares, or if he's just gone on with his life.

It's so easy to push things back in your brain, till it isn't.

"He asked me if I wanted a little brother. I said no, because I knew what he meant. I could see the wheels spinning in his brain. That's why he taught me how to drive," Sam says, tapping the steering wheel. "At first he said it was in case he got sick and needed to be driven to the hospital. But that was bullshit."

"What?" I ask, not following.

"The truck. He wanted me to drive the truck. When he took the kid." He looks over at me, then back at the road. "He wanted me to help him."

"Oh," I say.

"I said no way. But I knew he'd do it without me. And he did."

What was that kid's name? I can't remember. I can't even picture him, though I'm sure his photo appeared in some papers. He was a hero, I guess. "What would have happened, if he'd . . . if he'd actually taken that kid?"

"I don't know," Sam says.

"Would he have let you go?"

"Let me go?" Sam asks.

I nod.

"He was never going to let me go."

I turn and gaze out the window, the scenery rushing by an ugly blur. I think I might roll the window down. I need air. But I just rest my head against the cool glass, and I'm glad that we ride along for a few miles without any talking. Without any stories.

"Everyone thinks I must be so happy he's dead," Sam says, ending the silence.

"Are you?" I say.

"I mean, I am, in a way," he says, focused on the road. He's quiet for a minute or so, like he's remembering something. Then he says, "I'm also sad."

My stomach feels tight again. "Why?" I finally ask.

For a moment Sam focuses on driving, sticking to his lane. Then he exhales loudly. "There were times when . . . I don't know. He was all I had. And there were times when . . . Never mind."

"You can tell me," I say. He's told me so much already, but I know there's so much more he hasn't talked about. Might never talk about. So much that will only stay in his brain. That must be the loneliest feeling in the world.

"The thing is, there were times when he was good to me." His voice is soaked with emotion now, and I see his chest heave.

He sniffles, takes a breath, and slows the car and takes an exit off the highway. Anniston. We're here.

We drive along past a bunch of strip malls for a bit. There are hills in the distance, surrounding the city like a big high fence. Eventually, he turns into a neighborhood of small homes with hardly any trees. It all looks new, but not fancy. He pulls up in front of one house, redbrick, one story, with light yellow trim. Two cars are parked in the garage and one in the driveway. A wreath hangs on the front door. An inflated Santa Claus sways around in the middle of the yard.

Sam turns off the engine and we sit there a minute. He's not even looking at the house. He just gazes down the street.

"This is where she lives." He unbuckles his seat belt. "Come with me?"

"Yeah," I say. I know he's nervous. I am too.

We both get out and walk to the front door. He stands there for a second, then rings the doorbell. Another deep breath. It seems to take forever, he's about to push the doorbell again, but then we hear a latch being undone. The door inches open. It's a man, about Dad's age, maybe older, with buzzed gray hair and an angry-looking face. He's kind of bulky—a mix of fat and muscle—and he's wearing a checked button-down tucked into jeans, loafers on. "Yes?" he says, giving us both quick glances.

"Hi, Mr. Clarke. It's Sam."

"Sam?" he says, sounding confused. He gives him a closer look. "Oh. *Oh*." For a second I think he's going to slam the door on us. "What are you doing here, son?"

"I want to see Kaylee."

He just stares at Sam, then at me. "I'm his friend," I say.

Mr. Clarke steps out onto the little porch and pulls the

door shut behind him. "I don't think that's going to happen."

"Is she home?"

"How did you get here?" the man asks. "Your folks know you're here?"

"Please, can I see her?" I can see something rising in Sam—panic, sorrow, desperation, all mixed together.

"Please," I say. "We came all this way. Sam really wants to see her."

"That's not possible. I think you boys should leave." He gestures to our car. "Your parents know you did this? I don't think—"

"You have to let me see her." Sam's voice sounds high-pitched, a little crazy.

"Now, son—"

"Kaylee!" he shouts. He makes for the door but Mr. Clarke blocks him. Sam tries again, and this time the man takes hold of Sam by the shoulders and physically backs him away. "I told you, you can't see her. Now please don't make any more trouble."

Sam struggles, tries to push past him, but Mr. Clarke grabs Sam's arm and yanks him out into the yard. Sam's strong, but this man's stronger. I follow, tense with a readiness to do something if I need to.

"Kaylee!" Sam shouts again.

"Sam," I say, trying to talk some sense into him. Coming here was a bad idea. We need to leave.

Then we all hear the front door open. Everyone stops. A girl steps out. She's in jeans and a sweatshirt. She has this fake red hair with streaks of blue or green in it—it's hard to tell in the morning sun. She has a nose ring, a lip ring, multiple earrings. But she looks scared, not like some tough girl. She has her arms folded around herself, like she's trying to keep warm.

"Kaylee," Sam says.

"Go back inside," Mr. Clarke barks at her.

But she just stares at Sam. "What are you doing here?" she says. She has a high, little-girl voice that doesn't match her appearance.

"Kaylee," Mr. Clarke warns.

"I came to see you," Sam says. "I wanted to see you. I miss you. I wanted to—" His voice cracks. He's crying now. "You're . . . You're so beautiful."

Kaylee shakes her head, slowly. "No," she says. "No."

"I miss you," Sam says.

"No," she says, wiping her eyes, a dark mascara-stained tear running down her face. "I don't . . . I don't know you. Go away."

"Kaylee," Sam says, the hurt in his voice so raw that it makes my chest ache.

She doesn't say anything else. She just turns and walks back into the house. I think that Sam's going to scream and try to run after her, but he just goes down on his knees and gazes at the closed door. Mr. Clarke still stands there, glaring at us like we're intruders.

And maybe that's what we are. Intruders.

"You boys go on home now, before I call the police. You shouldn't be here. You should be home with your parents. Go on," he says, like we're stray dogs.

I walk over to Sam. "Sam, let's go. Please?"

Sam's face is wet with tears, but he looks calm. He stands and walks to the car. We both get inside.

"Let's go home," I plead. Mr. Clarke is still standing in the yard, watching us, waiting for us to go. "Sam."

He clutches the steering wheel and stares forward at nothing. I wonder if he's even heard me. But he finally turns on the ignition. "There's one more place," he says. "One more place I have to go."

CHAPTER *15*
Again

Beth

I wake up to Chita's snoring at a quarter to nine. I should sleep in, but I'm hungry. And thirsty. I scoot out of bed, leaving Chita on the air mattress that's pushed up against my closet. I open the door, softly as I can, and go to the kitchen. The house is quiet. Sam and Josh must still be sleeping, too. I open the fridge and grab a water bottle and take a few sips, walking back to my room. Maybe now I'll be able to get back to sleep.

But I just lie there. I keep thinking of the kiss with Donal, over and over again. I know he'll text me today, and I wonder what he'll say. I grab my phone and click, but there are no messages. Not yet.

Eventually, Chita stirs and opens her eyes and stares at me. "Morning," I say, and she groans. "Want some coffee?"

She sits up, her hair shooting off in a million directions. "Sure," she says.

I head back to the kitchen. I wonder what the weather is like, so I glance out the window of the kitchen door. That's when I notice that my car is missing from the driveway. My first thought is Earl took it, for some reason. But I can see his truck is gone, too.

I look at the key rack. My keys aren't there.

A panic rises from my gut. Did someone steal my car? In this neighborhood, it seems ridiculous.

But Sam also went missing in this neighborhood.

Sam.

"Where's my coffee?" Chita teases, coming into the kitchen. But when she sees my face, she says, "What?"

I don't say a word. I race down the hall. I don't even knock; I just barge into Sam's room. No one's in there. The bed is made. "Oh my God," I say, trying to push down panic.

Then I see the piece of paper on the bed with my name on it.

"Beth? What's going on?" Chita calls.

I grab the note and read:

> Beth,
>
> I went to Anniston with Josh. Please don't worry or freak out. I took your car. I'll be back tonight before Earl gets home, I swear.

I left my phone and Josh has his turned off.

Please don't tell on me. I'll be okay.

I'm sorry.

Love,
Sam

"Oh my God," I say. I keep repeating it: omigodomigodomigodomigod.

"What's going on?" Chita asks again, sounding as anxious as I am.

I hand the note to her. She reads quickly, then says, "Oh shit."

I sit on Sam's bed. I'm close to hyperventilating. This can't be happening. He can't be gone. I've lost track of him again. *Again!*

"Beth? Beth?"

I snap to attention. "What do we do?" I ask, barely stifling a desire to scream.

"Call your stepdad?"

"No! They can't know I let this happen. We have to go after him, we have to—" I can't even complete the thought. My ears are ringing. I close my eyes and lie back on the bed. In the background I hear Chita on the phone, nearly shouting. Finally, quiet. She sits down next to me.

"Donal's coming over."

"Donal?" I have a quick lift of happiness, hearing his name, before I immediately fall back to reality.

"Yeah. He has a car. You want to go after Sam, right? You have to calm down. Let's get you dressed. He'll be here in a few minutes."

So that's what we do. I dress. I grab my bag and make sure I have everything I might need. We sit in the den, Chita holding my hands.

"Listen," Chita says. "I'll stay here, in case Sam calls or comes back. Okay?"

"Good idea," I say, because I hadn't thought of that.

We wait. I try to stay calm. I *have* to stay calm. Chita tries to help, rubbing my hands, but my mind still races. How far away is Anniston?

Is Sam already there?

Why is he doing this?

When Donal pulls up in his Jeep, I hug Chita and she says, "You'll find him." She opens the kitchen door for me and I dash to the car and get in.

"You okay?" Donal asks.

"Let's just get going," I say.

"To Anniston," Donal says. He punches something into his phone and a computerized lady's voice starts speaking.

"Thanks," I say. I can breathe a little better now. It was the sitting and waiting that was making me crazy. Waiting for Sam, just like last time. This time I'm not going to sit around and wait. We're going after him, and I'm going to find him and drag him back home, and I'm never letting him out of my sight again.

Drive faster drive faster drive faster, my brain shouts. The minutes and miles tick by, but it still seems like we have a long way to go. Anniston's only two hours away, mostly a straight shot on I-20. But I want to be there *now*. I *need* to be there now.

"Why do you think he went to Anniston?" Donal asks.

"I don't know," I say. I don't know anything anymore. I thought Sam was okay. Christmas was so nice. He seemed so happy. I'm stupid for thinking that. So stupid.

"So, where do we go once we get there?" Donal asks.

"Damn," I say. In all the rush I hadn't really thought of that. I try to think—where would he go? All I can think of is the place where he lived with that man. "I can't remember the name of the complex where he . . . where that man held him. But I think that's where he might go."

"Can you look it up on your phone?" Donal suggests.

"Yeah, good idea," I say, my effort to stay calm like a constant battle inside my body. I whip out my phone and feel creepy but type in "Russell Hunnicutt apartment" and then a whole bunch of articles flash up. It's almost eleven. We have about an hour to go till we get there. I scan through the articles, picking through the details, hoping some will name the neighborhood or apartment complex, but feeling the panic wash back over me. What if we can't find him?

I know this is my fault. Living in my cocoon of ignorance. Not wanting to know anything about what my brother went through.

"Sam," I say, looking at my screen. "Where are you?"

Donal steps on the gas.

CHAPTER 16

Meadowbrook Manor

Josh

Sam seems to drive around with no particular destination in mind, despite what he said. He doesn't talk. It's like he's under a spell. A tingle of fear starts to spread through my body.

We drive past a strip of restaurants—Applebee's, Denny's, then a BBQ place called Smalley's.

"That's where Rusty worked," he says, sounding normal again, not crazy, not broken, but my belly still feels tight, like I'm on guard. "I got so sick of barbecue. He brought it home all the time. I never want to eat it ever again as long as I live."

"I hate barbecue, too," I say, even though I know it's not for the same reason.

Sam doesn't respond. It's like I'm not right next to him. All he can see are the places and people from his time here.

"That's the mall. Where I met Kaylee."

It looks like every other mall—a giant brick and glass fortress surrounded by a vast and half-empty parking lot. It's getting close to noon. My stomach growls. But if we ate, I know I wouldn't be able to keep anything down.

Suddenly he slows the car and takes a right, onto a street that goes up a hill. We pass a pawnshop, a shabby-looking beauty parlor, then a little church. After we pass a vacant lot, he turns left.

"Here we are," he says.

The name of the complex is painted in fading black letters on a white sign, hanging by two chains from a wooden post: MEADOWBROOK MANOR.

Sam drives into the lot, which is only half filled. Parking spots are marked with faded painted numbers. A sign warns that cars will be towed if parked in reserved spots. Sam pulls into one of them.

"Is it okay to park here?"

"This is our spot. His spot."

Where he would park the truck. The white truck he painted red.

He shuts off the engine and we sit there a minute, facing a gray-wooden wall that separates the parking lot from the road we just drove up. Finally, Sam opens his car door and gets out, and I follow him. He walks across the lot, toward a little set of cement stairs, which lead down to a courtyard. The complex is two-story, dirty white brick, and U-shaped. In the courtyard is a grill that looks charred and unusable, and two pocked cement picnic tables set on slabs of concrete. A deflated basketball lies on the yellowed grass.

Sam walks down the steps and veers right to one of the picnic tables and sits on the tabletop. He's facing an apartment, just staring. I sit next to him. The cement is cold on my jeans.

"You okay?" I ask, and the fear starts snaking through my bones again, fear because I no longer know what Sam is capable of. He doesn't respond to my question.

The apartments all have doors painted dark green. A black and rickety-looking metal railing runs around the second floor. God, this place is depressing. I try not to think of all the things Sam went through here, but all of the awfulness seems to hover in the air like a cloud.

Sam still stares, like he's waiting for someone to walk out of that apartment.

I keep expecting the neighbors to look out their windows at us. Maybe someone will recognize Sam. But it's like this place is abandoned. And wouldn't people want to move, I think, after they found out what happened here? Maybe they've all left. Maybe this place *is* deserted.

Sam bolts up and walks toward the apartment he'd been studying. He tries the knob and jiggles it, but the door's locked. He keeps jiggling, like going harder will make it open. Then he finally stops. He stands there in front of the door, and rests his head right where the peephole is.

I want to go home. I want to leave this place badly. My phone is back in the car. I could run to the car and call someone—Sam's stepdad, or my parents. Or Beth. She's probably awake by now. She's probably flipping out.

Sam starts knocking his head against the door, but not forcefully. Knock. Knock. Knock. Then, the fourth time, he bangs it real hard, slamming it again and again.

"Sam!" I shout. I leap off the table and run over to him. I'm about to grab him when he stops. I can hear him making these awful sounds. Moaning mixed with crying. "Sam," I say, but my voice is dry and weak.

Sam wiggles the knob again. Then he starts kicking the door. Kicking and kicking, still making that moaning sound. I cringe but creep closer and pat him on the back. "Sam." He spins around. His face is red and angry and he looks at me like he doesn't know who I am.

"Leave me alone!" He pushes me hard and I stumble back, but I don't fall down. He turns back to the door and starts kicking again.

"Sam," I plead, my heart pounding so hard I can almost hear it. "Sam, please, stop!" Tears start spilling from my eyes. Maybe he finally hears me. Maybe he hears my cry-soaked voice, or maybe he's worn himself out, because he finally stops kicking.

"Sam," I say. "Please, can we leave this place?"

For a few seconds he just stands there. I can hear him crying. We both are.

"He was right," Sam says faintly.

"Who was right?" I ask.

"Rusty." He rests his head on the door again. "No one will love me now."

I wipe my eyes. "It's not true," I say.

"You saw Kaylee. You heard her."

"Sam," I say, trying to steady my voice. He needs to hear me. "I wouldn't be here if it was true."

He lifts his head from the door and wipes his eyes with his shirt. Maybe he heard me, truly. Maybe he understands what I'm trying to say. He sniffles. He stands there, quiet finally. I feel relief pour over me slowly, like syrup.

A shout cuts through the drab air that surrounds us. My head is foggy, but it hits me that someone is yelling—someone is yelling Sam's name.

CHAPTER 17

Home

Beth

I'm still combing through those damned articles, and I can't find the name of the complex, and I think I might start crying.

Then my cell rings.

The number has a 205 area code, one I don't have programmed in my phone. I think about letting it go, but I realize—maybe it's Josh. Yes, it has to be Josh!

"Hello?" I shout.

"Beth? Is that you?"

The voice is familiar, but it's not Josh. "Who is this?"

"It's Tony. Tony Johnson. Do you remember me?"

"Tony?" Of course I remember. "Tony! I'm so—"

"He's here, Beth!" Tony says. "Sam's here! He's outside his old apartment, yelling and kicking the door and stuff, he's with some kid, he—"

"I'm on my way there now, Tony. But you have to tell me the address. Please, tell me the address!"

"Okay," he says. "It's 189 Meadowbrook Lane. And our complex is called Meadowbrook Manor."

"Meadowbrook Manor at 189 Meadowbrook Lane," I say back to him. I grab Donal's phone and type in the address as the destination, my shaky hands somehow hitting the right letters, and the GPS starts recalculating. "Tony, don't let Sam leave, okay? Call me if he does. I'm hanging up now."

Up ahead I see a sign for the exit to Anniston. Donal's free hand reaches over and takes mine and I hold on tight. *Please stay there, Sam.* I chant it in my head: *Please stay there, please stay there, I'm coming for you, I'm almost there.* Donal turns off the interstate onto the exit. He runs every yellow light, and I clutch his hand more tightly. Once he turns onto Meadowbrook Lane, he guns it up a hill.

I keep looking out the window for Sam, just in case, but mostly it's crappy old shops

"Here it is!" Donal announces, making a left into a parking lot.

I scan the lot, which isn't that big, but I don't see my car. My hand grips the door handle but then I see it, almost hidden next to a minivan. "Stop the car," I shout.

Donal hits the brakes. I unbuckle and run out across the lot and to a set of steps that lead down to a courtyard. That's when I see him, straight ahead down a concrete walkway, leaning against a door. *Sam.*

Josh stands facing him a few feet away, frozen in place. "Sam! Sam!" I yell. I rush down the walkway. "Sam!"

Sam finally turns and sees me, his mouth open in surprise. "Sam," I say.

His face is all red. He leans back against the door and slinks to the ground. I walk to him slowly, like I'm approaching a skittish cat. "Sam, I'm here." What I want to do is start bawling. I want to clutch him and hold him tight. But I keep it together. It's like my body knows I have to be strong.

I walk closer and kneel in front of him. The cement of the walkway is hard and cold, but it doesn't matter. "Sam," I say.

He looks at me like he recognizes me now. He closes his eyes and I see tears. "It's okay. Let it out." I touch his leg, and he doesn't flinch. I sidle up next to him, and he latches on to me like I'm a lifeboat, his head in my lap, and in my arms he cries and shakes and I hold him. "It's okay," I say, again and again, softly. "I'm here." Josh is crying, too, his arms clutched tightly in front of his chest.

Sam wipes his tears with his jacket sleeve, and, sitting up, puts his head on my shoulder. "I had to come here," he says softly. "I had to see it again."

"It's okay," I say. "I understand." Though I don't understand. I can only try to understand. All I can do is try—that's all any of us can do.

"I saw her," he says. "Kaylee. She, she . . ." and he starts crying again, and I move my arm around his shoulders and squeeze him more tightly. I don't even know who Kaylee is.

"She looked at me like she didn't know me," he says through tears. "Like, like . . . like she hated me."

"Shhh," I say. Kaylee must have been someone important to him, like Tony. "I'm sure that's not true. And if it is true, then you're better off without her. She just doesn't know how great you are. How strong you are."

He pulls back away from me, so that we're looking at each other face-to-face, eye to eye. "You really think that?"

"Of course I do," I say, fighting back the tears. Only someone strong could have lived through all this. We *both* lived through these awful years. And here we are. That's something, I think.

More than something. It's everything.

"I'm trying, Beth . . ." He takes a shaking breath. "I'm trying to move on, like Mom wants. But when I sit in bed at night . . . when I look in the mirror, all I can think about is . . ." His voice breaks, his lips quiver. He looks right at me then. "Who's . . . who's going to love me?"

If I breathe my heart will crack into pieces.

"Who's going to love *this*?" He glances down at his body. "This fucked-up, damaged—"

"I am," I say, grabbing his hands. "*I'm* going to love you. I *do* love you. Mom loves you, and Earl, and Aunt Shelley, and Dad." I turn to Josh, his face streaked with tears. "And Josh loves you." Hadn't I known that all along? I feel so grateful for him now, for being Sam's friend. His only friend.

I take one of my hands and rub Sam's cheek, wiping away the wetness.

His whole life will be difficult. This place—that man—will never go away, not entirely. Not for any of us, really. People always say, *Get over it.* Like you can make some leap and then move on. But it's not like that. Some things you can't get over, not completely.

"Everyone here, in Anniston—everyone who knew me thought I was this kid named Sam Hunnicutt. I just don't . . . I don't know who I am."

"You're not Sam Hunnicutt," I say, "you're Sam Walsh. And you're almost fifteen years old." I smile at him. "And you're an artist. And you have a whole life ahead of you. And I need you in my life." I take a deep breath, because I can feel the tears welling. "I need you in it badly."

With that, he sidles back over next to me and lets me put my arm around him. His head falls back on my shoulder. He seems tired. So tired.

I am too.

Donal is with Josh now, his arm around his shoulder, ushering him over to the concrete picnic table. He sits Josh down and pats him on the back, then nods over to me, like he's saying, *Everything's going to be okay.* And when I look upward at the second floor I see Tony, leaning on the rail, gazing down at us with those intense eyes. He gives a little wave when we lock eyes. Then he backs up, and quietly goes back into his apartment.

"Sam?" I say. "Sam, whatever happened here. What happened to you . . . It's not going to define who you are. You know that, right?"

I feel him nod on my shoulder. "I know," he says.

It's not going to define any of us, I think. Not me, not Mom, not Josh. Sure, we'll never forget it—how could we? And maybe it's made us who we are today. But it's not the only thing in life. There's so much more.

"We can talk about it," I say. "You can . . . if you need to, if you ever want to, you can tell me things."

"Bad things?"

"Everything," I say. I know it will be hard to for me to handle. But what I really can't handle is Sam not being there, for the rest of my life.

After a while, Sam lifts his head off my shoulder and stands up. He reaches out his hand and pulls me up and hugs me. We stand there like that for what seems like forever. And I truly feel it then: Sam's back. I have my brother back.

"Beth," he says, whispering into my ear. "Please get me out of here. Please take me home."

CHAPTER 18

Any Other Freshman

Beth and Josh

Beth

We're at the kitchen door, ready to go, and Mom is smiling even though I know she's nervous. Earl stands behind her, and he grins in a big, encouraging way.

"You sure you're ready for this?" she asks Sam.

"I'm *sure*," he says, letting out an exasperated laugh.

Sam got a haircut last weekend. He's wearing a new shirt that I helped him pick out, and his favorite jeans. It's April, and this is his first day of school. He'll have to take summer classes to catch up, but unlike anyone else I know he seems excited about this. Excited about school in general.

It took a while to convince Mom, though.

"It's too soon," she would say, even when Lane, Sam's tutor, told her he was making a lot of progress.

It wasn't the schoolwork she was worried about. Sam hadn't been around lots of kids his own age in years. But Josh was always around our house, and Donal and Chita and the girls had been coming around a lot, too—to watch movies, for game nights, an occasional sleepover. Even

Grace came over once for dinner, and Sam was shy around her and everything, just like old times. He's still getting used to being around other kids.

And they're getting used to being around him.

"I worry," Mom told me one night in March when we were talking about it, when Sam was back in his room. "I worry about how Sam will be treated. By his classmates."

"They'll be cool, Mom. They'll like him," I said, though I knew there might be some jerks. "He'll just be like any other freshman."

"But Sam's different."

We're all different, I wanted to tell her. Instead, I said, "Mom. He'll have me there, and Josh. And all my friends. We'll protect him."

It was Donal, of all people, who convinced her. He came over one day when the weather had finally gotten better and we all played soccer in the front yard. All those moves Sam had as a kid came rushing back.

"Sam could make the team if he tried out," Donal said in an offhand way, when we were back inside. "He's so quick on his feet. We need fast guys."

I could see Mom looking at Sam, like she saw something new about him. "You think?" Mom said.

"Oh, most definitely," Donal said.

Sam cracked open a Coke and took a sip, then let out a ridiculous burp.

"God, Sam," I said, but I was smiling.

A week later, Mom relented. She went to the school, talked to the principal, a few of the counselors, and then to Sam's tutor, his psychiatrist. It was decided that it would be good for him, for socialization purposes more than anything else. Lane the tutor is going to stick around, because he'll still need a lot of extra help.

"We're gonna be late," I say, wanting to avoid any emotional displays. I want this to feel just like any old day for Sam, though I know that's impossible.

"Okay, go," Mom says, hugging Sam, then me. "I'll see you this afternoon."

We hug Earl, too. "You kids have fun," he says, like we're going to a movie and not school.

We drive along, listening to the radio. Sam seems too nervous to talk. And I guess I kind of am, too. Or maybe it's excitement.

I pull into the Central parking lot and find a spot in the back. Sam gazes ahead at the school, and through his eyes I see that it's big and ugly and kind of imposing. But I can see an excited twinkle in his eye.

"You ready?" I ask.

"Yep," he says, his smirk bursting into a confident smile. A smile that I'm seeing more and more of. At times I'll still see flashes of darkness cross his face, too, like he's remembering something—or trying to forget. "Sam," I'll say, when this happens, "you okay? You want to talk?" Sometimes he does, sometimes he doesn't. But he knows I'm there for him either way.

Up ahead, I spot Josh, waiting by the back doors.

"You go on ahead. I mean, I don't want to cramp your style," I say, teasing.

I think about my first day of school as a freshman, and how alone I felt. How alone I *was*.

But Sam's not alone, like I told Mom. He already has more friends than I had on my first day.

"Okay. Here I go," he says.

"Remember, meet me at the soccer fields after school?" I say. Donal wants to introduce him to his coach, because eventually he'll try out for next year's soccer team.

"Got it," he says, but he seems suddenly wary.

"It's gonna be great," I insist. "It really is." I think about that first moment I'll pass him in the hall. Seeing Sam where he belongs. Seeing Sam leading the life he was meant to live. I feel like I might turn into a big sap and start crying, but I hold it in and smile.

Sam grabs my hand and gives it a squeeze. "I know," he says. He gets out of the car and I watch him walk toward the building, my hand still warm from when he touched it.

Josh

I have Dad drop me off at school on the early side, out front, and then I walk through the halls to the back entrance, where I'm supposed to meet Sam. I take a few breaths, hoping I can get rid of the butterflies in my stomach.

I try to not worry about how other people might act. It'll be the first time most people see me with Sam.

The first time most people realize we're friends.

I've been mentally preparing. I'm the class vice president, I keep reminding myself. Sure, maybe it's a dumb, meaningless role, but people voted for me. They look up to me in some way. And when they see me with Sam, maybe they'll think twice before they judge him.

The heavy back door of the school bangs open and I turn and see Nick step out.

"Oh, hey," I say, a little startled to see him.

"Hey," he says.

Last Friday, after tennis practice, I told Nick that Sam was coming back to school.

"For real?" he'd said, like he hoped I was kidding.

"Yeah," I said. "He starts on Monday."

However he really felt about it was plastered over by him saying, "Cool."

I'm about to acknowledge Nick, but then I see that he's staring out at the lot. At Sam. Sam, walking toward us, a confident smile spread across his face.

It's Nick who speaks to him first. "Hey," he says, a pitch of nervousness in his voice. "Welcome back."

"Thanks," Sam says. Like this is no big deal.

"Yeah, welcome back," I say, even though he's never been to this school. But maybe it's a welcome back to something bigger than a dumb building. I bump his fist, and I see Nick lift his arm but then drop it, but Sam holds his arm out and Nick bumps his fist, too.

"I'll, uh, see you later?" Nick says to me.

I can tell he feels uncomfortable around Sam. But at least he's making an effort. "Yeah, for sure," I say.

Nick nods at Sam and goes back inside.

Now it's just me and Sam, and somehow meeting him here feels like it's always been our routine.

"You ready?" I ask.

He nods. "Yeah. Let's do this," he says, surprising me by taking the lead. He grabs the door handle, swings it open, and walks inside. And I walk in right behind him, hoping he knows I'm there. That I always will be.

ACKNOWLEDGMENTS

Eternal Thanks

To the late George Nicholson, who gave me my start. I miss you and will always cherish our partnership.

To Francoise Bui, who read early chapters and gave me enthusiastic encouragement to push onward.

To these friends who were kind enough to read early drafts of the novel:

 Daphne Benedis-Grab, thanks for our Korean dinners, for your constant stream of helpful advice, and for always boosting my spirits. You're a wonderful writer, a lovely human being, and a great friend.

Bryant Palmer, I'm so glad we found each other all these years after college. Thanks for your insights and your friendship and your general awesomeness. I can't wait to read your books.

Helen Ellis, my fellow Alabaman-slash-New Yorker. Thank you for the margaritas and tipsy book shopping and for your exacting, wonderfully ruthless edits. You killed my darlings and helped make this a much stronger book. I'm proud to be friends with such a talent (and a badass).

To Patrick Ryan, for pointing me in the right direction, and for writerly encouragement when I really needed it.

To Amy Chozick, for always being there. Your fearlessness has always been an inspiration. Looking forward to toasting your book in 2018.

To Alessandra Balzer, for giving me the kick in the pants that I needed.

To Angela Weisl, for allowing me into your classroom and for reminding me of why I do what I do.

To Will Walton and Tyler Goodson, for cheerleading and doing the good work.

To David Levithan, for everything you do for so many of us.

To Reiko Davis and Erica Rand Silverman, for their helpful feedback on the manuscript.

To all my friends and colleagues at HarperCollins. I couldn't think of a better and more talented group of people to work with day in and day out. I can't single out everyone, but know that your support and collegiality mean the world to me. Tina

Andreadis, on that one dark day, you gave me your shoulder to cry on and told me everything would work out. You were right. Kate D'Esmond, Heidi Richter, and Sharyn Rosenblum, thanks for keeping me (somewhat) sane. Thanks to Team Ecco—Daniel Halpern, Sonya Cheuse, Miriam Parker, Ashley Garland, James Faccinto, and everyone else—for welcoming me into the fold. And to the Harperettes, for the love and the shade: Yasir Dhannoon, Paul Florez-Taylor, and Brian Perrin.

To my amazing friends who, as I wrote and edited this book over the past few years, put up with my whining and neuroticism, gave supportive pats on the back, and, most importantly, took me out of my head whenever I needed an escape: Damian Fallon, James Pritchard, Constantine Hatzis, Dennis Gesumaria, Chetan Nagesh, Jon Greenway, Jason Bentley, Wayne Chang, Jason Wells, Chris Shirley, John Sellers, Robert Ennis, Kate Runde Sullivan, Clay Smith, Temo Callahan, Christopher Oakland, Scott Landry, and many more.

To my pen pals and kindred spirits: Debra Berman, Julie Kapphan Davis, and Melissa Tullos.

To Duvall Osteen, the most amazing and fabulous agent anyone could hope for. Thanks for rescuing me. Thanks for putting up with me. Thanks for helping me get this book into shape. And, most of all, thanks for finding this book a wonderful home. I look forward to all the amazing years ahead. And thanks to everyone else at Aragi for their support and hard work on my behalf.

To Stacey Friedberg, editor extraordinaire. Your passion for this book and these characters has meant the world to me. Chapter by chapter, paragraph by paragraph, line by line, word by word, your edits have been nothing short of brilliant. This novel is the best that it can be thanks to your hard work.

To the entire team at Dial Books for Young Readers, including Kristin Smith and the rest of the Puffin design team, for the perfect cover; Nancy Leo-Kelly, for the gorgeous interior design; Rosanne Lauer, for her copyediting expertise; and Lily Yengle and the ace publicity team.

Finally, to my family. Thanks, as always, for your love and support and belief all these years. I'd truly be nothing without you: Mom and Dad; Avery and Conan; Eric and Julie and Ethan; Mandy and Mary; Tilla, Anna, Sam, and the Yother girls; and Valerie, Jeff, and Clare.

Martin Wilson grew up in Tuscaloosa, Alabama, where both of his novels take place. He is a graduate of Vanderbilt University and the University of Florida, and his work has appeared in *Tin House*, *One Teen Story*, and other publications. His first YA novel, *What They Always Tell Us*, was the winner of an Alabama Author Award and a Lambda Award nominee. He currently lives in New York City, where he works as a publicist at a publishing house.